Dark
Harbour

David Lewis Paget

BARR BOOKS

For Blake

to illustrate the fact
that strange events
can happen
to ordinary people!

Copyright 2001-2015 by David Lewis Paget
All Rights Reserved.

ISBN – 978-0-9596876-2-0

Set in 14 pt. Times New Roman

Chapter One

The cleaning lady arrived at the house on Third Street, just as the owner was leaving for the hotel. She was ten minutes late, and he was impatient to leave.

'I want you to pay especial attention to the kitchen today, Mary. The cupboards are in a hell of a mess. A bag of flour burst and went all over the place. You'll probably have to empty the cupboards out first, and then clean all the shelves individually.'

Mary nodded. She knew what she had to do.

'Then make sure the floor's mopped and go through the wet areas. Don't bother with the bedrooms today, you can do them next week. Just the kitchen, laundry, toilet, and run the Hoover over the lounge.'

Mary saw him off, and shut the front door behind him with a sigh. Men! They treated you as if you were a complete imbecile where it came to cleaning. It wasn't as if she didn't know what she was doing. She cleaned six houses in the town, and made a tidy little income out of it, not to mention the perks.

Once she was sure he'd gone, Mary lit a cigarette and wandered around the house, casually taking in any changes that might have taken place since the previous week. The owner was pretty well heeled, and she often came in to find a new piece of furniture, or a new carpet that had been laid during the intervening six days.

Often, this meant that the older stuff was outside, under the verandah, waiting to be carted away. If there was anything worth looking at she was often given first choice, before it was inevitably dumped. She'd got some nice occasional chairs, a kitchen table and some second-hand bedding that way. Mary didn't believe in looking a gift horse in the mouth.

Besides these quite legal perks, Mary also took it upon herself to filch various foodstuffs from time to time, and that helped to keep her own grocery bill down. She usually kept her eyes open for half open packets, or items that might be thought to be going stale, and when she left, her ample bag was often bulging a great deal more than it had been when she arrived. If the owner asked, she would say that an item had gone mildew, or moisture had got in and spoiled it. But it wasn't often that he asked. The beauty of cleaning house for single men, she had discovered, was that they rarely knew what they had in their cupboards.

This particular day, she knew she was in luck, because she had *carte blanche* to clean out the kitchen cupboards, which mean that she could quite legally go through everything he had, and take all the broken packets. As long as he had a new pack, ready to open, her conscience would remain clear.

She finally set to work, emptied all the cupboards and scored herself a quarter of tea, half a pack of sugar, the remains of the broken bag of flour which she sealed in gladwrap, some vegemite in a jar, half a pot of strawberry jam, and a quarter of a box of corn flakes.

There were also some out of date cake mixes, and a broken jar of lemon curd, which she thought she could salvage.

During the day she made three trips out to her car to stow these items, checking carefully first that there was no one in the street, watching. It wouldn't do to be seen, innocuous though these items were.

After cleaning down all the shelves and replacing the rest of the foodstuffs, she went through the bottom cupboards and found a variety of cleaning materials and half a bottle of bleach that hadn't been opened since Adam was a boy. So what with sponges, scourers, an old potato peeler, one of three, a quarter bottle of dishwashing liquid and some washing powder that had spilt into the cupboard, and which she rescued in a paper bag, she felt she'd had a good day.

She finished the kitchen, ran a vacuum over the lounge and threw a couple of old Home Gardening magazines into her bag, and was about to leave when her curiosity took her to the bedrooms. Only two were set up out of the three. One was the master bedroom, the other for guests, but the third bedroom was a general junk room, also used for storing dry goods if there was no room for them in the kitchen cupboards. She always checked that one out.

The owner quite often bought by the carton, and if the carton was more than half empty, she could quite often get away with the odd jar of honey, or coffee, which was a real plus because it was getting so expensive these days. She looked around the room and saw nothing really new except for a cardboard box, hidden behind a couple of plastic crates. When she lifted the lid, it seemed to be full of packets of jelly crystals, but they had been disturbed, and this prompted her to disturb them more and delve down into the box.

Icing sugar! Packets and packets of it; all sealed in clear plastic, with 'Delta Icing Sugar' stamped on them in red ink. Why would anyone need this much icing sugar unless they were going to make a stack of icing? She remembered the lamingtons she had agreed to supply as her contribution towards the Bingo night at the Masonic Hall, and realised she'd forgotten to get the icing sugar in. She decided that he couldn't possibly miss a couple of packs, and stuck them in her bag before leaving. That would save her having to pick some up at the supermarket after work.

That night she made a lemon meringue pie, and two trays of lamingtons. Everything went fine, except for the fact that the grated coconut she had in her cupboard had been invaded by mice. She phoned her friend, Patsy, and asked if she had some grated coconut she could loan her. Patsy was only too happy to help out, and told her to come around. Mary switched off the oven, walked out of the front door, and was never seen alive again!

II

Damien Curtis slowed down at the junction, and glanced at the map lying open on the passenger seat. He presumed it was the left fork he was supposed to take, and that would keep him on the coast road until he came to the turn-off. He glanced up again and peered through the gloom at the road ahead. On low beam his view ahead was limited. The lights on the car seemed to be unusually dim, and it didn't make it any easier that oncoming headlights conspired to half-blind him. Every time he had the opportunity to put the lights up, another car would appear in the distance, and he would be forced to dip them again.

He came to a dip in the road, and the trailer jerked on the towbar, reminding him that everything he owned in this world was being towed behind him in a six by four trailer. Everything he owned in this world! He glanced into the rear vision mirror to make sure that his packing wasn't coming adrift, and caught a sight of his own eyes in the mirror. They looked red raw and puffy, a testament to the fact that even grown men can cry when their lives crumble and fall into an unexpected pit, when the love of their lives suddenly appear in the arms of their best friend. That was what made it doubly galling, the fact that it was a friend, a trusted friend of many years.

How long had they been laughing at him behind his back? How long had they been exchanging knowing glances across the dinner table while he had been off to open the next bottle of wine, happily oblivious to the fact that *he* was the third person in that company, not his friend? Two's company!

Damien laughed harshly in the darkened cabin, and the tears welled again behind his eyes. His mind was overwhelmed with the sudden disclosure, the white-faced admissions. He had experienced a feeling like something solid sinking from his heart through to his stomach, something small, round, and made of lead. It sat now, in the pit of his stomach, an excruciating ball of physical pain that just would not go away.

Every now and then he would shake his head violently, as if to try and clear his mind of those same thoughts that kept returning to plague him like a broken gramophone record, the needle stuck in the groove. His dark, wavy hair stood up in tangles, reflecting the number of times he had run his hands up and backwards in disbelief, in horror, and in shame.

'You must have known that we were coming to the end of the road, Damien,' Andrea had said, walking over to a white-faced John, as if to protect him from her husband's incredulous rage. That was Andrea all over... turn defence into attack, belittle her opponent and refuse to give up the moral high ground. She had stood with her head thrown back, her violet eyes cold for once, cold and raking him with their discontent. She looked a picture, the brave little woman protecting her man. Only this time 'her man' was his best friend, and his best friend had suddenly become alien to him, an inarticulate bundle of impulses in a crumpled jacket and soiled jeans.

'You and I haven't really clicked for the last two years at least. You've been off selling your stupid novelties, chatting up the office girls every day while I was left sitting at home. What did you really expect?

I've never been one for sitting around, waiting, Damien!'

'No, I should have known… not with your track record, Andrea,' he had replied, bitterly. His face had taken on that look of incomprehension you see in a child, when told that his pet has been run over. The scar at the edge of his mouth turned white under the pale electric light, and he tasted blood in his mouth. Vaguely, he realised that he'd bitten through his lip.

'Oh well, marry a slut, and what do you get? A married slut, I suppose!'

'That's uncalled for,' said John Inglis, suddenly animated from out of his white funk. The two friends glared at each other across the room, unable to believe that their friendship could unravel so rapidly.

'Don't you fucking dare, you bastard! How long have we known each other, John? Fifteen years – eighteen! You call yourself a friend!'

'That's not the point, Damien. I didn't set out for this to happen! But you've treated Andrea abysmally, Damien, you really have. Why, she told me…'

'You've discussed our marriage, our problems, with this… this piece of pelican shit?'

Damien was outraged and humiliated. Andrea thrust her head back and tried to stare through him, willing the moment to go away, to sink forever into the abyss of uncherished memories. Her complexion was even paler than usual, though the particular lip gloss she used had turned vaguely purple, and made her look a little like a walking corpse.

'Don't you dare speak to him like that! John was always there for me when you weren't. He was just a shoulder to cry on at first, and I needed that, Damien, I needed it!'

'Oh, you needed it all right! You always needed it, didn't you Andrea? Don't think that you're the first, John! Andrea's little peccadillo's haven't gone unnoticed, even if she thinks they have.'

'What do you mean by that! I'll have you know…'

Damien's brow clouded over, and the worry and stress of the previous six months stood out in deeply defined layers above his eyes.

'Don't crap on Andrea, and don't take on that holier than thou tone with me. Last year it was Mark Holbrook, your so-called tutor in the ill-fated Fine Arts course that you never finished. Tell John why you never finished it, Andrea. It wouldn't have anything to do with Mrs. Holbrook, would it, coming around here and heaving a rock through the lounge room window?'

Andrea began to shake uncontrollably in rage and fear.

'That's bullshit, Damien, and you know it. He's lying, John,' she said, desperately clinging onto John's free arm.

'She told me it was the kids from around the corner, but Jane Holbrook came to see me privately, and told me all about it. She caught them at it on the couch, at her flat.'

'If that's true, why didn't you say anything about it at the time,' said John, heatedly.

'Because… you bloody idiot, I didn't want to lose her! Can you get your head around that? I knew if I said anything she would go off half-cocked, and probably wreck someone else's marriage in the process. Sometimes it's better to grit your teeth and keep your mouth shut!'

'Well I don't believe it!'

John turned to Andrea and put his arm around her shoulder, and made soothing noises to calm her distress. His crumpled jacket stood at odds with her immaculate black shift, and somewhere in Damien's subconscious he was comparing this apparition of them to the model and the nightwatchman, and the combination was ludicrous.

'Wait til it happens to you, mate! You think you've got her now, well let me tell you… you're just a fill-in until the next guy comes along. Why would you think she'd need a bag of bones like you? She's always been the same! I should have had my head read to even fall in love with her in the first place.'

'Love!' Andrea snorted. 'You wouldn't know what love was, Damien. Once I married you – much against the advice of my friends and everyone else I might add – you just lost interest. You went off selling your blasted candles and novelties and forgot that I had needs too.'

Damien shook his head in disillusionment.

'We had to live, Andrea! You never said 'no' to the money I generated. Everyone has to make a living!'

Andrea sought refuge in tears at that point, as she

always did when defending an untenable position. She left with John after telling Damien to get his stuff out before she would consider coming back to the house, and then they disappeared down the drive in John's wanky BMW. It was the only possession John had, but it was enough to give the impression that he was somehow rolling in it, which was all a certain type of woman ever looked for. The man of substance!

Damien pulled a bitterly ironic face at the thought, and peered into the night. It was starting to rain, which made visibility ahead even more restricted. He put the wipers on, but that just had the effect of spreading an opaque smear of bugs and mud across the windscreen, making it almost impossible to see.

Up ahead he could see a couple of standard lamps, indicating the little settlement of Dark Harbour, a small seaside settlement off the main road, north. He looked at his fuel gauge, and saw it poised just above empty. He must have driven nearly three hundred k's since leaving that afternoon, not really knowing where he was going to end up, but just knowing that he had to get into the car and drive... drive until he was far enough away to prevent him from weakening and going back to fall at Andrea's feet, to beg her to take him back. She'd humiliated him; she'd destroyed him! But be damned if she was going to see him humbling himself before her. And he certainly wasn't going to give John the opportunity to score off him again. That friendship was dead and buried. Eighteen years! It *was* eighteen years, because they'd met at year 10 in High School, and despite the difference in their outlook, their bearing and orientation, they had somehow been close friends ever since. Or so he thought. Friends didn't run off with each other's wives!

Damien had never seen John as a threat, because although he enjoyed his friend's company, he thought of John as an amiable fool, a scruffy misfit. The only time John paid any attention to his appearance was when he was at work, whereas Damien preferred to look the part both at home and at work. Where Damien wore a gold chain around his neck and a fifteen hundred dollar bracelet, John affected a ring with a skull and crossbones, as if his taste had never really matured. Small wonder then that the shock had been so great when his immaculately turned out wife had turned to the comfort of John's fumbled protestations of love.

Damien came to the Dark Harbour turn-off, and slowed down. He needed fuel desperately, or he wouldn't be able to make the next town. So he turned off, hoping that there would be somewhere in this little backwater that he could get fuel at this time of night. He looked at his watch – eleven thirty! His heart dropped! Not likely, not in a little place like this. Everything closed up at six in these little towns, so it looked as if he would be spending the night in the car.

He drove around a long, sweeping curve towards the sea, and the rain suddenly increased in intensity, and came battering down on the screen. Visibility was about ten feet, but he was so close now that he decided to continue on into the main street, if there was such a thing at Dark Harbour.

Another set of headlights appeared in the darkness ahead, and whoever it was had also set them on high, in an attempt to see through the rain. He screwed up his eyes and hoped that whoever it was would drop them shortly, once they realised he was ahead. Ten seconds later, the other vehicle was getting closer, but still on high beam. Damien cursed, and flashed his high beam on and off three or four times to give them the message. Suddenly the other vehicle was coming straight at him, as if they didn't see him at all. At the last minute he swerved to the left, and the other car slammed into the side of his trailer, picking it up and spinning it around behind him, and in the process dragging the tail of his car around with it.

It all happened so quickly! Damien caught sight of a concrete edging at the side of the road, and beyond that, the dark pit of the sea. The trailer jumped crazily as it hit this ledge, and turned over, ripping the towbar off the towball, and flipping noisily over the ledge into the water. Luckily it didn't take the car with it, but Damien sat there for a few moments, stunned. The other car had come to a stop behind him, and up against the concrete edging, and there was no movement there either. After a minute or two of shocked confusion, both drivers got out of their cars and stood motionless, looking helplessly at the trailer lying half submerged in the water. Damien watched as what remained of his life floated slowly out on the tide, or sank heavily to the bottom.

III

The red-haired woman saw the furniture removal truck arrive at six thirty one Monday morning, and her curiosity was immediately aroused. She peered through the kitchen curtains at her neighbours place, and watched as the truck was backed in alongside the cottage, and the back let down onto her driveway. It was the first sign of life there'd been at the old place for a month, and it was so early in the morning that it was almost suspicious.

The woman went to a drawer under the sink and took out a couple of dexy's that she'd managed to hang onto in case of an emergency, and swallowed them down with a glass of water. For some reason they not only got her going, but they gave her more confidence to deal with the world outside as her nervous disposition had always needed a drug of some sort in order to cope. When the dexy's ran out she smoked pot, and when that wasn't available she took Valium or Serepax, or any one of the dozens of uppers and downers that she had managed to collect over the years from visiting various doctors, with her imaginary ailments. She was naturally timid until she took something, and then she became unnaturally confident and aggressive.

She watched the activity at the neighbouring cottage with a gathering sense of unease. Mary's lounge suite, occasional tables and bedroom furniture formed a procession into the back of the truck in a steady stream, and the two men worked quietly, saying nothing to each other that she could see, but just grimly getting on with their appointed task. After twenty minutes she plucked up the courage to let herself out of the back door, and walk the fifty metres or so across the waste ground that separated one cottage from the other.

'Excuse me,' she called out, as one man disappeared into the back of the truck with an easy chair.

There was no reply. Liz stood in the driveway until the other one came out, and then tried again.

'Excuse me,' she said, more loudly this time. 'Could you tell me who authorised this removal,' she said, her voice rising in apprehension.

The man ignored her. He not only ignored her, but he didn't even acknowledge her presence by looking in her direction. The two of them walked straight past her and went back into the cottage, and when they came out again they were carrying a bed frame, which effectively stood between them and her.

'I asked you a question,' she said, beginning to flush. 'Who authorised this removal? Mary Burton hasn't been here for a month, so it wasn't her!'

The older of the two men flashed her a glance of disapproval, but still ignored her, as they both walked past and back into the cottage. This time she followed them, and stood blocking the back door.

'I'm not going to budge until I get some answers,' she said, as the younger man came towards her with an occasional table.

Using the table as a battering ram, he barged straight into her, pushing her out of the way and continuing on to the truck. One of the legs of the table caught her, and knocked the wind out of her.

'Well, I've never seen such rudeness in my life! Who the hell do you think you are? I want answers, and I want them now, or I shall call for the police,' she said, to the older man.

He tried to barge his way out, and she stood aside until he'd passed, but then she came up behind him and grabbed at his shoulder. At this, he threw his chair down and turned to face her. Pulling a face as unfriendly as it was ferocious, he muttered:

'Piss off, lady!'

Liz staggered back as if she'd been slapped in the face.

'Right, that's it! I shall go for the police!'

The younger man on his way back grabbed hold of her, painfully, by the upper arm. He walked her over to the dividing line between the two properties and pointed her in the direction of her own cottage.

'Do what you like, just piss off!' Then he pushed her.

Liz Capel turned and rubbed her arm, then ran, stumbling, towards her own cottage and the phone. But when she phoned the constable, Jack Izzard, he wasn't in… or wasn't answering, one or the other.

The cottage across the way was emptied out by 7.20am and the two men got in and drove off, heading south. Liz popped a Serepax, and considered her options.

Chapter Two

Cherry Reynolds had been attending a Hens' Night for Katie Carstairs at the Promenade Hotel, a rather fancy name for an establishment that consisted of a small lounge area and even smaller bar, frequented mainly by the locals. There were also eight guest rooms, usually untenanted. The hotel was in a shabby state of repair! The wallpaper was peeling off the wall in the narrow entranceway, and the overall smell of the place was that of stale beer. But it was the only pub in the township, and except for the old Masonic Hall, the only place suitable for a gathering.

The gatherings in Dark Harbour were never very large. The population of 88 was spread across an area of ten square kilometers, and except for the small town centre which boasted one main street and three smaller streets leading off this, the rest of the area consisted of remote farmhouses and a few cottages spread at intervals along the coast.

Katie was 29, blonde, rather heavy in the thighs, and about to tie the knot with Erin Lachlan, one of the fishermen from that part of the country. They'd already been living together for eight months, so the ceremony was a mere formality, an excuse to legitimise the child that Katie thought she might be carrying. She was ten days overdue, so had insisted on a hurried affair at the local church, and the banns had gone up the Sunday before. With only two weeks to the ceremony the locals had decided the Hens' Night couldn't wait another week, so Patsy Donaldson, Emily Longstaff, Doctor Ilse Hirsch and Cherry Reynolds had gathered at the Promenade on the Tuesday night, determined to get well and truly plastered while the opportunity presented itself.

The ladies had assembled in the lounge at eight o'clock, and Cherry had turned up a quarter of an hour later. She wore a brightly coloured skirt and top, suitable for the occasion, and wore her auburn hair pulled back into a ponytail. She was twenty-eight herself, but had pretty well given up on any ideas of finding that Mister Perfect herself. As a result she lived life to the full, which meant plenty of booze, cigarettes, and a strict regime of gardening.

'Ah, here she is at last,' said Patsy, thrusting a gin and tonic in front of her as she sat down. 'Get that down you, girl. You're two drinks behind us already. You don't want to be the only sober member of the Dark Harbour Pisspot Club!'

The others laughed, and talked frantically about Katie's dress, and who would be bridesmaids, and who would give her away. They were the only ones in the lounge at that time, which was one of the reasons they'd chosen the Tuesday night. Not many ventured out to the pub on a Tuesday, and with the added disincentive of the miserable weather, they thought they would be free from interruption.

'Who's going to give you away then, Kate,' Emily said for the second time.

Katie looked over and pulled a face.

'Well, not my old man, and that's for sure. He couldn't walk straight up the aisle if he tried – even if I was to ask him, which I won't,' she replied. 'No! I've asked Erin's grandfather if he'd do it, and he said he would. Said he'd be honoured,' she added as an afterthought. 'We've always got on pretty well.'

'Well that's one way around it,' said Emily. 'Has your father always been as big a soak as you make out?'

There was a sudden silence. Emily Longstaff wasn't exactly renowned for her tact. She was forty-eight, and the end result of a failing marriage. Katie shrugged her shoulders, and tried to look unaffected.

'He used to come home and fall in a heap on the lounge room floor, if that's what you mean... when he wasn't beating my mother up! I always knew when he'd been on the rum. He could drink whiskey until it came out of his ears, and he'd come up smiling. But after three or four rums... God! Watch out!'

'Funny that we never used to see him down the pub,' mused Emily. 'I suppose he only used to drink at home!'

'Oh, he'd come to the pub occasionally, but when he did, he'd always get into a fight, usually with the other boaties. Erin can't stand him! No, he did most of his boozing out on the boat. They all do you know, even Erin. I've told him that he'd better not turn out like my old man!'

'You haven't got any worries there, Katie. Erin takes life too seriously to give in to the demon drink,' said Cherry. She'd known Erin all her life, had even dated him until he'd objected to her drinking and smoking. With such a small population, most of the affairs in Dark Harbour bordered on the incestuous!

'It's a pity that Liz couldn't be here,' said Patsy, musingly, in an apparent aside to herself. 'She was a laugh and a half, once she got going!'

The others looked at her sharply, as if she'd raised a subject they didn't want to think about.

'Yeah, well… them's the breaks,' said Cherry, trying to make light of it.

Ilse Hirsch got up to get the next round of drinks, and carried her fancy leather purse over to the bar. She fancied herself as a cut above the others, and possessed a poise and grace that most women envied. She was also the only doctor in the area. Not a local, she'd arrived in Dark Harbour when she was twenty-eight, and had boarded with a cousin, also a doctor, who had gone on to work in the U.S. in some research facility or other. She'd bought his cottage, and taken over his little medical practice in the main street. At 32, it was a constant source of speculation why she had never married.

'Do you all want the same again, or do you want to experiment?'

'I'll have a Bundy and Coke,' said Patsy.

'Make mine a Cinzano Bianco,' said Emily, emptying her gin and tonic in one gulp. 'Just straight!'

She patted her greying hair into place, and looked at the younger ones with a hint of envy, as if life had somehow cheated her out of the last twenty years.

'What... no mixer? Hell!' said Ilse. 'I couldn't drink that straight.'

'Why spoil good booze with a mixer,' Emily replied.

'I'll have a Vodka and Lime,' said Cherry, turning back to Katie again.

'What shall I get Katie... a Mickey Finn?' said Ilse, dryly.

'Yes! Kahluah and Vodka and Bourbon for a start.'

'And Jack Daniels and Schnapps and Southern Comfort, with just a touch of bitters.'

'God! Do you want to kill the poor kid,' screeched Emily. 'That would fell an ox!'

'Well, you did say why use mixers,' laughed Cherry.

'Just give me a Bacardi and lemon, that'll do,' said Katie.

Ilse had to poke her head through into the bar to attract the barmaid's attention, and in doing so she noticed that the bar was occupied. She came back and whispered:

'Shush! Igor Morris is in there, and Charlie Fairweather and Lionel. We don't want them in here.'

'You mean 'Rigor Mortis' don't you,' Cherry whispered, and they all began to giggle. Rigor Mortis was the town's pet name for Igor Morris, a phlegmatic Welshman who seemed permanently under the weather, and whose favourite saying was 'Right, Boyo. I'll be with you in a crack o' the whip!' What wasn't generally acknowledged was that he was extremely well read in Celtic history, and had a fund of tales that he could trot out at a moment's notice, given the right sort of company. Emily Longstaff was his one secret admirer, and often drew attention to herself by sitting as close to him at gatherings as she could. Fascinated by his name, she had managed to elicit from him that it was the result of a Welsh grandmother's chance meeting with a Russian sailor, and the result, his own mother, had decided to continue the Russian tradition.

Emily's own husband had lost interest in her years ago, and spent his time following the horses, and fishing. They barely spoke at home except on a Saturday night, which was his night for sex. Emily complied without comment and without apparent interest, as long as he came at her from behind, and didn't force himself into her face. They hadn't kissed for years.

The women downed their drinks in three gulps, before realising that the previous order had somehow become mixed up.'

'That was a rather strange Bianco,' Emily muttered, taking swift, deep breaths.

'Oh! I think I must have got the Bianco,' said Ilse. 'You probably got my Johnny Walker on the rocks.'

'No... hell! *I* got that,' said Katie, pulling a face. 'God, I hate whiskey!'

Patsy looked at the group in distaste, and stuck out her tongue. She was often the joker of the group. 'Well I must have got the farking Mickey Finn,' she mumbled, and then hiccoughed to prove the point. They all fell about laughing, and the noise drew a couple of figures from the bar.

'Well look at this, the town's pride, all getting sloshed together. Maybe we're in luck tonight,' said Lionel Jury to Charlie, who came in behind him with a swaggering scowl on his face.

'Not tonight you're not! This is a Hens' party Lionel. No men allowed!'

'Oh, we wouldn't dream of imposing ourselves on you,' said Lionel, smugly. 'We'll just sit over there in the corner and make ourselves scarce!'

'We'd rather you pissed off back to the bar, Lionel,' Patsy hiccoughed again. 'This is private womens business over here!'

Lionel ignored her and led Charlie to a corner table some ten feet away. A silence fell over the group, and Cherry scowled at the intruders. Lionel was one of the trials of Dark Harbour, one of those people you put up with for the sake of peace. He had a supercilious manner which went together with his forty years and his pipe, and this he pulled out at the most inauspicious times to cloak everyone else in clouds of smoke. His drinking partner, Charlie Fairweather was Lionel's shadow. Five years younger, Charlie thought of himself as a tough son-of-a-bitch, but he became totally incompetent around women. He had a continuing infatuation with Cherry Reynolds, who took great pains to ignore his every fumbled advance.

24

'If you're going to Erin's Buck's night, you'd better piss off, Charlie, or we'll all come along and ruin it for you.'

'Ah, take no notice,' said Lionel. 'This is a public lounge, and we've as much right to be here as they have!'

'We'll remember this, Lionel Jury! You might just lose a few magazine orders after tonight.'

Lionel was the local newsagent; the only one for sixty kilometres, so he knew the threat was an idle one. Charlie sipped his beer and leered at Cherry, and she turned her back and ignored him. After that, the hilarity seemed to go out of the Hens' Night, and the women got down to some steady drinking. There was no point in going home sober.

'Are you on a promise tonight, Katie?'

'Do you mean is Erin on a promise? No way! I've told him to tie a knot in it until the wedding night.'

'Huh! My old man's had his in a knot for so long that he can't remember how to untie it,' said Emily, facetiously. They all laughed because they thought that it was probably true.

'Well I'm still looking for an old man,' said Cherry, blearily. 'And he'd better be young!'

'Me too,' said Patsy, shaking her blonde hair. 'But I've tried them all round here, and there's not one who knows how to tie his own bootlaces.'

'You're pretty full of yourselves, aren't you,' said Charlie, nastily. 'If Cherry wants a real man, she only has to turn around!'

'God… the monkeys *are* noisy tonight,' said Cherry, loudly. 'Throw him a banana someone!'

Charlie leant back and scowled, knowing that any riposte he was likely to come up with would be outdone by Cherry. Besides, he was determined to get her onside, and even he realised that to antagonise her was not the way to do it.

Cherry got in the next round, and to simplify matters they all went for a Bourbon and Coke.

'Halves or full,' said the barmaid.

'Fulls! Or fives full,' slurred Cherry, somewhat under the weather. 'Or ssould that be fives fulls?'

'Five fulls,' grinned the barmaid. 'I don't envy you lot tomorrow morning!'

Three more rounds succeeded the Bourbon, taken in order; Drambuie, Crème de Menthe and Southern Comfort. The last was too much for Emily Longstaff, who raced off to the toilet to be violently sick.

'Onesh down, an' foursh t'go,' Cherry slurred through her drink.

'Farking two if you don't farking mind,' said Patsy, and raced off to emulate Emily.

Charlie Fairweather saw his chance and cornered Cherry at the bar.

'One more for the road, Cherry,' he smirked. 'My shout!'

'Nope! My'sh shout… 'n you can fark arf!' she replied, emulating Patsy, not quite *that* silly yet.

Charlie blushed.

'No need to be bitchy about it! I was just offering…'

'I knowsh jush what you were offerin', Charlie…an' you can pusht it back in your troushers!' she squealed, laughing at her own joke.

'She's got your measure, Charlie,' said Lionel, grinning safely from his seat in the corner.

'Yessh! Two inches,' giggled Katie, who had once had a short but torrid affair with Charlie Fairweather.

Charlie retired in disarray.

Emily and Patsy appeared pale-faced from the toilets, and indicated that it was time to call it quits. It was eleven thirty. Katie staggered to her feet and helped Ilse to hers.

'Are you coming, Cherry?'

'I'sll be awright,' slurred Cherry. 'I jush want to try thatsh Ousho!'

'You'll be sick as a dog,' said Ilse in parting.

She was right. After the Ouzo, Cherry paid a hurried trip to the toilet and divested herself of the last five drinks. She felt better after that, at least until she walked outside and the cold air hit her.

She climbed into her car, and reflected that it was lucky that the local policeman never came out after eight o'clock at night, or she'd be done for sure. She started the car and moved warily out from in front of the pub, her lights on high beam. It didn't seem more than two minutes before this fool came at her in another car, flashing his headlights up and down in quick succession, and hypnotising her in their beam. She didn't have a single reflex left to call on, and when she hit the trailer it was pure instinct that made her slam her foot on the brake, or the car would have continued over the sea wall and into the water.

II

Erin Lachlan was also taking a drink that night, though not for social purposes, merely to keep warm. It was raining cats and dogs where he was, out on the deck of the 'Vagabond', a twenty-three tonne trawler powered by an old but trusted Perkins diesel. On nights like this he always kept a flask of brandy or rum in the wheelhouse to ward off the cold.

He'd powered out at seven o'clock that evening, meaning to set his craypots at hundred metre intervals, in a line running along the reef about three miles out. Pickings had been slim for a while, and with this wedding coming up Erin knew that he would need to raise as much as possible to see him through all the hidden costs that Katie had so cavalierly let them in for. There was the photographer for a start. Erin would have been happy to let his mate, Eddie Oswald, snap away with the old Kodak, and order a few enlargements from the results. But Katie had insisted on a professional coming up from the city.

'Now don't be mean, Erin! This is a once in a lifetime thing, and I'm not going to have all the other girls say that you were too tight to get a proper photographer.'

'I don't give a shit about the other girls, Katie. Have you any idea what it costs to get a professional photographer to drive all the way up here, stay overnight, and take scads of photo's?'

'It's either a professional photographer, or your child is going to grow up a bastard,' Katie had sulked. She got her way – as usual!

Erin figured he could be looking at anywhere between fifteen hundred and twenty five hundred for that little gesture. Then there was the dress. She'd picked out one with a long train, trimmed with lashings of lace for a mere twelve hundred.

'That's cheap! You've got no idea what these things run into,' she said, when he protested about the price.

'If that's ruddy cheap, I'm surprised that people can still afford to get married,' he moaned. 'The way you're going, the only thing I'll be able to afford is a silk jockstrap! How would you like that at your wedding?'

Katie ignored him. She knew what crayfish were fetching at the market per kilo, and had an idea that her future husband's finances were a bottomless pit, for her to dip into at leisure. What she didn't understand was the cost of diesel fuel, maintenance, seasonal variations and the long periods when it was illegal to drop the pots into the water at all. Women!

The caterers had come in with a deal at twenty-five dollars a head, and at that Erin had snapped. He grabbed the list of a hundred and ten guests that she had roughed out, and started to blue-pencil every name he wasn't familiar with.

'Who the frig is Donny Williams?' he said, peevishly.

'Oh, Donny! I've known Donny forever, Darl! We went to school together.'

'What? In the fifth grade,' he snapped. Donny hit the bin. 'And who's this Carla Johnstone... and Hetty Springfield, for god's sake?'

'Carla's my mother's second cousin from Norwood. They used to be real close until a few years ago...'

The blue pencil flashed in the light.

'And Hetty?'

'That's my great aunt on my mother's mother's side.'

'How come I've never met her?'

'Well, actually... I've never met her either, Darl. But she's family! My Mum would be real put out if she wasn't invited!'

'Well your Mum is going to be put out,' said Erin firmly, and refused to listen to any of her protests. 'If there's one thing you're going to have to learn when you marry me,' he said, heavily, 'it's that you'll have to learn to stick to a budget. That trawler out there didn't cost peanuts, and it's a long way from being paid for yet. Nearly half my income goes to the bank every month, for that, and for the house. Another slice goes out in diesel. Then there are all sorts of fees you don't even know about. It's not cheap, being a fisherman!'

'Oh, you do all right,' she sulked.

'Yes, I do! But I won't if you come in spending like a woman with ten pairs of hands. You've got to be reasonable, Katie! I haven't worked my arse off for sixteen years, only to go bust because of a woman's silly whims.'

Erin was thirty-two, and had been married before. His first wife had taken him to the cleaners, and he had been lucky to come out of it with just his boat. She'd got the house and car, and a cash settlement. That was six years before. Sometimes he wondered why on earth he would even consider going through all that again. But Katie had finally managed to get in under his defences, and he was lost.

He often talked to his crewman, Craig, about the lunacy that was mankind.

'Sometimes I think that men are the biggest idiots on the planet, Craig. We've got this appendage between our legs that sits up, points to the nearest female in sight and says 'follow me!' and like idiots, we do! We're slaves to our dicks, Craig. If you'll take my advice, you'll keep the bastard in your trousers and your money in your wallet, because as sure as shit you can't have pussy and money at the same time. The moment the pussy beckons is the moment the hand slides into your wallet, and it takes an operation to get it out again… the hand out of your wallet, I mean!'

Craig grinned. He'd not only heard it all before, but had experienced a similar condition in his own life.

Erin wandered out of the wheelhouse and went down on the deck to help Craig with a tangled line.

'How the hell did you manage that, Craig?'

'It must have been tangled up on deck, mate, because when I went to run it out it snarled. There's a bloody great knot in it. I might have to cut it.'

'Don't you dare! You'll lose the pot, and I can't afford to keep on replacing the damned things,' said Erin. Between the two of them they backed the motor off, and managed to untangle the line after about ten minutes.

'Now, for chrisesake, run it out more slowly next time. You're always in too much of a hurry!'

Craig could have rejoined that when he did take his time, Erin went off about how slow he was, and that he would have to buck up if he wanted to stay on as crewman on the 'Vagabond'. But it was a futile exercise, as well he knew, because Erin would deny it. Whichever way it went, a crewman on a trawler was there to take the blame for everything that went wrong. It might as well have been written into the job specs.

'Once all the pots are out, we'll throw out some lines and try for a bit of schnapper,' said Erin. 'We might have to go out another couple of miles.'

'Pity we can't throw a net overboard,' said Craig.

'Yeah. Well we can't. Fisheries would crucify me, *and* take the boat. Don't you know, their job is to make our lives as miserable as possible! They're pretty good at it, too. They got Kevin Jackson last week with fifty abalone... took his car, boat, trailer, and the poor prick's up for a heavy fine.'

'What... they finally got him? He's been poaching for years.'

'Yeah, well! He's going to be looking at a ten thousand dollar fine. Maybe that will slow him down a bit.'

Craig looked at Erin, quizzically.

'You haven't got much time for Ab poachers, have you?'

'No, I bloody haven't! There are two types of fishermen. Those who do everything by the book, and pay the piper, and those who try to cut corners and get away without paying anything. An abalone licence is now worth about one and a half million! How do you think the licence holders feel when they see these poachers getting away with their Abs?'

'I'm on the poachers side,' said Craig, rebelliously. 'Stuff the Fisheries!'

'Yeah, well you can say that, but if you were like me, and had to buy two line licences to get one, at twenty five thousand dollars apiece, you'd resent the poachers too.'

The last pot reeled out into the water, and Craig attached the orange float to the end of the line and cast it adrift. Then the rain came down again, heavily, and they both sought shelter in the wheelhouse. Erin cranked up the diesel while Craig rolled them both a cigarette.

'I'll head out past the light, and go to the old car drop. They should be biting around there.'

For years Erin had been taking pieces of old junk, fridges, car bodies, steel lockers and anything else he could find out to the same spot, and dumping them overboard to make an artificial reef. Once the molluscs and limpets had attached themselves to the resultant junk, and the weed had taken over, the fish used it as a shelter during bad weather, and as long as he kept the exact location secret, it was his own private fishing spot.

Erin was careful to phone the 24-hour Fishwatch service and de-register his boat from commercial activities before throwing a line in.

After a couple of hours out there they'd filled their recreational quota of schnapper, whiting and Tommy's, and pulled in a few squid before heading for home. It was while coasting in to tie up that Craig noticed the debris floating in the water.

'What do you make of that, Erin,' he said, pointing out the various pieces of clothing and suitcases half submerged in the water.

'God knows,' said Erin. 'See what you can snag!'

Craig used a long handled crab net, and managed to pick up an ornate carved wooden box that had been floating just under the surface. When they pulled it up on board, Erin waited until they'd tied up, and then spilled the contents out onto the deck. The box was full of old family photographs.

'Curiouser and curiouser,' said Erin. 'Stick them back in the box, and I'll have a look at them later.'

Chapter Three

Damien stood and looked at the other driver in the dark, who seemed to be standing, shivering in shock. He walked around to her, intending to give her a piece of his mind, but she continued to stare fixedly at the trailer in the water. It was as if she was unaware of his presence.

'Are you bloody blind or something? Couldn't you see me coming? I flashed my headlights at you to tell you to drop yours. I couldn't see a bloody thing,' he began.

She jumped, and staggered dangerously close to the edge as she spun around to face him.

'Don' you tush me,' she said, fearfully, putting her hands up to protect her face.

Damien took a step back and put his hands up in a gesture of peace.

'Don't worry! I'm mad, but I'm not *that* mad,' he said. He looked at her more closely as his eyes adjusted to the darkness, and saw an attractive woman with long, auburn hair, aged in her late twenties and obviously far more distressed than the situation warranted.

'Look, it's all right. I've lost a bit of stuff, but neither of us are injured, so it can't be that bad. Calm yourself down!'

'I don' know you! You'sh not from round here,' she mumbled, slurring her words.

'If I was a cop,' Damien said, 'I'd swear that you were as drunk as a skunk!'

'A cop! Is you a copsh?' she said, fearfully. 'I'sh just goin' home. Really offisher! I'sh only live up the road.'

Cherry peered at him through what seemed like a mist, and he swayed and blurred in front of her eyes. She found it hard to keep her balance.

Erin saw her begin to stagger, and made to reach out and steady her, but she reacted and took a step back. The next minute she was in four feet of water, and coming up for air.

'You pusshed me,' she yelled, the moment she got her breath. 'You basshtard! You pusshed me!'

Damien knelt down on the edging and looked down into the water. She was about four feet below him and floundering around in the water. His first instinct was to laugh, but he suppressed it, as it didn't seem an appropriate reaction just at that moment. He looked down at himself, soaked to the skin already with the driving rain, and made a decision.

'Oh, stuff it!' he muttered, then jumped down into the water to help her. It was a little deeper than he thought it was. She was standing on the wheel of his trailer, so he found himself up to his armpits and struggling to keep his feet. The water was cold, and the shock of it to his system made him gasp. 'Hell, that's cold,' he wheezed, and reached out to help her get out of the water.

'Don't you dare touch me,' she screamed, suddenly sober with the effect of the dunking and the cold. 'You keep away from me!'

She swung her fist and caught him on the jaw with an uppercut that knocked him flat back into the water. He came up spluttering with rage.

'You stupid bitch! I'm just trying to help you. What do you think I jumped into the water for?'

'You might be trying to kill me,' she cried out, shrinking back into the safety of the underside of the trailer.

'Why the bloody hell would I want to kill you, you stupid cow,' he yelled, pushing his saturated hair back out of his eyes. 'Now we're both bloody soaked!'

'Well I'm not Liz Capel, and I'm not Mary Burton! You figure it out!'

Damien stood back and looked at her as if she was demented.

'I don't know what the fuck you're talking about! I've never heard of these people. I'm a stranger here. I'm just passing through, trying to get some petrol for god's sake!' He glared at her, and she glared back. Then she seemed to become unsure of herself.

'You what... petrol? At this time of night?'

'Yes, at this time of night. It may not occur to you country bumpkins, but there are people out there, travelling, driving along the great highways of this country at all hours of the day and night. Just because they don't all end up in Dark Harbour, this bloody madhouse, doesn't mean that they won't, occasionally, run out of petrol near here, and be forced to drive in looking for new supplies.'

Cherry was silent for a minute, trying to adjust her eyes so as to bring him into focus. Once she did, she realised that he wasn't bad looking, and on top of that he was also reasonably young. About thirty-two or three at a guess! And he was as mad as a cut snake!

'Well... if you say you're all right...'

'You mean, if I'm not a mad killer,' said Damien, a slight smile creasing the edge of his mouth. He had an old scar at the edge of his mouth that whitened when he smiled. Now he really looked attractive, she thought.

'Well get me out of here,' she said, holding out her hand.

They had to walk hand in hand along the wall for about fifty feet before there was a set of stone steps leading up onto the road. Once out of the water they stood there dripping, and looking rather sorry for themselves. It was still teeming down, and they both looked a little like drowned rats.

'Is that your stuff,' Cherry said inconsequentially, nodding at his gear floating away in the dark. He nodded.

'It was! It isn't any more! I should really try and salvage some of it.'

They both looked at the water, and then shook their heads in unison.

'I don't think there's much worth saving there,' she said. She looked up and down the road, and then giggled. 'You wouldn't believe this, but I was going the wrong way, anyway!'

Damien stared at her, and shook his head in disbelief. She noted his dark look and recovered herself.

'I'm really sorry! I suppose it was my fault. I'd just been to a Hens' night at the local pub, and thought I'd still be all right to drive. I guess I was wrong!'

'I guess you were,' he said, agreeing with her. 'Anyway, my name's Damien Curtis.' He held out his hand.

'I'm Cherry Reynolds,' she said, 'the goodtime girl of Dark Harbour.'

'So there's a pub in the town! I think I'd better go and get a room, and get dried off. I'm shivering fit to bust. I can always worry about the trailer tomorrow!'

'Yes, you're right. I think I'd better get going too. I'd offer you a room, but…'

'But you don't know me, and I might stave your head in with an axe in the night!' he replied, grinning.

'Something like that,' she said, backing away. 'If you're still around tomorrow, I'll come and apologise properly.'

'Fair enough,' he said, and watched as she got into her car, backed up, and drove off in the opposite direction to which she'd come. He looked ruefully again at the wreck of his trailer, and walked around to the driver's side of his car. As he did so, a shape loomed out of the darkness, and a fist came crashing out of the night and landed on his jaw. Damien suddenly found himself lying flat on his back, looking up into the shadow of a man standing over him. It was too dark to see his face.

'That's just a warning! We don't like foreigners around here; get my drift? You'd better be gone tomorrow!' The stranger then turned and disappeared as quickly as he'd appeared. Damien could hear his footsteps heading off in the opposite direction to the township, but by the time he got to his feet there was no sign of him.

He put his hand up to his lip, and found he was bleeding. There wasn't even a handkerchief to stem the flow of blood, so he wiped it on his sleeve. Looking around to make sure there were no other surprises lying in wait for him in the dark, he got into his car and locked the doors. Then he turned on the internal light, and checked himself out in the mirror. He was going to have a fat lip in the morning.

He started the car and drove along until he saw the lights of the Promenade Hotel, parked his car outside and went in by the Guest Entrance. A surly man in his fifties gave him the once over before he managed to tell him about the accident, and that he'd had to jump in to pull a woman out from the drink.

'What woman? What was her name,' said the man, showing a spark of interest.

'Cherry Reynolds,' Damien replied.

The man grunted.

'That figures,' he said, and turned away to get him a key.

It was one o'clock in the morning before he'd managed to have a shower and warm up, wrapping himself in a blanket while he hung his sorry clothes in front of a one bar heater to dry. He was going to look a right mess in the morning.

He checked his wallet, tentatively pulling out a sheaf of notes and peeling them carefully away from each other to let them dry. His credit cards were plastic, so they were intact. Seven hundred and forty two dollars and sixteen cents, he counted, though that didn't include his savings or credit balances.

Even though his savings book had been protected in a plastic cover, the water had got in at one end and begun to smear the numbers. He opened it up to the last page and watched the total beginning to blur before his eyes. Forty seven thousand three hundred and fifty two dollars and sixty-four cents! His total worldly wealth, thirty thousand of which had been part of the inheritance he'd received from his father's estate the year before. Luckily, Andrea hadn't managed to get her hands on it yet, and he'd been still debating what to do with it when his marriage collapsed.

He laid the book close to the fire, and watched as steam began to rise from the pages. What a disaster! Sitting on the edge of a strange bed, naked except for an old grey blanket, he remembered why he was there, and thought of Andrea for the first time since the accident. But then he caught a flashback of Cherry landing in the water, and to his surprise found himself laughing out loud. What a crazy cow! So she thought he was an axe murderer.

He pulled out his mobile phone and tried to get a signal. No service. This must be one of those places where you couldn't use a mobile. He laughed at the incongruence of his situation.

He wasn't laughing the following morning when he went out to his car, to find 'Piss Off!' scrawled in white paint across his windscreen! When he walked out into the road to get a better look, he saw that both tyres on the driver's side were as flat as a pancake.

II

Cherry Reynolds was still asleep when Patsy Donaldson called the next day, to see if Cherry had survived *virgo intactus* from the night before.

'Wake up, sleepy head,' she called out, rapping on Cherry's bedroom window. 'It's eleven thirty, time to *bee* up and making honey, Honey!'

Cherry finally roused herself from what seemed to be a thick, dark blanket across her brain, and staggered, dishevelled to the door.

'Oh for chrisesake, it's you! I thought it was important,' she muttered, staggering into the lounge and collapsing on the settee. She was asleep again in twelve seconds flat.

'Come on, Sleeping Beauty! I'll make you a coffee, and you can tell me all about it.' Patsy wandered off into the kitchen and made herself at home with Cherry's utensils. She made a show of clattering and banging about with the cups and spoons, and after a few minutes of this Cherry gave up and came to, wandering out to the kitchen to reduce any permanent damage Patsy might be inflicting on her kitchen.

'Sit yourself down right there and tell me all about it! Who is he? Is he good looking, and are you going to see him again?'

Cherry looked up at her, uncomprehending, and then the events of the previous evening came flooding back.

'Oooohhhh shit!' she said. 'Oooohhh shit, oh dear!' She was silent for a moment, and then she covered her eyes, and said more vehemently, 'Oh shit!'

'I take it that's a euphemism for '*oh shit, oh dear!*' Was it that bad?'

'Yes, it was that bad! I socked him in the jaw... I remember distinctly. I hit something – his trailer. Oh shit! It landed in the water, and all his stuff floated away!'

'So you *were* the culprit. I saw them all down there a while ago, trying to hoist the trailer out of the water. It looked like a total write-off to me!'

Cherry looked up, hopefully.

'What about his stuff?'

'I think he got a few soggy underpants back, some disintegrating hard-back novels and a coffee plunger. Someone said that everything he owned in the world was on the back of that trailer.'

'Have you seen him? Was he down there with them?'

'No. He'd gone off to buy some clothes. Lionel Jury said that he looked like he'd just crawled out of a tumble dryer. Even the dye had run in his shirt.'

'So you haven't seen him, then!'

'No, I think we've covered that. I haven't seen him. No!'

'Oh god! From what I remember, he may be gorgeous, Patsy. I'm not sure... my eyes might have been playing up, but once I got over the frightfuls I have a distinct impression that he smiled at me, and he was gorgeous!'

'Well, given the Ouzo, the Bourbon, the Vodka, and the fact that every man around here is the equivalent of Darth Vader, that could mean that he's passable, hasn't got a hair lip and can speak in sentences of more than one syllable.'

'You don't sound impressed, Patsy.'

'No more impressed than I was with Mr. Wonderful. Remember him?'

'You mean Bob Everard? Yes, I remember. That was the week I thought I might have to be fitted with bi-focals. As it turned out it was just a bad case of myopia. God, you're getting cynical in your old age, Patsy. It must be terrible to be over thirty!'

'No... it's terrible to be over thirty and still looking for Mister Right! Very disillusioning. I've even considered going to the city to find a fella, but then I'd have to live there, and who could make that sort of sacrifice, eh?'

They both sat for a while and sipped their coffee. Shortly the colour began to return to Cherry's cheeks, and she perked up.

'I remember now! I said that if he was still around today I'd go and apologise properly.'

'All is not completely lost, then. I suggest you make it soon, because the Klan has already struck its first blow at Mister whoever's enthusiasm. Some intelligent scribe painted 'piss off' across his windscreen this morning, and let down two of his tyres.'

'Where did you hear this? Oh, for god's sake, not again. If we could only find out who's behind this sort of thing, maybe we could run *him* out of town, on a plank.'

'What makes you think it's a 'him',' said Patsy. 'Maybe it's a 'her'. Maybe it's a jealous Lezzo who wants to keep us for herself!'

'A harem of spinsters,' Cherry grinned. 'If things don't get much better, I might just join!'

'I'd have to be a lot more hard up than I am at present,' said Patsy.

Cherry sat back and thought for a minute.

'So someone's trying to run him out of town. Seriously, I wonder why? Remember that guy last year, Trevor… what was his name? Trevor Scholes? No one ever did find out who beat him up, did they? Even if *he* knew, he wasn't telling. He was out of town and gone the next day, wouldn't even go to the local doctor to get treatment.'

'No, that was a bloody shame, that.' Patsy had quite fancied Trevor Scholes.

'Well give me five minutes and I'll throw some clobber on, and we'll go down and see if we can run into him. Damien Curtis, that's his name. It comes back to me now.'

'It's a wonder, after the number of brain cells you killed off last night. I'm surprised you can remember your *own* name!'

Down at the scene of the accident, the trailer had been hauled up onto the roadway. As the two women approached in Cherry's battered car, Damien rolled up from the other direction. This time he was dressed in a new pair of Jeans and a new short-sleeved shirt. He even had new sneakers on his feet, so it looked as if he'd had to replace everything.

They got out of the car at the same time, and the moment he recognised her, he made the sign of the vampire, and staggered back, mockingly.

'Oh, charming,' said Patsy. 'He's a real card, this one!'

'Good morning ladies,' he ventured, once they got close. 'I haven't been introduced,' he said, indicating Patsy. Cherry hastened to correct the problem.

'Oh, this is my friend Patsy Donaldson. She was one of the guests at the Hen Party last night – and if she'd stayed to look after me, maybe this wouldn't have happened,' she said, accusingly.

'Listen to her,' said Patsy. 'She was doing a fan dance on the bar when I left, and about to sink another Ouzo and lemonade.'

'Liar,' laughed Cherry. 'Anyway, this is Damien Curtis, Patsy.'

'Pleased to meet you, I'm sure,' Patsy said, shaking his hand. 'Where did you appear from… is this a normal apparition, or do you always materialise in country towns at midnight, driving the poor inhabitants witless, and inciting them to ram your car?'

'No, I usually confine myself to the suburbs as a matter of fact. This is my first foray into the land of drunken Amazons and rampaging Commodores.'

They all laughed. Cherry adopted a more serious expression.

'You must have hit your lip last night, when you jumped into the water after me. You'll have to excuse me, I was suffering from galloping paranoia last night!'

Damien touched his lip, and grimaced.

'No, that wasn't it at all. Just after you drove off, some Crazy loomed up out of the rain and just about laid me out. He caught me totally off guard, and left me lying in the road.'

Patsy and Cherry looked at each other in shock

'Do you mean to say you were attacked?' said Cherry. 'How awful!'

'Not only attacked, but warned off,' said Damien. 'He stood over me and informed me in no uncertain terms, that strangers were not welcome in your little town, and that if I valued my health I should be gone by today.'

'You're joking,' said Patsy, aghast.

'Unbelievable,' muttered Cherry. 'What are you going to do about it… I mean; have you been to see the local policeman. He's only just around the corner.'

'Naah! Hardly worth it! Just some bloody looney from the pub, I suppose!'

'It wouldn't have been Charlie…' said Cherry, looking knowingly at Patsy.

'No! What for? He fancies you, but I don't think he really believes he has a chance… do you?'

'No, I don't,' said Cherry. 'What about 'Rigor Mortis'; he's a queer one!'

Patsy shook her head.

'I take it, then, that you're not married,' Damien said, looking at Cherry.

'You'd take it that neither of us are married,' said Patsy, preening herself. It's hard to get married where the women outnumber the men, and what men there are were left over from Noah's Ark!'

Damien grinned.

'You paint a very black picture of this town.'

'It's hardly a town, is it Patsy? Just a little settlement for dropouts and genuine nature lovers!'

'Well, can I interest you ladies in a spot of lunch at your local watering hole,' Damien grinned. 'Seeing as you're not married, and I won't find myself on the wrong end of a couple of irate husbands.'

'You mean the Promenade? That sounds all right to me, what do you think, Patsy?'

'They don't do a bad lunch,' said Patsy, 'and although our appointment books are absolutely bulging at this time of the day, I think we can spare you an hour or three.'

Damien grinned, and drove back to the pub, the girls following in Cherry's dented Commodore.

III

Craig Mortimer had been a busy boy, once he'd tidied up the deck of the 'Vagabond'. Erin had cued him up to be ready at seven o'clock the following morning for a quick trip out to empty the craypots, and normally he would have raced off home for a few hours of shuteye before getting up again at six. This time he made his way through the sleeping town in the rain, and hauled up at Ilse Hirsch's cottage at one-thirty in the morning. Ignoring the fact that the lady might be sound asleep, he tapped on the door, and after considerable persistence the door opened to allow him entry. No light was turned on, and the door was not shut firmly behind him. After fifteen minutes he re-emerged, looking rather pleased with himself.

On the way back he called in at the Promenade Hotel, and caught the licensee just before he turned in for the night. Frank Kelly wasn't exactly overjoyed to see him at that time of night, but after a few muttered sentences he led him back to the little office under the stairs, and they remained engaged in whispered conversation for just under fifteen minutes. By the time he re-emerged into the street, someone had scrawled 'Piss Off' across the Falcon parked outside the hotel, and had let down two of the driver's side tyres. Craig grinned to himself and made his way home to the little one bedroom cottage that he shared with his dog, on the south side of the township.

At 34, life had not been kind to Craig Mortimer. He had left school early, and spent time in the merchant service before irregularities in ship provisions persuaded him to look for other forms of work. He had tried his hand variously as a salesman, a factory worker, a mechanic and a night watchman, not to mention various storeman positions. His first wife had left him after eighteen months, alleging mental and physical abuse, including strange sexual practices that did not fit in with her respectable suburban upbringing. His next relationship was with a prostitute, and he lived off her income for a while until she became tired of him, and eloped with a Vietnamese pimp. His parents died in a light plane crash and left him just enough to put a deposit down on his cottage, but very little else. The majority of their property went to his sister. He had drifted in to Dark Harbour in a last attempt to make some sense out of his life, and just stayed. A fascination with the town's single woman doctor had helped to keep him there, and he had no plans to change his situation... not just yet, anyway.

Craig Mortimer didn't always crew on the 'Vagabond'. He hired himself out to anyone who would have him, which meant that on some days he would be out scale fishing, and on others he would be assisting on a prawn boat. All the boaties knew him, and as there was a lack of regular labour in and around Dark Harbour, Craig was rarely out of work. When the boats weren't out, he'd work in the fish processing plant, along with up to twenty others from the town. It was all casual work, but it was an income.

He wasn't a popular figure, nevertheless. There was something shifty and vaguely untrustworthy about him, and he was seen as a last resort except for the most menial of tasks. He'd bought his cottage two years before, and even though he'd earned good money on the boats, he constantly seemed to be in financial difficulty. Twice the bank had threatened to foreclose on his mortgage, and he'd lost his car to a bailiff only a month before. He was constantly on the lookout for a new source of income.

The following day, as Erin steered the 'Vagabond' out into the bay, Craig stood beside him in the wheelhouse.

'What are you going to do with those photographs, mate? Did they all stick together, or did you manage to get them pulled apart?'

Erin looked at him in surprise.

'What made you think of them? To tell you the truth, I carted them home, put them down on the bench outside the back door, and clean forgot about them. I suppose they'll be one big soggy lump by now!'

'That's a shame,' said Craig, staring fixedly out to sea.

'Why's that?'

'Oh, it's just that I think I know who all that stuff belongs to. Some new bloke; just passing through town last night! Cherry Reynolds was with your missus last night, wasn't she?'

'Yeah, that's right. They had a Hens' Night at the pub. Why?'

'Oh nothin'. Just that she had a prang with this guy, knocked his trailer over the edge of the seawall, and tipped all his stuff into the water. I reckon he'd be pretty pissed off!'

'So that's where all that stuff came from! So you reckon they're his family photo's… shit! I should have separated them. I was just so bloody stuffed; I went in and straight to bed. I couldn't be pissing around half the night with someone else's old photo's!'

'No, mate, I can understand that. What if I offer to do them? I can pick them up on the way back and soak them apart, then dry them out.'

Craig looked at Erin, hopefully. Erin returned the look, but with an element of suspicion.

''Why this sudden philanthropic urge? What's in it for you? I've never known you to be the Good Samaritan type. Do you know this bloke?'

Craig pulled a face, as if embarrassed.

'No, I don't know him. But the poor sod just lost everything he owned, and you know what people are like about old photo's. There might be a reward!'

Erin nodded his head in enlightenment.

'You cunning bastard! You're the only bloke I know that would even think about something like that. Yeah, sure… take the bloody things. It's no skin off my nose!'

Craig smiled, but stuttered a reply.

'Oh, th.thanks! You know what it's like… I just need every cent I can get, mate. You have to keep your eye out for the main chance!'

'Yes, I know what it's like,' said Erin.

Privately, Craig slipped even lower in his esteem than the place he already occupied, which was just about rock bottom. There was something a little distasteful about Craig's endless pursuit of the almighty dollar. He was a bit of a prat, really.

They went on to pull the pots, all twenty-four of them, and managed a haul of 96 crays, ranging from Jumbo's to mediums. Erin was well pleased. This should go a long way to keep Katie in the manner she obviously expected. He was in a good mood all the way home.

Chapter Four

Katie Carstairs woke up that morning in a similar condition to Cherry. Erin had gone, long before she opened her eyes, and the hammer pounding in her brain forced her up and out to search for the aspirin in the kitchen drawer. She took two, then drank two cups of coffee in a row, and smoked four cigarettes. This got her sluggish metabolism to the state where she was able to fall into the shower, and complete the restoration process.

'Never again,' she mumbled.

When Emily Longstaff called in, bearing gifts of vitamin C, Katie was looking almost human, though she still had to put her head under the hair dryer. Emily waited patiently while that was accomplished, and read a magazine to pass the time. When Katie walked out all fresh and blooming, Emily put the magazine aside.

'Did you hear about Cherry?' she said.

Katie looked at her quizzically, and shook her head.

'No, I didn't think so. We all missed the drama last night. When Cherry left the pub – only about ten minutes after we did, or so I heard – she was so cut that she drove straight into some visitor to the town who was coming in, looking for petrol.'

'What? At that hour of the night?'

'Seems he was about to run out. Anyway! She hit his trailer and knocked it over the wall into the sea. Luckily it didn't take his car with it. But all his stuff broke loose and floated out into the bay. They reckon he lost everything. He was on his way to live in some new place, and the road stopped here.'

'God! Is Cherry all right?'

'She was all right this morning. As a matter of fact, I saw her and Patsy going into the Promenade with this fellow in tow. So he can't be too cut up about the accident.'

'Maybe they were just going for a goodwill drink.'

'No – to lunch, I think. He's not a bad looking fellow!'

'Not as good-looking as Erin though,' said Katie, coquettishly.

Emily looked at Katie speculatively.

'Your Erin isn't everyone's cup of tea, Katie. He can be a little brusque at times! Still, he's what you want, so there's an end of it.'

Emily didn't get along with Erin. She'd been Katie's confidante all through the marriage saga, and had been privy to conversations that were really none of her business. His hard-headed brand of common sense smacked of a lack of malleability, and if there was one characteristic that reminded Emily of her own husband, it was a lack of malleability.

Katie sighed.

'Oh well, that's probably a good thing. If all the loose women in Dark Harbour were after him, I don't suppose I'd stand a chance.'

Emily bristled at that.

'Hey! Watch who you're calling a loose woman! I'll have you know that I'm pretty tight where it counts. Ask my old man!'

Katie grinned, and lit a fifth cigarette.

'So what's the plan for the day,' she went on, trying to remember whether or not they'd already made plans.

'You haven't forgotten! God, girl, it was only last night. You said you were going out to see your mother today, and to brave your father's wrath. Don't you remember... you asked me to come along for moral support!'

'That's right. So I did,' said Katie, looking troubled. She wished now that she'd kept her mouth shut. Her father was a surly drunk, who had wiped her off his welcome list years ago. In her late teens she had been a vociferous protector of her mother, every time that he came home drunk. On more than one occasion she had locked him out of the house until he sobered up, and on one horrendous night when he had kicked the door in, she had called the police. That had resulted in him spending a night in the cells, for which he had never forgiven her.

'I don't know why she never left him, you know,' she said to Emily. 'He was a right bastard when I was young. If ever a woman should have left a man, that woman should have been my mother! I could never understand it.'

Emily raised an eyebrow, which was always a preparatory to some cynical remark.

'She obviously loved it, Katie. Some women are built like that. They need the drama; it gets the old adrenalin flowing. So much better when you're making up in bed, later!'

'What, with a black eye? Sure!'

'You're pretty naïve sometimes. I tell you that there are a lot of women out there who have put up with a lot worse than your mother, yet would never testify against their husbands in court, even around here. I don't know why it is. Maybe they lead such humdrum lives that it at least gives them something to break the monotony, something to bitch about to their friends. There's something about being seen as a martyr!'

'You think they thrive on other people's sympathy.'

'Something like that! It also places them frequently as the centre of attention. Haven't you ever seen a group of women vying with each other to tell the goriest tale about their health, or their operation? Women are always trying to outdo each other – you should know that. What did you just say about Erin, and loose women, just a while ago?'

Katie nodded.

'Maybe you're right. But that doesn't make me feel any better about going out there and braving my father's sneers.'

'You're lucky to have one,' said Emily. 'My folks died years ago.'

Katie looked at Emily, with her greying hair and her sad eyes, and suddenly thought that she had never figured on Emily having parents at all. She had always just been!

'Did you get on with *your* father?'

'You mean, did *he* get on with *me*? Sure he did! Every time my Mum was asleep, he'd sneak in and stick his fingers up you-know-where, then bend me over the bath tub and sodomise me with the soap.'

Katie looked at the older woman in horror.

'*You're joking*!'

Emily looked at her appraisingly.

'I don't joke about things like that!'

'But that's terrible,' said Katie, sidetracked for the moment from her own concerns. 'So why would you say I'm lucky to have one – a father, I mean?'

'Well, I still loved him. He was my Dad, you know, and you only get one. So he had a few flaws in his character – don't we all?'

'Yes – but *that*!'

'Oh, I don't know! He gave me a taste to be sodomised when I got older, which is fortunate as it turns out, because that's all my old man is ever interested in. That's probably the only reason my marriage has survived as long as it has.'

'You surprise me, Emily,' said Katie, blushing. 'I never think of you in relation to having sex, especially kinky sex.'

'Is there any other kind,' said Emily, smiling sardonically. 'Just because I'm twenty years older than you doesn't mean that I've given up living. Though I must admit, I wouldn't mind an affair. I quite fancy Igor, you know!'

Katie suppressed a giggle.

'What on earth could you see in him? He's weird!'

'No, he's Welsh – there *is* a difference. I love his accent. It's so musical! He could sodomise me any time he likes!'

'Emily!' Katie squealed, holding her ears in mock horror. 'You're corrupting me!'

As it turned out, the visit wasn't anywhere near as bad as she'd feared. After answering the door of the small, neat cottage where they lived, Katie's father retired to the shed, and didn't come out again until after she'd left. She was actually able to spend a bit of quality time with her mother, without them being interrupted all the time.

'I just came out to invite you to the wedding Mum. I'm finally getting married!'

Mrs. Carstairs looked a little troubled.

'Are you sure this is what you want, Katie? There's no shame these days in just living together, you know.'

'Yes, I know that. What do you think we've been doing for the past eight months? But... I've got something to tell you, Mum. I think I'm pregnant.'

Mrs Carstairs face lit up, and after the congratulations and mutual hugs were over, she said: 'Perhaps I should go and tell your father that he's going to be a grandfather, Katie!'

Katie shook her head, firmly.

'No! You tell him nothing, Mum. I don't want him near my child! You can come over on your own, occasionally.'

Mrs Carstairs put on a brave smile, and looked somewhat troubled again.

'Maybe it's time that you two put your differences behind you, dear. You know, he doesn't show it, but your father is terribly hurt by your attitude to him.'

'Is he, really? Well, he brought it on himself. He should have kept off the booze, and kept his fists in his pocket, shouldn't he.'

Katie refused to go and say goodbye to her father when she left. Her mother drew her aside at the door, just as she was leaving.

'It wasn't really as bad as you think, Katie,' she said. 'Not really!'

II

Andrea was standing, staring out of a first floor grimy window when John returned to the pokey one bedroom flat. She turned to look at him as he entered, but she could tell by his downcast expression that he had struck a blank. She looked out again at the factory wall, blocking their view.

'Can't you get these windows cleaned, John. This place is putrid!'

John was distracted.

'What... windows? Oh, those! I've never really bothered. I'm not here most of the time anyway. It's just a place to hang my hat.'

'Well I hope you don't expect me to put up with these sorts of conditions. It's not exactly what I'm used to.'

'No, that's right. You're more the Buckingham Palace type, aren't you,' he replied, facetiously.

The close, loving relationship, that Andrea had deserted her marriage for had taken exactly three days to disintegrate into a litany of name-calling, backbiting, and scorn. It was one thing to get caught up in the excitement of secret rendezvous and clandestine love-making in untenanted office blocks, quite another to wake up in a dismal flat, with no creature comforts, and a partner that had to keep disappearing to earn his daily bread.

'So you couldn't find him,' she said. 'He's gone!'

John Inglis nodded his head, and looked glumly about him.

'Yeah! It seems he loaded the trailer up yesterday, and took off, destination unknown. I feel bloody terrible about it.'

Andrea nodded.

'How do you think I feel? I had a year and a half invested in that marriage!'

'But you told me you loved *me*!'

John sank into an old armchair, and looked at her uncomprehendingly. Andrea walked purposefully over towards him, and crossed her arms.

'Look, John, I think we'd better admit it, before it goes any further. This has all been a dreadful mistake. You miss your old friend; I miss my husband. We've been a couple of idiots between us, and now we've made a right mess of things and Damien's gone off somewhere – god knows where – and we're going to have to find him and sort things out. It's the only thing to do!'

'He'll never talk to me again!'

'Oh, don't be soft. He'll be so glad to have me back that he'll soon get over any animosity he holds towards you. You're his oldest friend, after all. Be positive!'

John shook his head, sadly.

'He'll never talk to me again!'

Andrea shrugged her shoulders impatiently, and went back to the window.

'I don't know how you can live like this, John. I had you picked for a smart, upwardly mobile executive. But look at this; you're a slob!'

'That's what my mother always told me,' John said, not caring now, one way or the other. He had chanced his arm, and lost. Whatever happened from now on was purely academic.

'Well, I'm going home. Of course, I might not *have* a home for long, because the one who paid the rent is no longer with us. You're going to have to put your hand in your pocket and help me out until Damien gets home.'

John looked at her, incredulously.

'You're not serious!'

Andrea rounded on him, angrily.

'Of course I'm serious, John. What do you think? I don't have an income! You got me into this mess, now you can help me get out of it.'

John shook his head, and Andrea felt a sinking feeling in her stomach.

'Even if I could, I would hardly fork out for a woman who has just left me. Be real! Anyway, the pure economic facts of the matter are that I can't. That BMW out there takes sixty per cent of my income. It's all that I care about!'

'Well the BMW might just have to go, John. I have to be able to survive!'

'Oh yes,' said John, sarcastically, 'we can't have little Andrea put out, can we? The fact that she's always lived like a leech on the backs of others, and has never contributed so much as an hour's work to her own upkeep... well, that's only her due, isn't it, babe? Believe it or not, there are a million housewives out there who lie on their backs and wave their legs in the air every day, and not one of them expects to get paid for it!'

Andrea went white with rage.

'Why, you little bastard! How dare you talk to me like that!'

'How would you like me to talk to you? Maybe it's time you listened to a few home truths. There's a four-letter word, Andrea, that you never seem to be able to get your tongue around. It's called 'Work!' Go out and get a job, Andrea. Get out there and become a useful member of society, make your own way. If you had, maybe Damien wouldn't have had to struggle so hard to make ends meet. After all, you never thought to curtail *your* spending, did you?'

'I refuse to listen to any more of your disgusting babble. How I could ever see anything in you is beyond me. I must have had a brainstorm.' She sat down heavily, and burst into tears.

'Oh, here we go. Daddy's little girl isn't getting her own way, so on with the waterworks. Is that what you used to do as a kid, Andrea? Did you always get your own way?'

As if in answer, Andrea got to her feet, grabbed her bag and headed for the door. She paused for a moment at the threshold and looked back, delivering a scathing look at her erstwhile lover. Perhaps he would call her back. Maybe he would panic, have a change of heart.

John looked at her sullenly from his chair, then raised his hand and put one finger up. His meaning was more than clear, and Andrea turned and left, slamming the door behind her.

III

Cherry and Patsy excused themselves to go and see to their war paint in the ladies, while Damien sauntered over to the bar to order for the three of them. He ordered drinks first.

'I'll just have a beer, and the two ladies would like lemon squashes. They tell me they had a bit of a wild night here last night, so they're on the wagon for a few days.'

Frank Kelly just grunted, as if he didn't feel like discussing locals with a stranger. He was a big, surly man, built like a rugby player gone to seed.

'That'll be four-eighty,' he said, took Damien's note and turned to the till. When he turned back, Damien ordered butterfish and salad for the three of them.

'I suppose you'll be moving on this afternoon,' said the Hotelier, looking up at him, searchingly.

'Moving on?' Damien laughed. 'Oh, hell no! I'm just beginning to enjoy myself. I was going to ask you if there were any cottages to rent around here, preferably near the sea?'

'No – nothing,' the barman replied. 'Never has been! The only way you get to live here is if you buy one!'

Damien nodded.

'Well, that's not beyond the bounds of possibility! I've got nowhere else to go. What do they run into around here? How much, I mean?'

'I don't think there's any for sale,' Frank said, staring at him with what appeared to be undisguised hostility. 'In fact, I'm sure there's not. The last cottage sold here was about eighteen months ago, and that was to a local who'd been away for a few years, and was just coming home.'

Damien picked up the drinks, and looked the barman squarely in the eye.

'Are you trying to tell me something? I've already had one message, scribbled on my car.'

'That was nothing to do with me, mate,' said Frank, shaking his head. 'But I can tell you, the locals here are a provincial bunch. They like each other's company, and they don't like outsiders. It takes twenty years to be accepted around here. Believe me, I've been here for twenty-five.'

'Typical country town, you reckon!'

'No – not typical! It's a one-off, this place. Mainly fishing and farming, and if you don't fit into one of those two brackets, then it stands to reason you're not going to fit in. Let's just say that we don't have the problems of other towns, and we want to keep it that way. Why import a problem?'

Damien nodded, and returned to the table. Cherry and Patsy were just returning from the ladies.

'Well, I've just been warned off again,' he said, in a low voice. 'What is it about this town?'

Cherry shook her head.

'You mean Frank? Don't take any notice of him. He's like a bear with a sore head most of the time. If there was another pub in town he'd have gone broke by now.'

'She's right,' said Patsy. 'He just runs with the pack. There's a hard core of them that get together every Thursday night, get drunk and talk about what's good for the town. They never ask us, do they, Cherry?'

'That's for sure... but of course, we're just women, what would we know?'

'Sounds like a bit of a male hierarchy,' said Damien.

The meals were delivered, and they were three-quarters through them when the questions regarding Damien's background began to surface.

'What's your story, then,' said Patsy. 'You didn't just materialise at the town limits, so where did you come from?'

'Do you really want to know,' said Damien. 'I told you, I came from the suburbs!'

'Yeah, we know that, but… other things. What do you do – for a living, I mean? What brings you to Dark Harbour?'

'What you really mean is, are you married,' said Damien, with a devilish grin.

'Yeah, well… we did wonder. Are you married - or something?'

'Yes I am married; no we are not together; yes I am looking for somewhere new to live; and yes, I am nursing a broken heart. My wife ran off with my best friend!'

'That was a mouthful,' said Cherry. 'How long ago did this happen? Years, months, weeks?'

'About three or four days ago! She took off with a friend of mine I'd known since High School!'

Cherry and Patsy exchanged glances.

'Baggage!' said Patsy.

'Definitely!' said Cherry. 'What a shame!'

Damien laughed.

'Hang on; hang on! What are you on about - baggage?'

'You're carrying too much baggage at the moment to be of any use to us. We thought you might be a genuine proposition, but it'll take a couple of years before you're marketable again.'

'Is that right,' he laughed. 'You've really got it all worked out, haven't you, down to the 't'?'

'That's life,' said Patsy. 'After a break-up, you've got too much crap in your head to be able to concentrate on forging a new relationship, so the new woman in your life usually spends months listening to your tale of woe, then you go off and marry someone else.'

'True,' said Cherry. 'We see it all the time!'

'Or you go back to *the bitch* for another dose of misery,' said Patsy.

'Is that why you're not married,' he asked.

'Pretty much,' she replied. 'There's not much point in expending that much energy on the other half's past relationship, with no chance of future reward.'

'Whatever happened to no pain, no gain?' Damien smiled.

'It's a crock,' said Patsy. 'Invented by men so they can dump on women!'

'You really are cynical,' said Damien, shaking his head. 'Are all the women here like you?'

'Most of them... the unmarried ones, anyway! Or should I say, those not in a relationship, and there's plenty of *them*!'

'In answer to your next question, about fifteen! We added it all up once, didn't we Patsy?'

Damien shook his head.

'I tell you what, I'll just sit back here, and you two can supply the questions *and* the answers… it seems to work better!'

'Cheeky bastard,' Cherry grinned. 'Well, what are you going to do now? Bugger off I suppose, like all the new blood ever does around here.'

Damien sat back and put his hands behind his head, and stared at the ceiling for a while. Then he sat up again.

'No! Stuff it! I'm getting too many warnings, and that tends to put my back up. Besides, if there are fifteen vacant women around here, that might just be what I need at the moment to soothe my tortured soul! I like what I see so far, so if I can find somewhere to stay, I might just do that!'

'That's another problem,' said Patsy. 'Lack of accommodation!'

'I don't know,' said Cherry. 'There's not much to rent, admittedly, but there are a few places for sale. They've been on the market for a long time now, for obvious reasons, but… if you approached the executors you might just be able to convince them to let you rent them.'

'What do you mean, for obvious reasons? Are they rat infested or something?'

'No – nothing like that!'

'What then – haunted? Your happy barman over there just told me there was nothing, not even for sale!'

Patsy and her friend exchanged glances, and Cherry raised one eyebrow as if to say, *'should I?'*

There was an ominous silence. Finally Patsy spoke.

'We don't usually talk about it! It's a bit of a sensitive subject around here, and we don't want it in the newspapers or we'd have hordes of sightseers plaguing the place, and that's something none of us want.'

'I can assure you that I have no interests in Fairfax, and no desire to spread rumours. I just want a place to live!'

Cherry spoke.

'Well, if you promise to keep it to yourself. There's the cottage that Liz Capel used to live in. That's still empty, but I think her furniture's still there. She disappeared about, what, Patsy, eight months ago?'

'Yeah, about eight months!'

'Liz Capel! Isn't that the name you yelled at me the other night, when we were in the water? And another one…'

'Mary Burton! Yes, that's right. You were freaking me out. Both of them disappeared from this town without trace. We think they were murdered, but no-one's ever found a body.'

Damien pulled a face.

'Maybe they just moved. Maybe they just went off to live in the city?'

'What… and leave all their stuff behind. Not likely. Mary Burton was on her way to Patsy's place one night, about twelve months ago. She'd just spoken to her on the phone, hadn't you Patsy?'

Patsy nodded her head.

'It was nine o'clock, and Mary phoned me up. She was trying to make lamingtons, and she wasn't having much luck with the icing. She'd also run out of grated coconut. I had a spare packet in the cupboard, and she said she'd just pop over and pick it up. Anyway, she didn't turn up. I phoned her at nine-thirty, to find out what had happened - no answer! I phoned again at ten - no answer! In the end I walked around there, at about twenty past ten. The front door was wide open; the oven was off. All the lights were on. No Mary!'

'So you knew her well, this Mary?'

'Oh, hell yes! We'd known each other from kids. So did Cherry!'

'So what happened?'

'Well, the next day I called the local copper out, Jack Izzard - there's only one around here – and he made enquiries. That's when it got scary!'

Damien waited for her to continue.

'He came back and said that there was nothing suspicious about it. Mary had just decided to take off for somewhere else, and had exercised her right to privacy. She didn't want anyone to know where she'd gone. He said she'd been upset over a love affair, but we knew that she hadn't had a love affair for at least six months, because we girls know these things. We talk… you know?'

'So where did the policeman get his information from?'

'He said that he had reliable information from sources in the town, and that the matter was closed.'

'Didn't anyone press the issue,' said Damien. He could feel the hairs rising on the back of his neck.

'Cherry tried. She was pretty well told to mind her own business, weren't you, Cherry?'

'Yes, true! Every time someone brought it up they got pooh-poohed by the Klan, so in the end it just got brushed under the carpet. A month later, a moving van pulled up at her cottage, and emptied it out. When her neighbour asked one of the removalists where they were taking her stuff, he refused to answer. She phoned the local policeman, but he wasn't there at the time. Later, she went to see him and he said not to worry, he knew all about it, and everything was all right. That neighbour was Elizabeth Capel!'

'You're joking – the other one that disappeared?'

'That's right! She disappeared a couple of weeks later, after she had been making noises around town about Mary Burton, and that she was going to go to the authorities in Adelaide.'

'God! This sounds terrible. Do you think this local copper is behind it... and if so, why for chrisesake? It doesn't make sense!'

'You're right about that! But it's put the female population on edge around here, I can tell you that!'

'So both of these cottages are vacant?'

'Yes. Like I said, Liz's still has her furniture in it. She was officially listed as a missing person, not like Mary. I don't know whether it's for sale yet, or not, but I could find out. Mary's is empty, and I think you might be able to rent that, if you can contact the executors. I believe it's being handled by a solicitor, who also acts as a real estate agent. A guy, name of Raymond Massey! He's got an office in the main street, but he's only here one day a week. Fridays, isn't it, Patsy?'

'Yeah – Fridays!'

'That means I'll have to hang about for another couple of days at the Hotel.'

'It'll be worth it, if you can get a cottage.'

'Well I'd certainly like to. I just hope the locals don't make a habit of defacing my car every night.'

'That was probably just a one-off. I can't see it happening again. Here! ... if you like, we'll go for a drive and show you around town, and some of the local sights. We can also show you the two cottages. It might help you to make up your mind.'

'So you want me to stay then, despite the baggage.' He was looking directly at Cherry when he said this, and she blushed slightly and looked away.

'Of course we do! Just don't go running off with any of the others,' said Patsy. 'We were first, and we want first crack at you.'

They all started laughing, and Cherry looked even more embarrassed.

'You really come out with things at times, Patsy,' she said. 'You should wear a sash with 'Miss Blabbermouth' plastered all over it!'

'I'm beginning to like this, being the centre of attention. It's a nice change for me,' said Damien. 'You know, I haven't thought about *the bitch* for over two hours. Keep this up and you might have me cured.'

'Down boy,' said Cherry. 'There's a way to go yet!'

Damien went up to the bar to settle the bill, and while there decided to pay up front for his room.

'How much for another two days in the room? I'll want it at least until Friday, maybe longer.'

Frank Kelly looked at him grimly, and shook his head.

'Sorry mate, no can do! I've got the Pest Controllers coming in this evening. You'll have to be out of your room by six o'clock tonight.'

Damien looked aghast.

'Well, haven't you got another room. Surely they're not doing the entire Hotel.'

'They are, as far as you're concerned, mate! Sorry, but that's the way it is!'

'Well, that's a bloody ridiculous way to run a business, isn't it? Who's leaning on you – the same bloke that hit me last night, or the coward that smeared paint on my windscreen?'

'Nothing to do with me, fella! Just pick up your bags and go!'

'You've been a real sport,' said Damien. 'I'll recommend you to all my friends!'

Frank Kelly turned his back and disappeared through into the bar. He wasn't going to be drawn any further on the subject.

When Damien caught up with the girls in the street outside, he told them what had just transpired.

'You what? You can't stay there? I'll bloody see about this,' said Cherry. 'Pest Controllers my eye!'

She stormed back into the Hotel, leaving the other two bemused on the pavement.

'What's all this crap about, Frank? You won't rent Damien a room 'til the weekend!'

'What I do in this pub is my business, Miss Reynolds.'

'I can't believe you would be so petty. What have you got against him? He's perfectly innocuous, hasn't done anything to anybody. Why try to get rid of him?'

Frank leaned over the counter, and stared her in the eye.

'If I were you, I would keep out of things that you don't know anything about. It's healthier that way.'

Cherry took a step backwards.

'Are you threatening me? That sounds like a direct threat! How would you like me to go around the corner and see Jack Izzard, and tell him what you just said?'

'If that's what you want to do, go for it. But don't forget that you have to live in this town, and if you start to give me any trouble I'll bar you from this pub… for life! And don't think I can't. You'll have to go a long way for a drink!'

Cherry came flying out of the door of the pub and into the street, as white as a ghost. Patsy looked alarmed, and when she went over to Cherry to find out what was wrong, Cherry just shook her head, and swallowed hard.

'Let's get out of here,' she muttered, and they climbed into Damien's car and set off for a tour of the area.

Chapter Five

Wilf Carstairs stayed out in the shed until his daughter, Katie, and her friend, had gone. He gave it ten minutes then went back into the house and sat down at the kitchen table to read the paper. When his wife walked in a few minutes later to put the kettle on, he affected an air of disinterest about the visit.

'That was nice dear, to get a visit from our Katie!'

Wilf just grunted, and turned to the sports page. Meg looked at him nervously, out of the corner of her eye. She didn't dare push the issue, but she desperately wanted to impart the news, and try and talk him round so that she wouldn't have to attend the wedding on her own. Wilf was a difficult man to deal with, but over the years she had usually found a way to get through to him, though occasionally it had backfired, and she'd paid the price.

'Would you like a cup of coffee while I've got the kettle on,' she ventured. It always paid to soften him up first.

He looked up.

'Yes. Why not? That would be nice!'

Despite his crusty exterior, Wilf could be extremely generous, and in his sober moments he was always courteous and affectionate to his wife. That was what Katie always overlooked, Meg thought. The good times! When she weighed everything in the balance, the reason she hadn't left him was that Wilf was a good provider and a good companion, as long as he stayed off the grog. These days he confined his drinking to the times spent out on the Prawn Trawler that he had operated from Dark Harbour for the past thirty years. Of the six trawlers in the Fishing Fleet that operated out of the Harbour, his was the only Prawn Boat. That was probably because prawns were not plentiful in their part of the gulf, and others who had chanced their luck there had moved on to better grounds, some going as far up the east coast as Sydney. He had decided to stay, and it had paid off because, with only one boat operating, there was always enough for a decent catch.

Mind you, there had been hard times, and plenty of them. Back a few years, when the competition had been tough, and he had sometimes been too drunk to take the boat out, they had almost gone bankrupt. In those times the bailiffs had just about set up camp in their garden, and Meg had spent the days terrified that they were going to force their way in and take the television and the washing machine. Thank god those days were behind them.

Over the past two years, fortune had seemed to smile on them. Wilf didn't have to go out as much as before, and yet there was always plenty of money coming in, and she lacked for nothing. She even had her own car these days to take for long shopping trips into the city, and Wilf didn't seem to begrudge her the money. If only he and Katie could patch up their differences!

'Katie was saying that she's finally going to tie the knot,' she said, conversationally, as she put his coffee in front of him. She put her tea on the table, and sat down opposite him. Wilf looked up with a thoughtful look on his face.

'You mean marriage... to that Erin wacker? Oh that's great!' he said, sarcastically.

He and Erin didn't exactly get along. Erin had heard enough about Wilf's earlier antics from Katie to give him a jaundiced view of her father, and that was in addition to a philosophical divide when it came to the subject of fishing. Erin maintained that the Prawn Trawlers were destructive to the gulf, in the way that they dragged chain along the bottom to induce the prawns to rise into their nets.

'It's your bloody chains that are killing off the habitat on the floor of the gulf, Wilf. You do inestimable damage down there! The chains rip up the weed, and turn the bottom into a desert. Another ten years of that, and there won't be any fish left to worry about.'

Wilf waved him away, impatiently.

'What the hell would you know, you Johnny-come-lately's! I've been fishing this gulf for nearly forty years, thirty in a Prawn Boat. Nothing's ever changed. If anything, it's all these bloody recreational fishermen with their pissy little tinny's who are depleting the fish stocks. There's bloody thousands of them! It stands to reason that if they all take their quota, that's all the less for you to pull out of the water. Anyway, why should you care? You've got twenty-four craypots. What do you want with scale fish?'

'You don't see it, do you? You can't take anything in isolation down there; it's an interdependent fishery. Scale fish, prawns, rock lobsters, blue swimmer crabs, abalone; they all depend on their environment being protected. You're the only bugger tearing up the bottom!'

'Well tell Fisheries about it, and stop bleating in my ear. Their studies tell me you're wrong. It's not the chains, mate!'

Meg sipped her tea, and tried to gauge how far she could push the subject. Wilf gave her an opening by wading in with his age-old criticism of his daughter.

'The trouble with 'our Katie' as you insist on calling her, is that she's all out for herself. She's a greedy little cow... nothing's ever enough for her. She was half the problem when she was living here with us. I couldn't keep up with her incessant demands. She seemed to think that we had a bottomless pit of money to be splashing about, when in actual fact we were going through pretty hard times.'

'But all that's in the past, dear,' said Meg, reaching out tentatively to touch his hand. 'I wish that you and she could make it up. She is your daughter, after all, and it looks now as if she's about to make you a grandfather.'

'What's that? A grandfather! Well I'll be...' Wilf almost smiled, but caught himself in time and put his head back down to his paper. 'I'll be damned, eh?'

Meg smiled to herself. The shot had hit home! She didn't say any more, but decided to let him brood on it for a few days. He might come round yet, she thought. The problem was, would Katie?

Wilf looked up at his wife, briefly and surreptitiously, and noted the anxiety that was reflected in her eyes. Her mouth too, was drawn down at the edges in a semi-permanent state of despair. She'd always been the same, as long as he could remember, anyway, and somewhere deep inside him a voice told him that he was the cause. That knowledge made him feel alternately angry and guilty, and he addressed it by asserting to himself that Meg was naturally masochistic, and that she was only really happy when she was miserable.

'That's a nasty-looking cold sore you've got there,' he said, noting the effusion at the corner of her mouth. She had attempted to cover it with make-up, but it was still noticeable.

'Yes, dear, I don't know where they keep coming from. It'll be gone in a few days.'

That evening Wilf received a long telephone call, after which he announced that he was taking the trawler out for a couple of days. He was going to try new grounds, he said, and it might be an extended trip. Just as he was pulling anchor on the 'Sea Horse', the 'Vagabond' went cruising out past him with Erin Lachlan at the wheel. Erin deliberately avoided looking in his direction, but Craig Mortimer made a point of walking over to the side and giving him the thumbs up as they passed. Wilf put his hand up in salute, and three fingers to tell Craig the number of days that he would be away.

Craig nodded thoughtfully, waved again, and then went back to his duties on the deck.

II

Damien pulled away from the pub, and then under direction from Patsy followed the road along the coast, heading north.

'There's Cherry's place,' she said, pointing out a little cottage situated on the right hand side of the road and back amongst the trees. A few hundred yards further on, and she pointed out her own. 'Just pull up outside, will you,' she said.

She turned to look at Cherry in the back seat, and told Damien to switch his motor off. Cherry sat quietly, looking out of the window.

'Okay, what happened in there? You looked like you'd seen a ghost when you came out.'

Cherry shook her head.

'I'm getting frightened, Patsy. This place is changing! People are getting weird. Frank just about threatened me when I went back in there. He said I should mind my own business, and not meddle with things I know nothing about.'

'Yeah, well you know Frank…' said Patsy, pulling a face.

'No, Patsy! I said what if I went to Jack Izzard and told him that he'd threatened me, and he said go ahead, but that he would bar me from the pub for life!'

'Now *that's* a threat,' said Patsy, whistling. 'God! No more social club booze-ups, no more quiet drinkies on a Saturday night. What a bitch!'

'It's that serious, is it?' said Damien.

'It is around here,' said Patsy. 'The whole social scene of a little town like this revolves around the pub. If you get cut out of that, your social life evaporates. Kaput!'

'I can't believe that he would even *think* of doing that to a local,' said Cherry. 'After all, I've lived here all my life. I've known Frank forever, or just about. What the hell's going on around here?' She turned to look at Damien. 'What exactly do you do? You're not a policeman or something, are you? Or a secret agent! You're not something to do with the disappearance of Liz Capel or Mary Burton?'

Damien shook his head, bemused.

'I'm buggered if I know. They just seem to have it in for me for some unknown reason. I'm a salesman! I sell novelties, mainly candles, whatever I can get. I take them around to all the offices in the city, and the girls come and see me in their break, and buy things from me. I do pretty well out of it, too – or at least, I did!'

'So, you've given that up as well as your marriage.'

'I didn't have any choice, did I? I felt that I just couldn't stay there where I'd be likely to run into one or the other of them, or both, at any tick of the clock. It was too painful!'

Cherry nodded, sympathetically.

'Well you can't stay at the pub, and there's nowhere else immediately available. What about it, Patsy?'

Patsy shrugged.

'It's all right with me. I was just thinking of you! I wouldn't want you coming around green-eyed and jealous at three o'clock in the morning, just to see what we were up to.'

Cherry laughed.

'Is that what you thought? You're barmy, you know!'

Damien looked from one to the other of them, bemused.

'Would one of you care to let me in on this conversation. It seems to be passing right over my head!'

'Patsy's got a sort of granny flat behind her place, left over from when the last people had it. She's only ever used it for a junk room, but if it's all right with her, and all right with you, you could rent it for a while until you sort yourself out.'

Damien looked at Patsy, and raised an eyebrow.

'Well don't look at me like that. We didn't offer it straight away, because we had to be sure you weren't the guy behind the 'Texas Chainsaw Massacre'. Now that you've bought us lunch, you appear in a much rosier light.'

They all laughed.

'Well let's have a look at this facility,' said Damien. 'It certainly seems like an answer to a prayer.'

'You won't say that when you see it,' Patsy laughed. 'It's a junk tip! You'll have to help me empty it out and clean it up a bit. We'll have to transfer all my crap into the shed for the time being.'

'That's all right,' said Cherry, getting out of the car. 'I can help too. I'll just have to get some old clothes on. I wouldn't want to do it dressed like this.'

They walked around the back of the cottage, and the granny flat was thirty metres further back, standing in the shade of the surrounding trees. It was overgrown with weeds, and there was no garden fence to speak of. The property just sprawled.

Patsy fumbled around in her bag for the keys.

'It's not badly set out, really. You'll see!'

Inside, Damien surveyed the devastation of piles of clothes, blankets, large cardboard boxes of indeterminate origin and purpose, and a sewing machine set up in the middle of the mess. The main room doubled as a lounge room and kitchen, and there was still some furniture there, albeit covered in piles of junk. There was one bedroom, similarly cluttered, with a divan double bed; a toilet and even a small laundry.

'It looks all right,' said Damien. 'Why didn't you think to rent it out before?'

'Who to,' said Patsy with a shrug? 'No one ever stays here. It's not as if we have a roaring tourist trade in the town. The harbour's too deep, so there's not even a reasonable beach here. There's no caravan park, and as you can see, no accommodation. Only one pub, and an unfriendly population! Everyone who's ever thought to stay here has had an unfortunate accident, or has been somehow persuaded that there are better pickings up the road.'

Damien turned to her in the middle of that jumble, and stuck his tongue in his cheek.

'Unfortunate accident! How many unfortunate accidents?'

Cherry looked at Patsy with a frown of disapproval.

'You're going to put him off if you don't shut up! I don't know… Miss Blabbermouth is about right!'

'Don't you think that I'm entitled to know the full extent of what I'm getting myself into here,' said Damien, searchingly. 'This place is starting to sound like Nightmare on Elm Street!'

'Well if you must know,' said Cherry, 'there have been quite a few accidents here with visitors to the town. One guy fell off the wharf where one of the trawlers was tied up, and as he tried to climb back out, the trawler drifted across and crushed him against the pier. Another one drowned over at the point. He went over in a boat, intending to climb the Knoll, and abseil down it. The Knoll is that big hill you can see on the northern side of the bay. He fell! The cliffs rise up at that point very steeply, and I suppose that if you're into mountain climbing, it would be a good practice climb. But it's been forbidden now, by the council! No one's been allowed to climb it since the accident.'

'Not much in that, I suppose. Could happen to anyone!'

'Then there were the two guys who went out fishing in a small boat, and never made it back. The boat was found half submerged about a mile out, and it looked as if it had been run over by a much bigger boat, because it was all chewed up.'

'Not one of the trawlers?' said Damien.

Cherry shrugged.

'Nothing that anyone could prove, anyway, though Fisheries came down and checked all the trawlers out, just in case.'

'What about the body,' said Patsy? 'Tell him...'

'How did I know that you were going to come up with that one,' said Cherry, sardonically. 'All right! But it was a hell of a long time ago. Erin Lachlan was coming back in one night - one of the trawler men - about three years ago, and he saw something floating in the water. It was the headless body of some guy, aged in his twenties or thirties they reckon. But no one had seen him around town, not even passing through. The body could have come from anywhere. It was floating about two miles out.'

'No wonder they call this place Dark Harbour,' said Damien. 'Are you sure Stephen King doesn't live here?'

'No – it's not that bad,' laughed Patsy. 'Nothing ever happens to the locals.'

'Well, that's very reassuring,' said Damien. '*Very* reassuring!'

'If you're interested in where the name comes from,' said Cherry, 'you only have to look at the shadow cast by the Knoll in the late afternoon. There's a great shadow falls over the harbour, so I suppose the early seamen around these parts thought it might be an apt name for the place.'

'It's even more noticeable in the winter. It gets really dark then,' said Patsy.

'Well, I suppose we ought to attend to present business first,' said Damien. 'How much for the flat?'

'I don't know. How about thirty dollars a week? It's not exactly the Ritz.'

'Sounds all right to me! Are you sure that's enough?'

Patsy pulled a face.

'Hell, yes! It'll be quite a change having someone living out the back. Then if I hear strange noises in the night, I'll be able to scream, and you'll come running, of course.'

'Part of the service,' he grinned. 'With my trusty broom handle.'

'Just as long as she doesn't make a habit of it,' said Cherry, squeezing his arm. 'You'll know if she's genuine or not by what she's wearing. Anything other than her neck to ankle fluffy Pooh-Bear nightie, and you'll know it was a put-up job. Then you have my permission to head for the hills.'

'Party pooper,' sniffed Patsy.

Damien pulled out his still damp wallet, and counted out a hundred and twenty dollars into Patsy's hand.

'There you are… a month in advance. It'll probably take that long to sort something out with one of those cottages.'

The trip around the area was put on hold while they travelled back to the Hotel to pick Damien's things up. Frank was nowhere to be seen on the premises, so Damien was denied a last shot at him. Then they went to Cherry's place, and waited outside while she went in and got changed. She came out in bib and brace overalls and a headscarf to protect her hair. It took three hours to sort out the flat, and by the time they'd finished the three of them looked quite disreputable.

'Time to call it quits,' said Cherry, smearing the dirt on her face.

'Yeah, I think that'll do,' said Damien.

'I tell you what; you get a couple of bottles in, and the two of you can come around to my place for dinner.'

'Good lord,' said Patsy. 'A dinner invitation! Don't pass that up, Damien, it's the equivalent of getting a telegram from the Queen.'

'Don't push it, or I'll serve you up beans on toast,' Cherry said, with a sniff.

'Even beans on toast would go down all right with a Chardonnay,' said Damien, smiling.

III

At eleven o'clock that night, Igor Morris, sober for a change, backed a refrigerated truck out from the side of the large processing shed near the wharf, and drove along the dock to meet a trawler coming in with its catch. It was the 'Wavefarer', a thirty tonne scale fish vessel that had been out for the previous thirty-six hours. He backed the truck up to the side of the boat, and the two deckhands opened the back of it and began to load fish that had been laid down in ice, while the trawler was still on its way back in. Part of the catch went into the truck, the rest into the Cold-rooms of the processing plant, where it would be filleted and packed the following day.

The catch was considerable, and was weighed before it left the boat. The master of the vessel stood by with a clipboard, and recorded the various categories and weights of the fish before it was loaded onto the truck. On the way back to Patsy's house, Damien and Patsy noticed the activity from a distance, and Damien pulled over to the side of the road, and switched his lights off.

'What's going on over there,' he said, peering through the darkness.

'Oh, that's just 'Rigor Mortis', getting ready for a trip to town. That's what he does. He carts fish, usually overnight to the city, in time for the markets the next day. He keeps some queer hours, but so does the fleet. He's got a radio link to them, and they let him know when they're coming in. Once he's loaded up, he takes off and gets back the following afternoon. He probably has a sleep when he gets down there. Does that satisfy your curiosity?'

Damien looked over and grinned at her in the dark.

'This place *makes* you curious. It's like a pond, a pool of stagnant water. On the surface, nothing appears to be happening, but if you take a microscope and go down, under the water, the pool is a hive of activity!'

He started the car, but didn't switch the lights on again, just pulled out from the side and travelled slowly along the road at about twenty-five kilometres an hour.

'What are you doing,' said Patsy, puzzled.

'I can't tell you why, but I just have this feeling that I don't want to be seen out here tonight. I think it would be better… for us both.'

'Now you're really beginning to freak me out,' Patsy said, and shivered in the cold night air.

If they had waited another twenty minutes, they would have seen Igor board the trawler and confer with the master. The trawler man went to a storage bin and pulled out a large schnapper, wrapped in plastic, and obviously intended for Igor's personal use. Igor put it under his arm, and disappeared with it into the back of his truck. Then he got out, shut the rear doors, and drove out onto the main highway for the city. By eleven forty, Igor was speeding along the highway, heading south, and talking to someone on his mobile phone.

IV

Doctor Ilse Hirsch was sitting at the rear of her cottage, enjoying the night air and spending some quality time observing her snake collection. She sipped her favourite Moselle, and luxuriated in the fact that her rear garden was so private that she could wander around with impunity, with little or nothing on. This evening she wore only a loose robe; open at the front, allowing her body to breathe and feel the cool air on her skin.

Though born in Germany, she had been brought to Australia by her parents when in her early teens, and had managed to improve her English to the point that she exhibited no trace of a German accent. The only signs of her heredity lay in her name, and in a haughty arrogance that she struggled, on occasion, to control.

She was a sensuous woman, with a tinge of refined cruelty in her make-up. As a doctor, she tended to view other people as specimens, or as laboratory animals, suitable only for experimentation and observation. There was something missing in her overall psyche that enabled her to overlook the individual humanity of others, and as a result she was coldly observant of human traits, emotions and reactions.

She had managed over the years to affect an artificial friendliness that attracted others, and she certainly socialised with the other women in the town, albeit only on a basis of drinks on a Saturday night. But she was cold where it came to men in general, and only used them sparingly to satisfy her physical requirements. These could range from sadistic game-playing with whips and high heels, to self abnegation and erotic punishment.

Her interest in snakes came from their cold-blooded nature, their continual pursuit of prey, and the lack of any conscience in their cruelty. In this, she probably identified with them, and she revelled in watching the way they moved, sinuously and silently in some orchestration of evil versus innocence. It intrigued her how evil invariably triumphed.

She sat now, watching them in the Perspex pen she'd had erected in her garden, where they could enjoy a relatively normal environment of rocks and undergrowth, places to hide from the harsh sun and a pool to swim in. The top of the pen was angled inwards to prevent them from escaping, and the base was solid concrete, covered over with natural elements, so they couldn't burrow out. At the side of this were other enclosures in which she bred rats and mice, similarly enclosed. These provided two further elements of her hobby, food and sport.

Sipping her Moselle, she pressed a button that opened a small door into an antechamber, allowing three or four rats to enter. This was then closed, and a door into the main pen was activated. The rats fled unknowingly into the larger pen, and the doctor sat back to watch the ensuing action with pleasurable anticipation.

The initial reaction of the rats on finding themselves in this larger space was to make a bid for freedom, and they ran straight into the Perspex wall, scrabbling at the smooth surface in an attempt to get through it. Within half a minute, this sudden activity in the slumbering pen brought out the inhabitants from their hiding places, and six foot browns like 'Axis Sally' and 'Goebbels' slithered out to investigate the commotion. Ilse experienced a rising excitement as the snakes pin-pointed a target and began the chase. She slipped her free hand down, stroking herself slowly as the terrified rats squealed and rushed backwards and forwards, looking for sanctuary. As quick as they were, once the snakes' cold eyes addressed the prey, there was no escape, and the sudden darting strike of the head brought both the terror, and Ilse, to a climax simultaneously. It was all over in two minutes and thirty-five seconds. Ilse sank back into her chair, exhausted, with fine beads of sweat on her upper lip. A few minutes later, she filled her glass again, and went inside.

Chapter Six

John Inglis woke the following morning, and lay for a while, attempting to get his bearings. He was in his own flat, but something was missing. He rolled over, and instead of Andrea, the beautiful Andrea, lying there beside him, the bed on that side was undisturbed. He groaned out loud, as the events of the day before came back to haunt him.

The scene that stuck in his mind was that of Andrea at the door, flashing daggers at him through her angry, violet eyes, and he raising one long finger at her as she swept out of his life. He groaned again, and then picked up the alarm clock as a tool to help his eyes begin to focus for the first time that day.

Seven-twenty! Lucky! The alarm had gone off and run down at seven, and it suddenly occurred to him that today was a workday, after a week taken off for compassionate reasons. The compassionate reasons had not been entirely evident when he had first applied for the leave, only that the desperate situation he had found himself in, the third part of a triangle between his best friend, and his best friend's wife, was coming to an ugly head. He had been expecting an explosion of atomic proportions for some time before the finale was actually played out, but when it was, it was something of an anticlimax.

John had expected more, a black eye at the very least, and a rampaging Damien closing on him with a cutlery knife, or an empty bottle of Riesling at the very least. Instead of that, most of the verbals had occurred between Damien and his wife, and John had stood there tongue-tied with apprehension until forced, finally, to protect Andrea's honour.

After leaving Damien's house with his prize, Andrea wept on and off for the next six hours. He had known that she was sensitive, that she suffered somewhat from temperament, but he had also thought that her relationship with Damien had been over for some months. He'd thought that the necessary adjustments she would have to make would be minimal, and that she would settle in with him in no time. He soon learned, to his cost, that a woman does not give up her affiliations so easily. There had to be an element of drama involved, and if Damien was not going to provide it by chasing her up the road, then she would have to provide it for herself. Consequently, by the evening of the second day, John was emotionally exhausted, without the energy to give the same answers to the same questions, repeated ad infinitum by his, by now, rather soggy lover.

The following day he had sought relief by going around all of Damien's friends, to try and discover where his erstwhile buddy was hiding out. He struck a blank. Not only didn't the friends know about his appalling break-up, or John's part in it, but Damien had not even had the bad taste to phone everyone up and badmouth his wife before she could beat him to it. This made John even more apprehensive. He found himself staring into a pit of the unknown, where the expected did not materialise, and the unexpected did.

In a moment of weakness John pulled out his mobile phone and dialled Damien's mobile number. It was unsuccessful. Either he had it turned off, or it was out of range.

Damien's sudden disappearance with what amounted to a few pitiful possessions loaded into the back of a trailer, had been entirely unexpected. John had expected him to fight to keep his home, and attempt to prevent Andrea from claiming the lawful ownership of anything they had shared together. He had expected the house to be locked up like a fortress, but when he arrived, faint-heartedly, to check the place out, he had found the front door open, and the remainder of the contents of the house strangely in their proper places. This was not par for the course!

He had also, timidly, been expecting Damien to be waiting for him with a small axe, or some other implement of bone-crushing destruction, and to jump out on him from the shadows with a courage-withering yell. But that hadn't happened either! Damien had, to all intents and purposes, disappeared!

John rolled out of bed and staggered into the shower. Though he had overslept, the sleep had been shallow and troubled, and had left him weak and devoid of energy. As he stood under the revitalising streams of heat and steam, he cast his mind back along a relationship that had lasted for almost two decades, only to be undone by the twin sins of lust and envy that he had been unable to overcome, even for an old mate.

'Stuff it!' he swore, and kicked the tiles hard enough to bruise his toes. He hopped around on one foot and said 'stuff it' again.

'How stupid can one man be?' he announced to himself, aloud. 'Stupid!'

He went back to scrubbing his back with the loofah, hoping to take enough skin off his back for it to constitute some form of Lutheran penance. He was suddenly overwhelmed with a sense of his own disgust, and for the first time allowed himself a glimpse of the enormity of what he'd done. But it was too late! There were some things in life that you could never take back, and sexual congress with your best friend's wife was one of them.

Stepping out of the shower he dried himself off, then went to the wardrobe to take out the uniform he'd just got back from the cleaners. That at least made him look and feel like a worthwhile member of the human race. He looked at himself in the mirror, combed his hair and put his hat on, noting how the gold braid glittered on the peak. Then he dashed out of the flat, jumped into the BMW that set him apart from his neighbours, and headed off for another day as a servant of the Department of Customs and Excise.

II

Andrea had no sooner arrived home than she was on the phone to her close friend, Veronica Walters. Her first query was a rather aloof aside about Damien, and whether Veronica had happened to see him lately. There was a touch of suspicion in her tone, which Veronica was quick to pick up on. Mutual distrust between best friends is endemic in the female of the species, especially where it comes to possession of the male. If Veronica had replied that she had indeed seen him, and that he was in fact sitting not two feet away from her at that very moment, drinking a mug of warm chocolate, then nothing in creation would ever have convinced Andrea that Damien had not wasted any time in sowing his wild oats, and that she would have to cut all her old friends dead, and start again. Such is the frailty of woman!

Veronica, however, was too wise to make any such admission, even though she had waved to Damien as he passed her house some days before, burdened down with an overladen trailer and heading in a northerly direction.

'No, chicken… I haven't seen Damien since you both came to dinner that time. Let's see, that was about six weeks ago. I've seen *you* since then, of course!'

Andrea was silent for a full thirty seconds, and Veronica began to count down, in anticipation of the inevitable outburst.

'He's gone away and left me,' Andrea sobbed, once she'd made her impression with the heartfelt silence. 'We had this terrible argument, and he said some terrible things to me and now he's gone, and I don't know where he is.'

This came over as an almost unintelligible babble to Veronica, in between sobs and sniffles, but the context was obvious.

'Oh, you poor thing! Men are such beasts, aren't they – though I must admit, I would never have thought it of Damien. He always seemed so devoted to you.'

'That's just it, he always was,' Andrea wailed. 'And now he's gone and we're two weeks behind in the rent. He was always so dependable, and he's left me in a terrible mess. What am I going to do?'

Veronica looked down sardonically at the phone, as if Andrea was staring out of the earpiece at her.

'Well, doll... I suppose you'll just have to do what we all do in situations like this. Pick yourself up, dust yourself off and point a brave face at the world. Believe me, it works!'

'That's not going to pay the bills though, is it?'

'No... no it's not! You'll have to get yourself up to Social Security and apply for a deserted wives pension, or whatever they call it these days. It's the only option you've got, outside of getting a job, that is!'

Veronica herself had always worked, in a dress shop, and had little sympathy for the Andrea's of this world who thought that men in general owed them a living.

'But that's... that's like... charity!' Andrea replied, aghast. The very idea of living on government handouts was an anathema to her.

'Like I said, or get a job!'

'I'm temperamentally unsuited to the rough and tumble of the common herd,' Andrea retorted, snappily, 'I would have thought that you understood that, Veronica. My analyst would be horrified.'

I'm sure he would, Veronica thought to herself. You wouldn't be able to afford his fees if you had to work for what I work for! She didn't say that, of course. Her reply was more down to earth.

'Needs must when the devil drives, Andrea! But look, have you thought of getting in touch with John Inglis, his best mate. He's probably staying with him until all this blows over.'

Andrea burst into a flood of tears once more.

'That's just it! Damien has fallen out with John as well. He's got this silly idea that I fancy him, and want to go off with him. Nothing could be further from the truth! He's a slob, an absolute slob! You should see his flat…'

Andrea pulled herself up short, suspecting that she might have let a little too much out of the bag. Veronica, on the other end, put two and two together and made five.

'I see! Well I must be going now, Andrea, I have guests coming to tea. Lovely to hear from you my dear!' And with that she dropped the phone into the cradle.

III

Damien dropped Patsy off at her door, parked the car in the driveway, and made his way out to the flat at the rear. Once inside, he turned on the lights then drew the Venetian blinds in the front, and pulled the curtains at the back. No need to feel more vulnerable than he already did.

They'd cleaned the junk out earlier on, and that was all right as far as it went, but he would have to do a hell of a lot more to the place before it was truly liveable. The furniture needed a good vacuuming, there was so much dust embedded in the fabric. He went into the kitchen, and idly ran the hot water from the tap. It was only lukewarm at this stage, as Patsy had only turned the heater on a couple of hours ago. Still, he broke out an ancient bottle of dishwashing liquid, and set to work to clean down the sink, the kitchen table and the cupboard shelves. He was tired, but didn't feel like turning in until he had at least made an impression on the place. He'd decided that he wasn't going to budge from there until the place was gleaming, even if it took all the following day.

As he scrubbed the sink, he tried to think of all the items he would have to include in a major shop, and then found a pen and paper and made notes from time to time as he thought of more items he would need. By the time the kitchen area was at a passable stage it was already one o'clock in the morning, and he decided he'd had enough. Looking in his bag, he found his mobile phone and turned it on, thinking in a moment of weakness to phone Andrea's number to see if she'd gone home or not. But the dial still said 'no service', and he was to discover over the next few days that Dark Harbour was in a dead zone where it came to mobile phones, and that it was impossible to make a call from there. He threw down the phone, turned off the light, and made his way into the bedroom.

Almost immediately he sensed that there was something wrong. They'd only been in there a couple of hours ago, and the place had been shut up tight. Now, however, he could feel a definite breeze in the room, and when he turned the light on he saw that the sliding aluminium window was open about a foot. The window faced to the rear of the property, and Damien was just about to step over to close it when he detected a movement in the corner, on the floor. Looking down he saw a large brown snake, backed into the corner, and just beginning to lift its head. There was nothing wrong with Damien's reflexes. He took a step back and was out of the door before the snake made a move, slamming the bedroom door behind him. Then he broke out into a sweat.

Four feet! That's what he estimated. A four foot long Brown! It could have killed him! He looked around for something to tackle it with, and then shook his head. No way was he going to tackle a Brown Snake at one o'clock in the morning, feeling as tired as he did. On the other hand, he wasn't going to spend another minute under the same roof, either. That left him two options. Either spend the night in the car, and he didn't fancy that, or knock Patsy up and beg the loan of her couch for the night.

He decided on the latter option, and headed for the house. He knocked on the door three times before he got any response. Finally he heard movement, and a voice whispered, 'is that you, Damien?'

'Yes, it's me, who do you think it is?'

She opened the door, looked quickly around and then literally pulled him in through the door, slamming it behind him.

'Thank God for that,' she said, and Damien could see that her hands were shaking. He couldn't help smiling as he noticed she was wearing her fluffy neck to ankle Pooh-Bear nightie, just as Cherry had described it.

'Here, what's the matter with you. I didn't think you were the nervous type,' he said.

'We've had a prowler, stalking around the house. I couldn't call out because you would never have heard me. But he was there all right!'

'Do you want me to go and have a look?' he replied, now nervous himself.

'Yes, but take something with you... here!' She walked over and grabbed the poker from the fireplace.

Armed with this not very substantial weapon, Damien began to walk around the outside of the house, checking carefully at each corner before venturing around it. When he got around the back, he looked down towards the flat and thought he saw a shadow, disappearing into the trees at the end of the garden. He looked again, but whatever it was had managed to slip away. He lost no time in regaining entrance to the cottage.

'You've fairly put the wind up me,' he shivered, as he handed her back the poker. 'If there was anyone there, they're not there now. But I do have an unwelcome guest in the flat out the back, which is why I came. Can I borrow your couch for the night?'

Patsy looked troubled, and ran her fingers nervously through her hair.

'What do you mean, an unwelcome guest?'

'A bloody great Brown snake, in the bedroom! I don't know whether it got in by itself, or whether someone put it there, but I'm telling you, I don't intend to tackle it until tomorrow.'

Patsy shivered.

'God – I don't blame you! Do you think it was put there deliberately?'

'Well, you were working in the bedroom at one stage tonight. Did you open the window for any reason?'

'I did, as a matter of fact, just to air the place out. But as I was finishing in there I slid it shut again.'

'You're sure of that?'

'Yes, I'm sure. I didn't actually put the slide in place to lock it, but I did close it. Someone must have been here!'

Damien nodded.

'I'd say you're right. After all the other things that have happened to me since I got here, I'd say that someone has got it in for me, and they're not going to let up until I give in, and leave.'

'Well this is great, isn't it? I'm wide awake now – feel like a game of snap?'

He laughed, and shook his head.

'I wouldn't mind a cup of coffee though. I didn't have anything out there, and I'm busting for a drink. I'll go shopping tomorrow and buy in coffee, sugar, milk, tea, all the good gear. Once I've dealt with the snake, of course!'

Patsy went into the little kitchen and put the kettle on. Without the make-up and in her old nightie, she had lost her blonde, glamorous edge, and now looked like a frightened schoolmarm. They were sitting down to coffee at the kitchen table, when they both had the same thought, at the same instant - Cherry!

'You don't think she's in any danger because of me, do you,' said Damien. 'I'd never forgive myself if my presence here brought any harm to either of you.'

'I don't see why it should, but I must admit, I am worried! Do you think I ought to phone her, just to make sure?'

Damien nodded, and watched while she went to the wall phone, and dialled.

'You risk waking her from her beauty sleep, of course,' he said.

Patsy shrugged.

'Stiff! It's in a good cause.'

She stood there for a good thirty seconds while the phone rang at the other end, and then, by Patsy's body language, Damien could see that Cherry had picked up.

'Are you all right, girl? I've been worried sick over here. I thought I heard a prowler, and Damien found a bloody great Brown snake in the bedroom. What's that?'

Patsy was silent for a minute, while Cherry spoke.

'You're joking!' she said, in a surprised tone. 'What? I don't believe it!'

She turned to Damien, and relayed the extent of the message. 'Cherry had a visit from Charlie Fairweather. He tried to push his way in, but she slammed his fingers in the door.' She turned back to the phone. 'Yes... he said what? I think we'd better come down and pick you up, and you can stay here for the night. We'll go and see Jack Izzard in the morning and put in an official complaint. Yes! That's right! God, what a nerve.'

Patsy put the phone down and grabbed a coat off a hook on the wall. As she put it on, she told Damien what had transpired.

'It seems that bastard tried to push his way in, and Cherry slammed the door on his fingers. She said he was jumping about, yelling and cursing, and he said that if he saw her again with you, she would live to regret it. She said he made all sorts of veiled threats that Dark Harbour wasn't such a safe place as she thought it was, and he mentioned Liz Capel.'

'Oh yes, what did he say?'

'He said she wouldn't want to go the same way as Liz Capel.'

Damien pursed his lips, and looked dangerous. The scar at the side of his mouth turned white.

'We'll see about that,' he said. 'Come on, let's go and get her.'

They piled into the car, backed out and drove the hundred yards or so to Cherry's place. Her little cottage suddenly looked vulnerable, perched on the side of the road, and as they pulled up the lights went out, and Cherry came hurrying out of the door and leapt in behind them.

'Let's go,' she said, 'I'm going to sort that bastard out tomorrow if it's the last thing I do. He won't threaten me again!'

They drove back and piled into Patsy's place, locking the door behind them. Cherry laughed, once the tension began to drop.

'The folks around here are going to think we've got a three-ringed circus going on. Any more of this and tongues will begin to wag.'

'Too late for that, I think,' Damien said, grimly. 'They already are. Though what on earth they're talking about is anyone's guess.'

'Well, you have a choice,' said Patsy. 'You can either share the couch with Damien here, or you can share my bed and we'll make mad, passionate love all night.'

'You can stick a couple of pillows down the middle, that's what you can do,' said Cherry, laughing. 'And if so much as one toe strays over the line, watch out!'

Damien slept on the couch, and wondered what Andrea was doing for the first time that day.

IV

In Ilse Hirsch's cottage, further back along the road, she sat at her mirror and painstakingly applied an excess of makeup to her already beautiful features. She sat with her gown open, so that her breasts were reflected in the mirror, and she stopped occasionally and caressed herself so that her nipples stood out in anticipation. Craig Mortimer sat cross-legged in the corner, and watched her preening herself.

'More mascara,' he said, 'I like your eyes black, like deep pools.'

'Sit quietly, little man. Your slut is making herself beautiful for you. I have to pay very close attention, or I won't get the effect I want.'

Ilse shivered deliciously along the length of her body as she lingered over the word 'slut'. She came from a background where the word was never heard, let alone spoken, so it held an erotic fascination for her that she could only experience with someone of a lower caste.

Picking up a lipstick of a particularly dark shade of red, she applied it to her lips generously, and was impressed with the effect of it against the pale contours of her features. She now looked like a whore.

'Do I look like a prostitute? Tell me what you'd like to do to me again,' she said, looking at him though the mirror. 'Tell me all the grotesque positions you'd like to see me in, and what you'll do to me if I don't do as I'm told.'

Craig's eyes glittered in the darkened room. He hadn't been able to believe his luck when the doctor first responded to his drunken overtures, over a year ago. She had the reputation of being an untouchable, a vestal virgin. She had never been out with any man from Dark Harbour that he knew of, though she had often made clandestine trips to the city where she would go into hiding for a week at a time, and no one knew what it was that she did there.

Ilse had taken him home on that first occasion, and laid down the rules of their relationship. It was to be clandestine, he was not to approach her in public, nor appear to be on intimate terms with her. He was not to mention her to his friends, and he should not have any expectations other than sex. She had no intention of becoming emotionally involved, and she made it plain that he was a cut or so beneath her, and that she would probably treat him with contempt in public. There was never any question of an open relationship.

'I'd like to see you down on your hands and knees,' he whispered, 'with a dog collar around your neck, and lead you out into the middle of the main street where people could stare at you.'

Ilse shuddered on her seat, and writhed on the cushion. Her nipples rose up of their own accord, and she raised her hands above her head to make her breasts stand out in the mirror. Craig got up and came up from behind, reached over and fondled her as she watched, breathlessly, in the mirror.

'And if I resisted you, what would you do then,' she asked, half-fainting.

He told her, in no uncertain terms.

'Let's do it,' she said, and led him off uncomplaining into the lounge room.

Chapter Seven

Emily Longstaff looked over the breakfast table at her husband, and suppressed a sneer. He was reading the paper, ignoring her as usual, and she often felt like grabbing him by the throat and shaking him, to ask him what on earth their relationship was all about. He rarely spoke to her except about items of trivia, day-to-day essentials, and to announce that he was either going to the pub, or off on another fishing trip with the trawlers. She put her coffee down with a clatter, thinking that it might break his concentration and cause him to look at her. It didn't, except for a momentary glance of irritation, after which he went back to the sporting columns.

'When are you going away again, Gordon? I need to be able to plan my days.'

Gordon pulled a face, then reluctantly put his paper down, and tried to recall what she'd just said.

'What was that?'

If he'd said, 'what was that, bitch?' it would have had the same effect. Emily sneered at him, and shook her head.

'God, you annoy me, Gordon! What am I, just the decoration around here? You never bloody listen to me.'

'What the hell are you on about? I was reading the paper, I just didn't catch what you said, that's all.'

'You never do, Gordon, that's your trouble. You never listen to me, ever!'

'What's got into *your* knickers this morning,' said Gordon, annoyed. 'I'm just trying to read the paper, what's so wrong with that?'

'Well, you could put the damned paper down for a change, and take notice that you're not alone in this house, that's what! I feel like the wallpaper around here sometimes.'

Gordon sighed heavily.

'All right! Just tell me what you said and we'll start again.'

It was always the same old argument. He wasn't paying her any attention; he lived in a cocoon! He had no respect for her; he should never have married, because he had no idea about how to live with other people. He'd heard the same old phrases trotted out so many times that any feeling he'd once had for his wife had long since evaporated. It had got so bad the previous year that he had joined the line-up outside Liz Capel's cottage, and had the usual fling, just to enjoy a recrimination-free relationship for a while. Liz had been totally undemanding, and totally accommodating. She made it plain from the beginning that your fetish was her fetish, and that wherever you wanted to put it was all right with her. It saved a lot of embarrassment.

Emily, on the other hand, had made it quite plain by various manipulations and mumblings during their twenty-year marriage that the only way she ever got anything out of the act was by rear penetration, and although that wasn't really his thing, she had made it the staple diet of his sex life. If confronted, Emily would have said that it was *his* preference, but she knew, deep down that it wasn't. Funny how a little thing like that could taint a marriage, and alienate the protagonists through a wall of silence! Because they never discussed the matter, never breathed a word about sex. He had attempted to raise the topic on a few occasions, and had been met with a barrier of obfuscation. The only thing she'd ever mentioned was that she'd been abused as a child, and didn't like to speak of it. So they didn't.

'I merely asked you when you'd be going away again… fishing! I need to be able to plan my days.'

'Oh! Is that all? Well why make such a big deal about it. I'm off again tomorrow, probably be gone for two or three days.'

'Well I won't be here tonight. I've got a meeting with the Bardic Society, so you'll have to sort yourself out regards a meal.'

'Yeah, well that's all right! I'm capable of feeding myself! What is this Bardic thing, anyway? What do you do there?'

'It's a traditional thing – Welsh! If you'd listened, you'd know all about it. I've explained at least three or four times, you just never pay attention.'

'Well if you don't want to tell me…' he muttered, and his eyes strayed back to his paper.

'No, I don't think I'll bother,' said Emily, and got up to wash the dishes.

II

Damien slept fitfully until eight o'clock, imagining faces at the window in his mind's eye, and dimly aware of various mutterings and scufflings that prevented him from falling into a deeper sleep. He was a city boy, and not yet used to the different noises of the country at night. The girls didn't wake until nine fifteen, by which time Damien was outside, searching the yard for something to tackle the snake with. He finally donned an old pair of waders to protect his legs, put on a pair of thick gardening gloves and took an old-fashioned rake with steel prongs and a flat steel backing plate. Entering the flat cautiously, he listened for a while outside the bedroom door, before plucking up the courage to fling the door open.

The snake was on the floor, not two feet away from him and he slammed the rake down in the middle of its back, causing the head to come rearing up towards him. He jumped backwards, and in a blind reaction pulled the door sharply towards him, slamming the snake's head in the doorway. He held it closed until the snake stopped thrashing around on the other side of the door, then perspiring madly from the shock and the exertion proceeded to pick it up with the rake and carry it ahead of him, like a trophy, out into the back garden.

He was met by the unexpected sound of clapping, and saw Patsy and Cherry, cheering his efforts at a safe distance. But that was not what caught his eye. Behind them, and advancing purposefully along the driveway was a policeman in uniform. Not young, Damien estimated that he was in his early forties, with a barrel chest and weather-beaten skin. He held a clipboard in his left hand, and he came up so quietly that the girls didn't hear him until he spoke.

'Cherry Reynolds,' he began, in a voice that sounded suspiciously official. 'I need to talk to you regarding an assault that you committed on the person of one Charles Fairweather, at approximately twelve fifteen this morning.'

At that point he suddenly noticed Damien, strangely attired in his boots and his gloves, dropping the snake on the ground in front of him. He took his cap off and scratched his bald head, replaced it and assumed a grim scowl, which made his jowls stand out even further than they did already

'Excuse me for a minute,' he said, leaving Cherry standing with her mouth open. He walked down the garden to where Damien stood, and stopped, looking down at the snake. 'And you are?' he said, grimly, pulling his pen out.

'And you are... what?' said Damien, not in the mood to be spoken down to by officialdom, whatever form it took.

'Name,' grunted the constable, preparing to write on his clipboard.

'Damien Curtis, for what it's worth. What's the problem, constable?'

Constable Jack Izzard waved his pen in the direction of the dead snake.

'You killed this, I take it?'

Damien nodded.

'Well I didn't invite it to supper, if that's what you mean!'

'If I were you, I would moderate your tone, sir. Are you aware that it is an offence to kill a Brown snake, under any circumstances, under the Native Conservation Act?'

'Oh, is it? Another idiotic law that our legislators have brainstormed, no doubt, along with protecting sharks, and encouraging burglars to sue their victims!'

'Be that as it may, the law is the law, and you have broken the law. I'm going to have to issue you with a summons, I'm afraid.'

'Maybe you'd be better taking a long, hard look at what's going on around here before you get stuck into innocent people, protecting themselves,' said Damien.

'I don't care for your tone. I'm going to have to caution you that if you persist, I will have to charge you with interfering with an officer in the performance of his duty.'

'Maybe that's what we need, eh! Something to bring this little town out into the glaring spotlight of the world! Amazing the things that can come out in court.'

Izzard continued writing, and tried to ignore this final parley.

'You will be required to attend the local magistrates court on a day to be appointed. What is your home address?'

'You're standing on it,' said Damien, indicating the granny flat behind him.

By this time both Cherry and Patsy had decided to wander over to find out what was going on.

'That's right, Jack. I'm renting him the flat,' said Patsy. 'Any problems with that?'

'I haven't, but the council might have,' said Izzard, grimly. 'Do you have a Certificate of Habitation for this building?'

'What the hell is a Certificate of Habitation? I've never heard of it,' said Patsy, angrily.

'If I were you I would ask Councillor Kelly. He might be able to enlighten you.'

'I hardly think that Councillor Kelly would be capable of supplying an unbiased opinion, considering the fact that he has already refused to rent Damien a room.'

'This is not a question of an opinion, Miss Donaldson,' he said to Patsy. 'It's a question of a council byelaw, and at a guess I would say that you are in contravention of one, by using these premises for habitation without a certificate.'

'Isn't amazing the way there's always some petty law that pops up, whenever you want to harass someone?' said Cherry, shaking her head in exasperation.

'If I were you, Miss Reynolds, I would worry about how to face your own charge.' The constable turned to her and consulted his clipboard. 'A complaint has been filed against you for assault. I am merely here to see if there is any substance in the complaint, and if it warrants further action.'

'If you're talking about Charlie Fairweather last night, Jack, then I'd like to file a complaint of my own. He came to my place in the middle of the night with the express purpose of threatening me. He tried to force his way into my house, and when I resisted him by slamming the door on him, he got his fingers jammed. That's the long and the short of it!'

'Mr Fairweather described it as a domestic disturbance that got out of hand. He informs me that you and he have had an understanding for some time, where he often comes around, at your insistence, and stays the night. In which case, it's obvious that you lost your temper for some reason and assaulted your partner. That's a very serious offence, Miss Reynolds!'

Cherry couldn't speak for a moment, she was so overcome with disbelief.

'Charlie... Charlie Fairweather! ...and *me*? You have got to be joking! I have never so much as looked at Charlie in that way. He's a creep... not only a creep, but obviously a congenital liar as well. Ask anyone!'

'He maintains that you and he have had an intimate relationship for about eight months!' said Izzard, a sardonic expression on his face.

'Well you can put that idea right out of your head, constable! I have never, ever, had a relationship with Charlie Fairweather, and if he were the last man on the planet, he wouldn't get any closer to me than the road out there.'

118

'I find that difficult to believe…'

'Why! Because a man told you so? That's right, we women don't count in this town, do we, Jack? Our word isn't enough. We're just a pack of scatter-brained idiots who don't even know who we're going out with half the time. I'm telling you that he came around and verbally assaulted me last night, threatened me, and tried to force his way into my home. I want him charged!'

'Well, that's not going to happen,' said Izzard, putting his pen back in his pocket. 'I'm not interested in payback – *he charged me so I'll charge him!* We'll see what the outcome of this assault charge is in court first. But I think you'd better have a better story than that if you want the magistrate to go easy on you. Charlie has witnesses willing to swear that they've seen you and he together, and that you were all over him, and obviously his lover.'

'They're bloody lying then, I tell you! How the hell do I get through to you? I have never so much as spoken to the man, except to tell him to piss off.'

'I would moderate your language if I were you…'

'Why? Those were my exact words…. Constable!'

Damien reached out and touched Cherry on the arm, drawing her away from the confrontation before she got herself into more trouble.

'Don't worry, Cherry. There might only be one constable in this town, representing the law around here, but I know a few higher-ups in the force who would be very interested in a constable who refused to take details of an alleged assault, and took sides in a dispute.'

Izzard went red in the face, and the veins on his forehead stood out in rage.

'Just you come with me. You and I need to have a little talk!'

Damien indicated to the girls that it was okay, and to stay where they were, while he walked down to the driveway behind the cop. The moment they were out of earshot, and around the corner of the house, Izzard turned to Damien and grabbed him by his shirtfront. He thrust his face into Damien's, who put his arms up in surrender so that he could avoid any allegations of assaulting a police officer.

'Be very careful, constable! I think this constitutes assault!'

'You bloody listen to me you drop kick! I don't know who the fuck you are, or where you came from, but you start messing with me and you'll find you've bitten off more than you can chew... understand! The most sensible thing for you to do at this point is to get into that heap of shit of yours, before I defect it permanently, drive it out of town and keep going. Then forget that Dark Harbour ever existed – get me!'

'I get you all right,' said Damien.

'You've got until three o'clock this afternoon.'

'You can go and take a running jump,' said Damien.

'I'm fucking warning you!'

'And I'm warning you, you pitiful excuse for a Police Officer. Get your fucking hands off me, or I'll be onto your Internal Investigations Branch, and I'll have your job. Don't you dare try to order me out of town!'

Izzard let him go, and pushed him roughly away from him.

'The next time I see you on the street, I'm going to run you in. Then don't be surprised if you end up the victim of a horrible accident. You might even take it on yourself to hang yourself in your cell. People do strange things when the balance of the mind is disturbed.'

'You'll have two witnesses to deal with then, won't you Jack?' said Cherry, appearing suddenly around the corner of the house. 'Then we might even get a few questions asked about Liz Capel, after all this time, and even Mary Burton!'

'You've got nothing,' said Izzard, scowling. 'Maybe you should go with him. You're just trouble, anyway!'

'And me?' said Patsy, appearing behind Cherry.

'The three of you had better keep right out of my face,' said Izzard, scowling, then strode off down the driveway and climbed back into his patrol car.

'Well,' said Damien, elaborately dusting himself down. 'Now that's how to deal with a died-in-the-wool pig! You didn't tell me the local cop was a Nazi!'

Cherry shook her head.

'I've never seen him like that before. It's like he's gone crazy!'

'Obviously, he's got his orders from whoever is behind this push to get me out of town. That bullshit about Charlie Fairweather was a farce, and he knew it. I doubt if it will ever get to court.'

'Well, I certainly hope not,' said Cherry, thoughtfully. 'I don't need this in my life. I don't need it!'

'You and me both, kid,' said Patsy. 'I suppose I'd better see what he's on about though, this Habitation Certificate!'

'You know what Frank Kelly is going to say,' said Cherry, 'so why bother? Let them come to you!'

'Yeah, I might just do that,' said Patsy.

III

If Damien's distractions were allowing him to get over his break with Andrea with a minimum of fuss, John's weren't. After work he decided to go around and see her, and try to work out their problems. He was infatuated with her, though she, obviously, had not felt the same degree of involvement. He had a sneaking suspicion that Andrea was a good deal shallower than he'd taken her for, when she'd been whispering hot words of love in his ear during their various assignations. What he failed to understand was that Andrea thrived on the forbidden, the sinful, the act of cheating itself. She needed the added spice of the gambler, in knowing that she might at any time be caught in the act, and lose all in this bizarre game of chance. The moment her behaviour was legitimised in any way, as it had been now by Damien flying the coop, she lost all interest in the game. As a result she had spared barely a thought for John since her angry departure from his flat. When he turned up at the house, she was not exactly overwhelmed.

'Andrea, let me in. We have to discuss this, once and for all. I love you madly, you know that!'

With bad grace, Andrea unlocked the security door, then turned her back on him and stomped into the lounge.

'I think you said it all this morning, John. It's just not going to work.'

''It *will* work, if only you let it work, Andrea. We both have to get used to the idea that everything has changed; Damien's gone! He's gone out of my life, just as much as he's gone out of yours. He was my mate for eighteen years, you know. Don't you think it's just as much a wrench for me?'

'The difference is that I'm still married to him, John. He can't just walk away from me that easily. And I can't walk away from him! I've been thinking about it all day, and I'm worried, I know what Damien's like. He's probably pining away for me at this very moment, and there's nothing I can do about it.' She began to cry.

John flopped down into an easy chair and glanced momentarily up at the ceiling. Not again!

'He's a good man, John, and I've injured him terribly. What really freaks me out is that he might be lying somewhere, right now, bleeding to death, his wrists slashed to pieces with a rusty razor blade. Even if he survived, he'd probably catch some terrible disease and die from that, instead. We need to find him, John!'

John shook his head, bemused. Why on earth Damien would want to slash his wrists, and especially with a rusty razor blade, was beyond him. He still hadn't twigged that it was indicative of the drama with which Andrea cloaked every action, in order to make her own mundane existence more bearable.

'I'm sure Damien's off having a good time, thinking stuff us, and letting us get on with it. He's probably bedded someone by now, and is off on a new romance. So you don't have to worry about anything. Believe me, Damien is not the type to pine.'

This was not the message Andrea wanted to hear.

'He's devoted to me! You just don't know him at all. He often said he'd die if anything happened to me.'

'We all say things like that,' said John, dismissively. 'It's what you want to hear, and it gets the right response.'

Andrea stopped sobbing for a moment.

'What do you mean by that,' she demanded.

'Weeell....' John said, nervously, 'it gets you into bed, doesn't it? Every woman wants to think she's Cleopatra. Julius Caesar's never enough, she wants the whole Legion lusting after her.'

'Are you talking about me,' she said, angrily, 'because if you are...'

John backed hastily away from the edge of the pit he was digging.

'Noooo.... I'm just talking about things in general. But Damien's no different to the rest of us, you know. He'll get over it!'

'He won't… he won't!' She stamped her foot in vehemence. 'He'll never get over me! I'm the love of his life!'

'Until he finds somebody else,' said John. He was becoming a little weary of the subject matter. 'What about us? You swore blind that you were over him, and that you loved me! You said I made you feel alive again, that I made you feel cherished!'

Andrea got up and paced backwards and forwards across the room, as if she were caught in a trap of her own making.

'I know I said that, and I meant it at the time. I was so confused! I *had* fallen out of love with Damien, and I *did* find comfort in our times together. But it was all physical, wasn't it? I mean; there's more to a relationship than just sex. There's caring, and feeling comfortable together, and being cared for and looked after – and Damien looked after me better than anyone I've ever met. He saw to all the bills and made sure that I always had enough to spend. That's important too! I always felt secure with him.'

'And you don't with me, I suppose.'

'To be honest, no, I don't. Look at you this morning when I asked you for help. You turned me down flat.'

'You told me I'd have to sell the BMW,' said John, heatedly. 'That was hardly a reasonable request.'

'If that had been Damien, he would have gone out like a shot, and sold it! That's the difference. He cared!'

'I think you're dreaming a bit there. The trouble with you, Andrea, is that you're incredibly selfish. Every thought you have revolves around you; how *you* would feel, how *you* would be affected. You never give a thought to how someone else feels, or how much *they* have to put themselves out to satisfy *your* constant whims. Damien often complained to me that taking you on was like taking on a hire purchase agreement, only there was never a final payment date. He used to make a joke of it, but it was obvious to me that behind it all there was an element of truth.'

'You're just saying that! I bet he never said that at all. You're just making it up!'

John shook his head, slowly.

'He said it all right, and a lot of other things too, which I won't repeat because they would be too hurtful. But the fact is, he wasn't so infatuated with you as you seem to think.'

Andrea took out her hanky and blew her nose.

'You're really hateful, John, when you talk like this. I don't know why I even listen to you. You'll be saying next that you didn't love me either.'

John was quiet for a moment.

'No – I wouldn't say that. I love you all right, but you drive me crazy with this sudden obsession about wanting Damien back.'

Andrea looked at him, and suddenly realised that without John she was devoid of transport, devoid of company, and devoid of even the slightest chance of getting her rent paid.

'I don't want him back for my sake,' she sniffed. 'I want him back for *his* sake! I want *him* to be happy, and

I know he'll never be happy without me. Once everything's settled down again, you and I could still see each other, and go on just like before. After all, he's out all day, and I get dreadfully lonely.'

'So you don't want to live with me, but you'd be quite happy to just carry on a long-term affair with me! You want the best of both worlds, in fact!'

'If you put it that way, yes! I'm worth it, aren't I?

John had to begrudgingly admit that, to him, she was worth it, even if admitting it rankled.

Suddenly there was a dramatic shift in Andrea's stance. She went over to him and allowed herself to be cradled in his arms. Then they were kissing, and in the heat of the moment she found herself pressed down into the settee, tearing at his clothes and pulling him down on top of her for the pure comfort of holding someone, anyone. At that moment even the plumber would have found himself in luck, and Andrea was away somewhere where she wouldn't have known the difference.

Chapter Eight

Ignoring the constable's warning, Cherry and Patsy decided to follow their original plan that afternoon, which was to take Damien on a tour of the local area. Using Cherry's car, they headed out of town in a northerly direction, aiming to show him the Knoll. This huge hill dominated the harbour. It was densely forested up the one side, but at the top fell away into sheer cliffs, some two hundred and fifty metres above the bay. Though technically on the northern side, the way it fell, in fact, was more north-west, but it didn't take more than ten minutes to get them to the foot of the hill, and then they began to follow the narrow dirt track that ran up through the trees, which would take them to the top of the cliff.

'Are you sure this old crate will make it,' said Damien, dubiously, as the nose of the car began to adopt an ever more acute angle.

'Don't you knock my car. She's been up here hundreds of times,' said Cherry, 'haven't you old girl?' She reached out and patted the dashboard, as if to reassure the shuddering motor that everything was going to be all right.

'Yeah, for God's sake, don't say things like that, the old girl will lose confidence,' said Patsy. 'If we have to walk back, all the way down, guess who'll be carrying me!'

'Hey! Watch who you're calling an old girl!' said Cherry, grinning.

'Not you, you bloody idiot! I was talking about your car,' said Patsy.

'I know, I know,' said Cherry. At that moment the motor stalled, with the nose up at an angle of about forty-five degrees. 'Oh, bloody great! Now look at what you've done, you two and your big mouths.'

'I didn't mean it,' Damien said, holding his hands up in mock surrender. 'Really – I'm sorry for what I said about you!' He looked back over his shoulder at the way they'd come, and the slope looked horrendous, especially if it had to be taken in reverse.

Cherry turned the ignition off and opened the door.

'Come on, we might as well walk the rest of the way. It's only about fifty metres to the top.'

'What about the car,' said Damien.

'She'll be all right! She's just a bit hot, that's all. We'll give it half an hour to cool down, then it'll start again, no worries.'

'I wish I had your confidence,' said Patsy, getting out of the car. 'I still remember walking back from Longvale, on a dark night in the rain.'

'She always brings that up,' Cherry said to Damien, laughing. 'So once we had to walk a few kilometres. It was probably good for our figures.'

'A few kilometres, she says. Hah! Try forty two kilometres, and the only reason we're not lying out there, a couple of bleaching corpses, is that some kind soul picked us up and drove us the last twenty kilometres. I was just ready to expire,' Patsy replied.

They were making heavy weather of the hill, making their way up through the trees on a sharp incline. Damien wasn't used to anything more strenuous than climbing a few office stairs every once in a while, and was beginning to pant.

'Are you sure it's only fifty metres and not fifty miles,' he said.

'Don't be a pussy,' said Cherry. 'We'll be there in a tick.'

'Can I be the pussy?' said Patsy, stopping and leaning against a tree. 'If you want a volunteer for the pussy, I'll be the pussy, please, please!'

Both Cherry and Damien fell about laughing, and it took an extra three minutes to finally come out on the top of the cliff.

The forest was so dense, that before they knew it they were on the edge of a precipice, heading straight down, two hundred and fifty metres into the clear glass-calm waters of Dark Harbour. Damien took one look down, then staggered back, away from the edge.

'Good God! You wouldn't want to come wandering up here blind drunk, would you? You'd be over that bloody cliff and in the water in the twinkling of an eye.'

'Yes, but what do you think of the view? See the township, over there.'

She moved aside to let him look, and the view took his breath away. It looked so tiny down there, little toy houses and little toy cars, and people walking who looked like tiny specks, ants on the landscape.

'Oh look, I can see Constable Plod, with his little bald head and his little toy police car,' Damien said, jokingly. 'Look, he's attacking an old lady on a tricycle.'

'Oh, come on,' said Cherry. 'Don't let's talk about him. That whole scene left a really bad taste in my mouth.'

'How do you think I felt when he suggested that I might hang myself in his cell,' said Damien. 'I tell you. There's something going on in this town, something…. Evil!'

'That's a bit melodramatic, isn't it. There's a few dunderheads who have decided, for whatever inane reason, that they don't like you, and they'd rather you left town… but that doesn't make the place evil! Does it, Patsy?'

Patsy was standing near the edge of the cliff, her blonde hair blowing every which way in the rather solid breeze.

'I don't know, Cherry baby. You know, I think I'm coming around to agree with Damien here. I mean it's not just this business of trying to get rid of him, there's also the thing about Mary Burton, then Liz Capel. Neither of them explained. I'm sure they're dead, because Mary would never have left like that, and Liz, well, she was a bloody good friend of mine, and if she could, she would have been in touch, even if it was just a short telephone call to let me know that she was all right.'

Cherry stood for a while, thoughtful, and stared down at the town.

'I've tried to put it out of my mind. I think the implications of trying to work through what really happened to them are just too horrendous for me to cope with. I mean; it could have been you, Patsy. It could have been me!'

'Yes… well that's the sixty four thousand dollar question, isn't it. Why Mary Burton? Why, in the middle of making a batch of lamingtons would she suddenly disappear off the face of the earth? What could she have known around here that was dangerous to someone? Try and think what it was in her daily life that she could have discovered, or overheard, that meant she had to disappear!'

'What did she actually do, this Mary Burton,' said Damien, sitting down with his back to a tree. 'I mean, workwise! Did she work? Was there a boyfriend, girlfriend, anyone she was closely involved with?'

Patsy came over and joined him at the tree.

'She cleaned… people's houses. She was a bit of a homebody really, would have made someone a great wife. She didn't seem to mind things like vacuuming, doing the dishes, the washing… she was one of the few women of our age group that I ever knew to regularly do ironing. And she never complained, did she, Cherry.'

Cherry shook her head.

'No. She was always cheerful. She was a bit of a klutz with her recipes, sometimes, but with ordinary home cooked meals, nothing fancy, she cooked up a treat. We went to dinner there a few times, didn't we, Patsy?'

'Yeah! It was a shock when she disappeared.'

'If she cleaned houses... then whose? How many houses did she clean? I take it that was how she made her living.'

'That's right, she had about six houses that she cleaned on a regular basis. Two she did on a Friday only, so they'd be right for the weekend. Four she did twice a week... no, that's three. The fourth she did every weekday except Friday.'

'Whose house was that?' Damien asked.

'Frank Kelly's!'

'What... the guy in the pub? Doesn't he live at the pub then?'

'He does sometimes, depending on how late he finishes. But he's got a house on Third Street as well, and he prefers to spend as much of his own time as he can, there.'

'In the light of recent events, I find that very suspicious,' said Damien. 'He's obviously hand-in-glove with the local copper, and they're both desperate to get rid of me. We don't even know why.'

'I think that's stretching it a bit,' said Cherry. 'Frank's a town councillor, so obviously he'd have a pretty solid tie-in with the police. They tend to work in together.'

'That may be so, kiddo,' said Patsy, 'but that doesn't mean that they haven't got something else going on between them, a secret agenda! What better ally to have than the one local cop, especially if it's illegal.'

'What on earth could be illegal around here,' said Cherry, scathingly. 'This is Dark Harbour, for god's sake, not Chicago.'

'How about fish?' said Damien. He was staring into the distance, straight down at the dock where the trawlers tied up. 'Have you any idea how much money is tied up in fish these days.'

Cherry shrugged.

'Oh, they make a good living, I suppose.'

'Millions!' said Damien. 'Literally millions, if you count the abalone divers! How often do the Fisheries Inspectors come around here and check the trawlers? Every week... on a regular basis?'

'Come to think of it, they pretty well leave our fellows alone. They must trust them to do the right thing, or something. We do see them from time to time, but the boaties always seem to know they're coming before they actually arrive.'

'So they must be getting their information from somewhere,' said Damien. 'They're getting tipped off, which means a contact in the Department of Fisheries itself.'

'Must be I suppose,' Cherry shrugged. 'But what do you suggest, that they're smuggling illegal fish?'

'The only one who would know that would be Igor Morris. He's the one that drives the catch to the cold stores, at the market. I don't know whether his load is checked as it's unloaded, though.'

'Even if it was,' said Damien, 'what's to stop him unloading some on the way to the city. He doesn't exactly go under escort.'

'I think you might be onto something there,' said Patsy. 'It has to be something, doesn't it, and that's the most plausible answer.'

'So you think they're profiteering from illegal fish, and paying off Jack Izzard so he'll keep his mouth shut. That means that Igor Morris would have to be in on it, and Frank Kelly, and maybe even Charlie Fairweather and his mate, Lionel Jury. Not to mention some of the boaties.'

'You think the newsagent could be involved? Really?' said Damien, surprised.

'Put it this way, Charlie Fairweather and he are inseparable. Lionel is a bit like Charlie's mentor, and Charlie is basically a nasty piece of work who goes around being Mr. Tough Guy!'

'There would have to be a lot of money involved to pay off that lot!'

'There would be,' said Damien. 'Thousands at a time! Even hundreds of thousands if you're talking something like abalone.'

Patsy suddenly had a thought, stood up, and grabbed at Cherry's sleeve.

'Every one of those names we just mentioned are members of the Klan! Every one!'

Cherry nodded slowly.

'You're right! Yes, and a few more, too.'

Damien stood up as well, and stretched.

'You do realise we've strayed somewhat from the point. Mary Burton! What could she have discovered at Frank Kelly's house that made her dangerous?'

'Money! Piles of money, hidden under the mattress,' said Patsy.

Damien shook his head.

'Unlikely. Money a publican could explain away. Couldn't get it to the bank in time. Keeping it there for cash payments to suppliers. No, that's too easy!'

'What about a diary, amounts received, how the money was divided between the members of the syndicate, because it would be a syndicate, wouldn't it?'

'I think you're getting warm. Yes! Definitely warmer there.' Damien looked over into the forest that grew along the top of the cliff. 'What's in there, anything? I suppose bushwalkers go for treks through there. What's on the other side?'

'If you'd like to walk with me for about fifty metres, I'll show you.'

'What do you think, Patsy. Is this particular fifty metres reliable,' he said, grimacing.

Patsy laughed.

'Oh yes, it's not far. I'll even come with you.'

They made their way through the dense undergrowth, but it was slow going. To cover fifty metres took about ten minutes, and you were fighting it, every inch of the way.

'The rainfall up here must be pretty good, with all this new growth,' said Damien. 'It's unusual to have bush this thick in Australia.'

'It gets pretty misty in the winter, and very wet.'

Shortly there was a break in the trees, and Damien found himself staring at an eight-foot mesh fence, topped with an evil layer of barbed wire. At intervals of about twenty feet there were large signs made of metal, and painted with gloss paint in red and black.

'Department of Defence – Keep Out!' Another said 'No Entry – Trespassers Prosecuted'. Yet another, picked out prominently in red paint said 'Danger – Unexploded Bombs and Shells. Keep Out. $10,000 Penalty Applies.'

'What the hell is this place,' said Damien. Cherry pointed to another sign, further along in the other direction.

'RAAF Firing Range – Danger! Unexploded Missiles and Bombs in this area.' In smaller print on a sign immediately beneath this it said: 'Persons found trespassing in this area will be prosecuted under the provisions of the Official Secrets Act, and may be liable to imprisonment for a period of up to seven years.'

Damien read it carefully, and then nodded, as if satisfied.

'Well, that answers my question, doesn't it? Do they still fly over, blasting away with bombs and missiles?'

'Not any more,' said Cherry. It's been closed now for about seven years. I think the council fought to have it closed off when a missile came hurtling off a cliff face, and narrowly missed one of the trawlers at anchor in the bay. As it was, it exploded underwater, and split the trawler's seams. The Air Force had to fork out to fix it.'

'Nice one,' said Damien. 'Okay, well I suppose we'd better be getting back to the car. It should have cooled down by now.'

They turned and fought their way back to the path, then began to descend. As they were going down, they could hear the sound of a vehicle coming up the other way. They looked at each other, and Cherry shook her head.

'I thought it was too good to last,' she said. 'More harassment.'

'I think you might be right,' Damien said, peering through the trees.

II

As Damien and the two women hurried down the slope, they heard the vehicle below them stop, and there was just the sound of a motor, idling. It took some minutes before they got to a point where they could actually see Cherry's car, and when they did, they could see the other vehicle parked beside it. It was a jeep, an old wartime model painted in camouflage colours and badly knocked about.

'Charlie Fairweather,' Cherry muttered, breathing heavily.

Damien came out into the opening and saw Charlie, with Cherry's door open, doing something in the interior of her car. He yelled out to the intruder, and started to run, the girls following on behind.

'Hey! What the hell do you think you're doing?'

As he spoke, Charlie got out, and Damien could see that he was grinning, taunting them with a look. He slammed Cherry's door shut and her car began to roll backwards, slowly at first, and then gathering speed, back down the steep track and out of control.

'I warned you,' said Charlie as they approached. 'Now you can wear it!'

He stood there defiantly as Damien ran towards him, his fists clenched and ready to take Damien out. 'Come on then, smart arse. Come and get it!'

Damien went straight for him, then unexpectedly leapt into the air and, taking advantage of the higher ground, launched himself feet first into Charlie's chest. One foot hit him in the chest, the other smashed into his jaw. Charlie went down like a sack of potatoes, and lay there groggily, looking up to see Damien kneeling on his chest, a fist perilously close to his face.

'Right, you prick! Now you're going to tell us what all this is about. You're going to pay for any damage to that car, and if you give me a hard time I'll tie you to that jeep and drag you down the hill.'

Charlie looked up at him, and sneered.

'You don't know what you're getting yourself into, mate!'

Damien's fist slammed down into his face, and Charlie's nose spouted blood as it flattened against his face.

'Ow, you prick! Get off me, let me get up, I'll do ya!'

Damien let him have it again, and Charlie sank back and groaned.

Cherry had chased her car down the hill, and found it rear-ended up against a tree. It was driveable, but only just. She marched back up the hill and got there just as Damien was getting ready to punish Charlie with a rain of blows.

'What the hell do you think you're doing Charlie Fairweather? You've wrecked my car. It wasn't much to start with, now it's totally stuffed. What did you want to do a thing like that for?'

Charlie looked up at her, and sneered, his face covered in blood.

'Serves you right, you bitch! Aren't the local boys good enough for you, Miss hoity-toity? You have to get yourself involved with a jerk-off from out of town!'

'Who I go out with, and who my friends are, is no concern of yours, Charlie. Now you're going to pay for that car!'

'Like hell I am,' he said, and spat in her direction.

Cherry walked around, stuck her foot in between his legs and ground her heel into his groin. Charlie shrieked in agony, and tried to curl up to defend himself. Damien socked him twice in the jaw, and Charlie went spark out. Then they went through his pockets. In the back pocket of his trousers, Damien found Charlie's wallet, and stood up, opening it up for inspection. In the back of the wallet was a wad of hundred dollar bills, half an inch thick.

'What were we saying, eh? Look at this! Count it, Cherry.'

Cherry riffled through the notes and looked at Damien in disbelief.

'There's $8,400 there! I don't believe it.'

'Well, it's yours, Cherry! Stick it in your pocket and buy yourself another car. This idiot isn't going to pay any other way.'

Cherry hesitated.

'I don't know whether I should. It's like stealing, isn't it?'

'Not at all, not after what he's done to your car! And by the way, I think we'll sort his jeep out while we're at it. You go down and get the car started, I'll fix this!'

Damien jumped into the jeep and drove it through the trees, up to the top of the cliff. Then he slammed it in first, set it rolling forward and watched as it drove over the edge and disappeared out of sight.

He was running back down and past the clearing as Charlie was coming round.

'If you want your jeep back, you'd better get yourself a fishing rod,' yelled Damien as he careered past. He was getting into the car before Charlie struggled to his feet, wiping the blood off his face.

'I'll fucking get you for this!' he yelled, shaking his fist. 'You haven't heard the last of this. You're dead meat!'

Damien gave him the finger as the car lurched forward and went clattering back down the hill, the boot hanging on by just one hinge.

'Oh God,' moaned Patsy. 'This just gets worse and worse by the minute. We can't go to the police, because Izzard's in with the rest of them. It's just us against them, and there's too many of them.'

'You worry too much,' said Damien, who was still feeling the adrenalin rush after giving Charlie what for. 'We've done all right so far, haven't we? They haven't got us yet, and they won't as long as we stick together on this.'

'What if he goes to Izzard about the money?' said Cherry. 'He can have me arrested!'

'I don't think so, somehow. If we're right, and they are into some form of illegal activity, they'd find it hard to explain what Charlie was doing walking around with over eight thousand dollars in his wallet. After all, what does he do for a living?'

'He's on the dole,' said Cherry. 'That's what I couldn't understand. Where did it come from?'

'I bet the Tax Office would like an answer to that question as well,' said Damien. 'No, I don't think the money is going to be a problem. We're just going to go quietly out of town tomorrow, drive up the coast and find ourselves a car dealer. Then we're going to buy you a car for cash, and drive back home as if nothing's happened. I don't think either Charlie or the cop are going to visit us again in a hurry.'

'Not officially, maybe,' said Patsy. 'But they might pay us a nocturnal visit. I don't want to disappear like Liz Capel or Mary Burton!'

Cherry looked over her shoulder at her friend in the back seat.

'It's really getting to you, isn't it, Patsy? If you want us to stop hanging around together for a while, I'll understand. It's not going to interfere with our friendship.'

Patsy nodded, a look of relief on her face.

'Yes, well maybe that would be for the best. My blood pressure must have gone up ten points over the past few days. I need to chill out for a while, get over all this aggro.'

Damien threw a sideways glance at Cherry, as if to say, 'where does that leave me?'

'I think Damien had better come and stay with me for a while,' said Cherry, as if anticipating his question. 'That will forestall any question of Certificates of Habitation that they might throw at you, and I will feel safer now that I know Damien can look after himself. That was an incredible sidekick you pulled back there. Quite the Bruce Lee, aren't you Damien?'

'I had the advantage of higher ground,' Damien laughed. 'I was just so mad that I let instinct take over. Mind you, I wasn't a bad scrapper when I was a lad!'

'So much for tough guy Charlie Fairweather,' said Patsy. 'That was great!'

143

'And I don't think he'll be interested in me any more,' laughed Cherry, 'now that I've crushed his nuts for him.'

'It will certainly cool his ardour,' Damien grinned. 'I hope you don't ever get that mad with me!'

'It depends on how you behave yourself,' said Cherry, archly. 'Just don't ever take anything for granted.'

'I won't, I won't,' he said, and gave her a knowing look. She smiled to herself, and drove back onto the main road, headed for home.

III

An hour later, at the Promenade Hotel, a blonde woman disguised in a headscarf made her way warily into the entranceway, and avoiding both the bar and the lounge continued on along the passageway to the private rooms at the rear. Beyond the guest rooms there was another passageway, a short one, with a locked door at the end.

She took a key out of her purse and unlocked this, passed through and closed the door behind her. Ahead there was a set of stairs, heading down into a cellar, and at the other end of the cellar, stocked with barrels and litres of wine, was another locked door. She used another key to open this, then again, passed through and locked it behind her. There was no window in the room she found herself in, only a small ventilator for air, and a dingy light, no more than twenty five watts.

In the corner was a toilet, standing stark against the wall, and it needed cleaning badly. Next to it was an old laundry sink, and there was a mop and bucket in the corner. Someone had recently been sick, and had missed the target, fouling both the porcelain and the floor around it. On the other side of the room was a low bed, and lying on the bed was a woman who looked ravaged and worn. She could have been anywhere between thirty and forty-five, but it would be hard to tell. She had straight red hair, but it had not been combed for some time, and was tangled and shoulder length. There was a glassy look in her eyes, and she barely had the energy to turn her head, to see who her visitor was.

'I've brought you a beam of sunshine,' said the blonde woman. 'Aren't I good to you? I hope you've been behaving yourself!'

With an effort, the woman sat up on the bed, swung her legs onto the floor, and tried to sit up straight. It was an effort. Now that she was sitting it was more obvious how emaciated she was, her flesh hung in folds at the neck, and her once finely muscled arms had shrunk to skin and bone. To look at her legs, there didn't seem enough muscle there to support her weight, but she did manage from time to time to get to her feet and walk around her tiny enclosure.

She tried to speak, but her mouth was dry, and the woman passed her a glass of water for her to wet her lips before any intelligible word was spoken.

'How much longer,' she said. 'You promised... how much longer?'

'We have to be sure that you're going to behave yourself out there, and not give any of our little secrets away, don't we,' said the blonde woman.

'I don't know any secrets,' said the scarecrow on the bed. 'For god's sake, let me get some fresh air. I can't breathe in here.'

'There'll be plenty of time for that when you get your health back. You've been very poorly, and we don't want you catching any more viruses when we let you out, do we?'

'I just want to go home,' said the woman.

'So, you don't want your little beam of sunshine then,' said the blonde woman. 'In that case, I'll take it back with me and have it myself.'

'No, no... I need it! You know I need it or I'll go crazy again. I don't want to go crazy again,' she wailed, in a thin, high voice.

'Well, keep your noise down. There are patients next door who are trying to sleep, as I've told you before. You're lucky to have your own room! They're all sleeping four to a room out there. You wouldn't like that, would you?'

'No, I know you're looking after me,' she said, brokenly. She put her arm out for the other to take, and the blonde woman fumbled in her bag.

'Don't be impatient; I'll get it out, soon enough. First I'm going to have to clean up the mess you've made.'

The visitor took the mop and filled a bucket from the old sink. Then she laboriously cleaned up the mess and flushed the toilet.

146

'Now can I have it,' the other woman said, her hands shaking. 'I can feel it coming on… the cramps. I'm getting these terrible cramps.'

'Now you can have it,' said the woman. She pulled a syringe out of her bag and took the cap off the needle. As the contents were injected into the scarecrow's arm, she let out a long sigh of relief, then fell back on the bed and stared, unseeingly at the ceiling.

'That should sort you out until the morning,' said the blonde woman to herself.

She let herself out through the door and locked it behind her, crossed the cellar floor and ascended the stairs. Once through the second locked door, and on her way through to the entranceway, Frank Kelly suddenly appeared from the bar. He grabbed her by the arm, and pulled her into his tiny office.

'She's got to go. I can't keep her here any longer. It's getting far too dangerous!'

'Stop worrying, Frank! I told you everything would be all right, and it is, isn't it? We haven't had any problems up til now.'

'No… but we have now! The lid's about to blow off this mess, I can feel it in my bones. If what Craig said about that Curtis guy is right, we're in deep trouble.'

'I wouldn't worry about him. He's too caught up in chasing Cherry around the place to notice anything strange going on. Jack will sort it out, anyway!'

'Yeah, well Jack tried, and he's crapping himself, says this guy is real trouble!'

'Huh… men!' said the blonde woman, barely concealing her contempt. 'There's too much at stake to cut and run now. Just give it another couple of weeks, and we're home and hosed.'

'You heard about Charlie?' said the publican.

'No – what about Charlie?'

'He got his arse kicked earlier on, that Damien made a right mess of him. And he took over eight grand out of Charlie's back pocket.

The blonde woman stamped one foot in anger on the floor.

'For god's sake, Frank, put a collar on him! He's a walking disaster area, that one.'

'Well he certainly is at the moment. He's got a broken nose, bruised nuts and two fractured fingers from when he fell. I don't think he'll be around for a few days, at least.'

'Well thank god for small mercies, Frank! Keep him away from Cherry, will you. He just makes things ten times worse.'

'I'll try,' said Frank. 'But you'd better get that woman out of here soon. This week, if possible.'

'I'll do my best, Frank!'

With that, the blonde woman made her way out into the street.

Chapter Nine

Doctor Ilse Hirsch busied herself at her cottage that evening, taking orders for tea or coffee from the other five members of the Honourable Society of Welsh Bards. Though only of questionable Welsh connections, namely a legendary great grandmother who had married a German before the Great War, she had been the driving force behind the formation of the group after listening to Igor Morris and his endless fund of Welsh stories. That she had a hidden agenda was not general knowledge, except to one person. Craig Mortimer shared most of her secrets by virtue of the fact that he, unknown to anyone else, shared her bed. The group sat and chatted in her small lounge room, and examined the new robes for the Society that had just arrived up from the city, thanks to the efforts of Morris.

'Are these a standard design, Igor,' asked Ron Davies, whose welsh ancestry had been interrupted by three generations born and bred in South Australia.

'Oooh aaah!' said Igor. 'These date back to the times of the Druids, boyo! You know how far back that is, don'you? Two thousan' years! True! The Welsh met Julius Caesar on the beach, in Kent. They painted their faces blue and put on a show of charioteering that he later wrote about in his history, '*The Gallic War*.''

'Is that so,' said Emily Longstaff, impressed. As usual, she sat as close to him as decorum would permit, on a pouffé, to the left of his armchair, which meant that whenever she was passed something from the group she would have to reach across his knees and brush his thighs with her hand or arms. Igor never complained. He felt flattered that a woman such as Emily would show so much overt interest in a crusty old scholar like himself. He also had it in mind to take matters further one day, when the opportunity arose. But in groups like this, he was careful not to let his interest show.

When he wasn't drinking, he constantly had his head thrust into a book, and was certainly an authority on some things, though not necessarily anything that interested anyone else. A lot of his reading concerned ancient civilisations, and he was well informed about the history of his beloved Wales.

'So who wore the robes, Igor... not the charioteers, I trust.'

'Oh no, Emily. Only the Bards - who were, you might say, the poets and singers of ancient Wales. They were like a secret society in those days, and were more like high priests. Their function was to pass down all the old tales and histories from father to son, if you like, and preserve the culture of the ancient Britons. At Eisteddfods and special ceremonies, the Bards would appear in their robes and recite verses and sagas for the education of the people. As far as we know, the robes were designed exactly the same as these.'

He held one up for them all to see. It was made of a dark green material, designed to enclose the head and shoulders and the entire body, so that no part of the Bard might be recognised. It was trimmed with a black edging, which made the resulting figure look rather ominous, a little like the medieval depictions of Death.

'We're gonna scare the shit out of the townsfolk in these,' said David Owen, a trawlerman whose great-great-great-grandfather had been transported from Merthyr Tydfil for jostling a visiting magistrate in the street, and stealing his gold pocket watch.

'Just in time for tomorrow night, Ilse,' said Igor, laughing. 'This town's never seen nothin' like this!'

'Well, I hope they don't see them tomorrow, either,' said Ilse, sharply. 'It's better if we keep it low profile until we're ready to do the blessing of the fleet. Tomorrow's just a warm up.'

Craig Mortimer sat in the corner, and occasionally managed to catch Ilse's eye. He was an honorary member, even though his ancestry was purported to be the hated English. In actual fact, though, he had discovered that his family originated in Monmouthshire, and as that had always been a disputed county, claimed by the Welsh but ceded to England, that made it all right. Craig remained secretive about his relationship with Ilse Hirsch, and she ignored him completely. But they often met at those times when no one else was around, and if they hadn't shared membership of this group, any meeting would have been enough to raise eyebrows had it been general knowledge.

The fact that Ilse was so obviously a social division or two above Craig allayed suspicion. She was also a year older. Ilse had no intention of letting it become common knowledge that her sexual tastes ran to the bizarre, and that a 'tumble in the rough' was her idea of great sex. Despite her poise and grace, Craig was the one outlet for both her sadistic and masochistic impulses, outside of the snake pit in the back garden.

'Try it on, Ilse. Let's see you in character!'

Ilse took one of the robes and disappeared into the bedroom, returning some minutes later with her head covered, and her hands clasped together. She looked so ominous that a sudden hush fell over the group. They were impressed! No part of her was recognisable, nor indeed, whether it was a man or a woman.

'So what's the score tomorrow, Ilse? I understand that we'll be wearing these things down to the dock, to meet the trawler 'Sea Horse'. That's Wilf Carstairs tub, isn't it? Will he be expecting us?'

'Oh yes, he's all tee'd up. Craig here was talking to him on the radio earlier. He's been out a couple of days, and he'll be back tomorrow. Are you driving the truck tomorrow, Igor?'

'No, not tomorrow! Frank Kelly has offered to stand in. He needs to pick up some gear for the pub anyway, so he'll be bringing it back in the truck the next day.'

'That's good, because we need you in the procession. It's just a practice, really. We'll go down, stand alongside on the dock and Craig and I will go on board, bless the catch, bless the boat and all who sail in her, and ward off evil waters. Then we'll slow march in procession back up from the dock. Simple!'

'What time is he due in, Craig,' said David Owen.

All eyes turned to Craig, who shifted uncomfortably in his seat. Craig always operated best in the background. When the spotlight of attention fell on him from time to time, he always felt somehow exposed.

'Oh, err… at this point it looks like about eleven thirty p.m. There shouldn't be anyone around at that time.'

'Does it really matter if there is?' said Emily.

'No – not really,' said Ilse, from somewhere inside her hood. 'But as I said before, it might be better if we're not seen the first time out. We don't want a crowd around us until we get used to performing these ceremonies. Everyone else can have a look at us later on.'

The group had a break while sipping coffee and tea, and Ilse disappeared into the kitchen, calling Craig in to help her take out some of the tea things. They were gone for some time.

'Tell us a story, Igor; come on! Tell us about the old times.'

Igor looked gratified. He was the resident story-teller, and it was nice to be appreciated.

'Have I told you the story of Bethgelert,' he said. 'In welsh, the 'th' sound is spelt with a double 'd', so it's actually spelt B-e-d-d-g-e-l-e-r-t. Anyway! This story goes back to the time of Prince Llewelyn, and is set in the valleys near Snowden, the highest mountain in

Wales. The Prince was very fond of hunting, so it's said, and he came one day to stay in a hunting lodge near the River Glaslyn. He arrived with horses and hounds, various servants and his wife, Princess Joan, who brought their baby son along. The next day, he looked for his faithful hound, Gelert, to take him along on the hunt, but for some unknown reason he was nowhere to be found. Now the Prince was very fond of his hound, and usually would not have gone off without him. This day however, he did, leaving the baby behind, sleeping, at the hunting lodge. It was not long before he began to worry about the dog's disappearance, however, and finally ordered them all back to the lodge. On their return, Gelert came bounding out to meet them, but on them coming closer, they could see that the great hound was covered in blood. Llewelyn panicked, ran into the lodge, and found the crib empty, but there was blood smeared all over the floor, the walls, and the crib itself. With a heartrending cry, Llewelyn drew his sword, and ran it through his favourite hound, thinking that it had killed his child. At that moment, as the hound gave its dying yelp, they heard a child's cry from beneath a pile of bedclothes, and on drawing them aside, Llewelyn found his son alive and perfectly well. At the same time one of the party lifted a pile of bloodstained tapestry from the floor, and found the body of a giant wolf, its throat ripped out, obviously killed by the hound protecting its master's child.'

'The Prince was overcome with sorrow at what he'd done, and ordered that the body of Gelert was to be taken to the meadow called Dol-y-Lleian and buried with all honour. He ordered a great stone to be raised above his grave, detailing the story of the faithful Gelert. Many years came and went, and eventually a village was built nearby, and it was called Bedd Gelert – or Bethgelert! The grave of Gelert. The stone stands to this day, and if you are ever in Wales, you may still visit the grave of this unfortunate hound.'

'That's a really sad story, Igor,' said Emily.

'When's this supposed to have happened,' said Craig, having just re-entered the room with another tray.

'Sometime in the thirteenth century, boyo,' said Igor.

What none of the group in the lounge realised, was that when Craig had followed Ilse into the kitchen, and pulled the door to behind him, she had flung open her gown to reveal herself to him. Beneath the gown, she had been totally naked. While Prince Llewelyn was thrusting his sword through the vital organs of his great hound, Craig Mortimer had been attempting to emulate him in the next room, on the naked, hooded body of his hostess. They had both been spurred on by the imminent danger of discovery.

II

With Patsy's desertion, both Cherry and Damien were much quieter once they found themselves solely in each other's company. The following day, Cherry made them up a salad for lunch, and they ate it at the back of her

155

cottage, where she had an outdoor setting, sheltered by a canopy.

'Do you think Patsy will be all right,' said Damien, after they'd eaten.

They were sitting back, enjoying the afternoon, and working their way through a bottle of Riesling.

'Yeah, she'll be all right. Why shouldn't she? We've both lived in this town all our lives, so what could threaten her now?'

'You said Liz Capel had lived here all her life too, and Mary Burton.'

'That's true! But I can't see it happening again. Even if there is something going on, I don't know anything about it, and neither does she. What are *we* going to tell anyone…?'

'I know nothing, either, for that matter. Which makes it all the more strange why I should have been targeted in the first place. I mean… I just called in for petrol! What's so hard about that? Surely, people call in here for petrol all the time.'

'Not so many as you'd think! Most travellers fill up back down the road at Longvale, and that's only fifty k's, so they usually go sailing past to Port Flint, or even further to Abbeville. The same if you're going in the other direction! Dark Harbour tends to be bypassed.'

'Nevertheless, if it hadn't been for the accident, and for meeting you, I would have spent a most uncomfortable night in the car, got petrol the next morning and been gone by nine o'clock. I had no intention of staying, originally.'

'And now?' said Cherry, looking at him searchingly.

Damien glanced over at her and smiled.

'Well, now I like the scenery... and I'm pig-headed enough to dig my heels in whenever someone tells me I have to go!' He noted the look of disappointment on her face and added: 'and on top of that, I've met a woman that I'm very attracted to. I have this feeling that if I can hang around for long enough, she might just take her eyes away from her drink long enough to notice me.'

Cherry put her glass down, and laughed.

'I thought that you and Patsy might have made a fine couple, to tell the truth. She's good fun, and I don't think you could have resisted her for long if I'd left you in that flat of hers.'

'No, true! I found that fluffy Pooh-Bear nightie of hers overwhelmingly erotic,' he grinned, and Cherry almost choked on her drink, she was laughing so much.

'It's a beauty, isn't it! She calls it her passion killer. She reckons that by the time you've struggled to get the hem up past her knees, you've had such an eyeful of Pooh-Bear that it would be impossible to maintain an erection.'

'I think she might be right,' said Damien.

At that moment a figure came stumbling around the back of the cottage, tripping over some timber that had been left lying across the path.

'Craig,' Cherry said, looking at him in surprise. 'To what do we owe the pleasure of your company?'

Damien looked at Cherry to see if he could detect a note of sarcasm there, but Cherry kept a straight face.

'Hi, Cherry! Sorry to barge in, but I need to see your friend there for a minute.'

'Sure... is it private, do you need me to go for a walk?'

'No, no need for that! It's just that we were coming in the other night, and we saw all this stuff floating out in the harbour... clothes, suitcases, all sorts of things. We didn't know who it belonged to at the time, but I managed to snag a small wooden box and pull it on board. It was full of family photographs.'

Damien sat up at this and took notice.

'You've got it, you say. Great! I suppose the photo's are stuffed, though!'

'Well, they were certainly wet, and I had to take them home and rinse them off in the sink to separate them from each other, then dry them out. It's taken a couple of days altogether, and I just wondered...'

'What Craig is wondering, Damien, is if there is some sort of reward for their return,' said Cherry, seeing Craig begin to flush.

'Oh, for sure... certainly! They're pretty important to me, as you can imagine. I thought they'd gone for good.'

'Umm, well, how much is what I was thinking. I've spent a couple of days...'

'Yes, I understand that, about the effort you had to put in. How about a hundred bucks,' said Damien, feeling generous.

Craig's face lit up.

'Great! I'll go and get them. They're in the back of the car.'

When he had gone, Cherry said *sotto voce,* 'he would have been just as happy with fifty!'

Craig duly returned and put the box on the table. Damien opened it up and pulled the photo's out. There was quite a pile of them. He riffled through the pile and then asked, 'was the box open in the water? I mean, do you think you lost any as you were pulling it aboard?'

Craig shook his head.

'No... I don't think so! The clasp was on tight. But it was full of water, obviously.'

'Hmmm. Strange! Still, here's your hundred bucks, and thanks for saving them for me.'

Craig took the proffered notes, but seemed reluctant to go.

'When I was drying them out, I couldn't help noticing that guy in uniform. What uniform was that, Navy?'

'Oh, you must mean the picture of my mate, John. No, he'd just joined Customs and Excise. They've got a lot of gold braid on their uniforms.'

'Oh, I see. So you're not...'

'What? Customs and Excise! No... you wouldn't get me in a uniform. That was his bag, not mine.'

'Right! Well, I'd better go then. Thanks for the reward, it will help out a lot.'

'No worries, mate. And thanks for the photo's.'

When he'd gone, Damien stared down at the table for some time, and then glanced at Cherry.

'I thought it was strange,' he said.

Cherry looked at him, quizzically.

'Well, he mentioned the photo of John in his uniform, but as you can see, it's not here! The photo's not here!'

Cherry watched as he riffled through the photographs again.

'Yeah, that is queer, isn't it?'

III

Emily spent the morning restlessly wandering around the empty cottage, trying to work out what to do with herself. Gordon had gone off on his trip, and Emily, as usual, was expected to be the good little wife and stay at home, twiddling her thumbs until he came back again. But this morning, she was feeling rebellious.

She had sat at the feet of Igor all the previous evening while at Ilse's place, and her occasional forays across his lap with her hand had caused no end of erotic sensations for the two of them. Eventually, Igor had allowed his left arm to drop unseen, down over the arm of the chair, where his hand had found the top of Emily's leg. Instead of pulling away, she had manoeuvred his hand in towards her crotch and had sat there, her knees pulled up, and her arms clasped around her knees. Everyone else was on the other side of Igor's chair, so there was little chance of being seen. When he eventually withdrew his hand, she had managed to press it against her breast as he pulled away, and she had waited around while all the goodnights were said, and the group disappeared to their various homes.

Twenty minutes later, Emily found herself pressed up against a tree in the shadows, while Igor worked his hand up between her legs and kissed her passionately at the same time. For the first time in years she found herself reciprocating, as she pressed up against him and felt him rising to the occasion.

'I didn't realise the Welsh were so well built,' she muttered, as he kissed her again.

'It's been a long time, Emily. I've never been much for the women, you know. I wouldn't go off with just any woman – she has to be special!'

'Do I fit that category,' she murmured. 'That would be nice, being special for someone for a change.'

'I've had my eye on you for a long time,' he said, 'but you're married, Emily. Taken!'

'That's right… a kept woman, that's what I am, Igor! But I'm yours if you want me. We can't do anything here though… it's too exposed,' she said. 'I'd hate to get caught!'

'I hope you're not going to leave me like this! I'll never be able to sleep tonight!' His tone was vaguely recriminating.

'So what do you want me to do?'

Then it was daylight, she couldn't get Igor out of her mind. At one in the afternoon, with Gordon over the horizon in the 'Wavefarer', when it was safe to stroll along the main street in public without being thought to be out of place, she ducked around the corner and knocked on Igor's door. He had spent an excitedly restless night as well, and by the time he invited her into his cottage for the first time, he knew exactly what he wanted.

Chapter Ten

The following morning, Cherry and Damien took *his* car and headed off early to Port Flint. They had spent a wary night together, listening for any strange noises and checking outside at nervous intervals for prowlers. It had been an unusually quiet night, ominously so.

'Do you get the idea that something's changed,' said Damien at about eleven o'clock. 'No snakes, no warnings, and we haven't had to jam anyone's fingers in the door yet. Even Jack Izzard seems to have lost interest.'

'Yes, it is strange isn't it, after the past few days… I would have thought Charlie would have been here, after his money, with Jack Izzard in tow.'

'Either he didn't dare report it, or Jack Izzard is in - whatever it is - with them! I'd go for the second choice. I still think it's fish, probably abalone. There's huge money involved.'

'Well, maybe we should get in touch with Fisheries while we're at Port Flint tomorrow, and let them know what's going on.'

Damien shook his head.

'Pointless! They'd think we'd lost our marbles. Let's face it, we haven't got anything to go on at all, it's just surmise. There's no hard evidence, just a lot of disjointed happenings and a lot of aggro. If I *was* a

Fisheries Officer I could understand it. Though why they would think that…'

Suddenly Damien did a double-take. He thought for a moment, then reached out and grabbed Cherry by the shoulder.

'The photo! That missing bloody photo of me, and John Inglis! I *thought* Craig was a bit too curious, and then, of course, the photo was missing. John is Customs and Excise! Maybe that's what they thought I was, undercover so to speak. In which case we're looking at smuggling. They're smuggling something, and it isn't fish.'

'What the hell could they smuggle from Dark Harbour? It's not exactly the centre of the universe,' said Cherry, bemused. 'It's not even on a trade route. If we were up near Darwin, on the doorstep of Asia, so to speak, I could understand it. But here?'

'It's coming in on the trawlers,' said Damien, taking a mighty leap in the dark. 'It's the only explanation. The trawlers bring it in, and then it's transferred to the city.'

Cherry shook her head.

'I find that hard to believe! Erin Lachlan is as straight as a dye. He's almost boringly law-abiding, I've known him forever.'

'Yes, but there are six trawlers operating from here. He's not the only one. It might only be one trawler involved, or two, or three. What about drugs?'

'Drugs?' Cherry shook her head, and then was silent for a while. 'Though I must admit, Liz Capel was a bit off the beam. She was always popping something… but they were prescribed drugs, medical stuff. She was always going off to one doctor or another with some ailment, and I remember going round there once and seeing a drawer full of various pills and things. But that didn't make her a druggie!'

'It made her vulnerable, though,' said Damien, grimly. 'For some people, one drug is pretty much like another as long as it helps them to avoid facing up to life.'

The following day, while driving out of Dark Harbour he brought the topic of Liz Capel up again.

'You've never really told me much about her… what was she like; as a person?'

Cherry pulled a face, and then shrugged.

'She was a funny sort of person, really. She could be the life and soul of the party one minute, and then totally withdrawn and paranoid the next. I think she used drugs to control her moods. When she was high, she had a tendency to become aggressive. Patsy got on okay with her… I never did, really. Not my type! She wasn't the most popular person around here.'

'What about her love life? Did she have any boyfriends?'

'Oh, yeah… millions of them! She was one of those women that attract men like flies. Usually the wrong type! They'd have their wicked way with her, and then ditch her. She was always getting ditched. The only really close woman friend she had, besides Patsy, was Mary Burton, and it was only when she became too vocal about going to the authorities in the city about

Mary's disappearance, that she disappeared herself. But at least she got her name on the Missing Persons list, which is more than Mary Burton did.'

'So, Jack Izzard didn't try to explain her absence away?'

'No, not that time! He made a big deal out of going down there with a couple of visiting C.I.B., and going through the place to see if there was any clue as to why she'd gone. But they came up blank.'

'Who had she been seeing at the time?'

'She was on and off with Lionel Jury for a while, but he's a pompous little shit. I think she'd already shown him the door. Charlie Fairweather was hanging about there for a while. He might have still been seeing her on the quiet. She was quite secretive about her love life, because you never knew if she was off with someone's husband. It never seemed to bother her – or at least, maybe she just didn't know how to say 'no' to them.'

'I take it she must have been pretty attractive, to have all these men hanging around?'

'That's just it. She was a redhead, but not what you'd call a raving beauty. Maybe she just gave off a lot of pheromones!'

'I don't suppose she was charging for her services, by any chance?'

Cherry looked shocked.

'What... Liz Capel? If she had, I'm sure everyone would have known about it. Dark Harbour is too small a town to keep those sorts of secrets!'

'Well, how did she make a living? Did she work...?'

Cherry shook her head, bemused.

'You know, it's funny. I'd never thought about it. No, she didn't work. I just assumed she was on the dole, like everyone else around here. Those that don't fish and don't farm are generally on the dole.'

'So you're on the dole, too!'

'I didn't say that… Gee, you're nosey, aren't you, Damien? You'll be asking me what colour knickers I wear next.'

Damien grinned at her, and looked back at the road.

'Well? What colour knickers *do* you wear? I saw some pink ones and some green ones in the washing basket yesterday.'

Cherry punched him on the arm, and blushed slightly.

'You leave my knickers out of this,' she said, smiling despite herself.

They had been travelling for about twenty minutes when there was the sound of a police siren behind them on the road. Damien looked in the rear vision mirror, and groaned.

'Oh no, not him again!'

Cherry looked around, just in time to see them being flagged over by Izzard in the Patrol Car. Damien applied the brake and pulled over to the left, off the road. The Patrol car pulled up in front of them. Jack Izzard got slowly out of his car, and walked back towards them, pad in hand. Damien didn't wait for him to arrive, but got out of the car.

'What is it this time, Officer,' he said, sardonically. 'Did I run over a protected bunny, or is this just a social call?'

Izzard glowered at him, but refused to respond to his jibe.

'You were just clocked at 125 kilometres in a 110 zone. I'm writing you a ticket.'

'Oh sure! That would be par for the course. Got any idle threats for me today, whore-fficer?'

'Just keep it up, Curtis! You'll talk your way into one of my cells yet!'

'Is that right?'

'Yes – that is right! There's your ticket for a start. Now, where do you think you're going in that rust-bucket?'

'Out of town, what does it look like. Isn't that what you wanted?'

Izzard began a walk round of Damien's vehicle, checking everything as he went. Then he came back to the front of the car and began to write on a fresh form, and speak as he did so.

'Two worn tyres – rear. One cracked and faded lens cover on rear offside brake light. One deep chip on windscreen in line of driver's vision! Get in and turn the headlights on if you please.'

Damien grimaced, but did as he was asked. No sense in inflaming the situation. Izzard checked the headlights, tail lights, brake lights and indicators. Damien got out again.

'Are you aware that one of your brake lights isn't working?' said Izzard, making a note. Damien said nothing. 'Show me your licence please, and your registration papers.'

'Don't you think this farce has gone far enough,' Damien snorted, frustrated.

'I'll be the one to judge that. Licence!'

After writing down Damien's details on his form, Izzard handed the licence back.

'This motor vehicle is hereby defected, and may not be driven on a public road until this defect sticker is removed,' said Izzard. 'That means that you must turn around and drive it back to Miss Reynolds place and leave it there until it's fixed.'

'Now hang on a minute…'

'If you defy this order, I am at liberty to place you under arrest. Is that understood?'

'Oh, it's understood all right. First of all you order me to leave town, and now, for reasons known only to you, I am being prevented from leaving. What's the matter… are you worried I might run into a real policeman at Port Flint and put in a report?'

'I'd watch my mouth if I were you! You're treading on sticky ground, very sticky ground.'

Cherry got out of the car and slammed the car door.

'Right! That's it, Damien. We'll hitch hike. Come on!'

Izzard was taken aback.

'I've ordered you to return this motor vehicle to Dark Harbour – and that means now!'

Cherry spun on her heel and stared him down.

'We'll return it later, *Constable!* Right now we have an appointment at Port Flint.'

'You can't leave that on the side of the road... it's against the law,' Izzard blustered.

'Which particular law was that? You've defected the vehicle. It will have to stay there now until it's convenient for us to return it.'

'I'm ordering you...' Izzard said, but Cherry was already out in the road, flagging a car down. Before the constable could say another word, the car had pulled up alongside, and a passenger wound the window down.

'Damien, what are you doing here?'

'Hi Veronica! Going to Port Flint? Could you drop me and Cherry there... we just got defected!'

Veronica shot a look at the Policeman, and it wasn't complimentary.

'Sure kid, hop in the back.'

Damien and Cherry were in the car and off before Izzard could make a move. Damien looked back and saw him stamp his foot in frustration.

'You did well there,' he said, grinning.

'Well... the nerve of the man,' said Cherry. 'I don't know what's got into him lately. I'm going to put in a complaint of harassment.'

Damien turned to their hosts in the front. 'I want you to meet friends of mine, Veronica and Tim Watson. Von, this is Cherry!'

The two in front turned, and nodded politely.

'What was all that about, Damien? That cop didn't look too happy.'

Damien explained about the car, but refrained from going into details about prior events. 'We're just going to Port Flint to pick up another vehicle, actually. Hers has finally bitten the dust.'

The Watson's dropped them off in the main street of Port Flint, and then went on with their journey. Cherry and Damien walked along to the first Used Car Sales yard they came across, and went in.

II

John Inglis had barely arrived home from work when the phone rang. Suppressing a groan, he looked agonisingly up at the ceiling, and picked up. It was Andrea.

For the past couple of days their relationship had run along the brink of on-again, off-again so many times that John was heartily sick of the whole ménage. Andrea's *'poor little me'* routine had worn so thin that he had decided to seek some relief by returning to his flat for a couple of days, on the excuse that it needed cleaning up. Once there he had flung himself down on the sofa, turned on the television and lost himself in a new episode of C.S.I. It almost felt like luxury, not to have to listen to Andrea's whining voice going over, for the umpteenth time, what had gone wrong in her relationship with Damien. The physical satisfaction he endured this for was small compensation for the hours of repetition, and he had got to the stage of beginning to wish that the whole contretemps hadn't occurred in the first place.

'John, it's Andrea. Veronica has seen Damien, and he's with another woman,' she wailed over the phone line. There followed a torrent of sobbing and a barrage of snuffled words, not one of which did John manage to interpret.

'Hang on; hang on Andrea! You're going to have to stop crying and compose yourself, because I can't understand a word of what you're saying.'

Three or four minutes later, after the emotional outburst had died down, John managed to glean that Veronica and her beau had taken a few days off to holiday up north, and on the way to the little town of Port Flint had run into Damien and an attractive, auburn-haired woman.

'I asked her how he looked, whether he was all pale and piquey looking, and she said no, he looked quite relaxed and happy, and he had this woman with him. I think she was trying to make me feel better so I wouldn't worry so much about him. But you'd think that at the very least he would be fretful, John. It stands to reason! I think she's lying… with the best of motives, no doubt,' Andrea sniffed, 'so I wouldn't worry so much. But I know Damien. He couldn't just go off like that and meet someone else… I'm his whole life! He told me so!'

John raised his eyes to the ceiling once more, and mentally patted his old mate on the back.

'Well, if he did, you should be happy for him, Andrea. After all, he's only following your example!'

There was a stunned silence on the other end of the phone. Andrea hated to be reminded of her own shortcomings.

'That's not very nice, John. You know I'm only thinking about his welfare, and I'm sure that this woman, whoever she is, can't be good for him. Anyway, it seems that Veronica found out that Damien is staying at some place on the coast called Dark Harbour, and I think he's staying with this woman. You're going to have to go up there and bring him back, John!'

John stood stunned for a moment at the gall of the woman.

'What do you mean, I'm going to have to go up there and bring him back! What for? Number one, he hates me, number two, you're supposed to be getting over him by now. You swore that he meant nothing to you anymore, just last night.'

'Yes! That's true. But he has to come back anyway, to sort things out. You know, the house, some of his things are still here, and he needs to make me an allowance, John. After all, we can't just live on *your* money. I need an income of my own.'

John suppressed a laugh.

'What makes you think that he would willingly pay you anything, Andrea? After all, you've been unfaithful to him; you've ditched him! There's no such thing as alimony any more, not in this country, at least.'

'It's not a question of law, John. It's his moral responsibility. I'm his wife, and he has to support me, at least until the divorce.'

'I can assure you, Andrea, that he doesn't have to do any such thing. If there were children involved it would be different, but there's not.'

'But he's got money, John... thousands! I know, because he inherited last year from his father's estate. But he wouldn't put the money in our joint account. I thought it was rather mean of him at the time, and said so.'

'Oh yes... and what did he say to that?'

'He said he hadn't decided what he was going to do with the money, that he might buy us a house. I thought that would be a bit of a waste myself. Who wants to be tied down to a house? Besides... all that money, land rates, maintenance, replacing things that go wrong. Let the landlord worry about all that.'

'Some people regard home ownership as a sign of stability, Andrea.'

Andrea didn't reply immediately, and John knew her well enough to know that the poignant silence indicated the onset of either a tantrum, or the sulks. His bet was on the sulks.

'I don't care what other people think, John. I'm too young to be tied down to mortgages and kids and land rates, and all that other boring stuff. But that's beside the point. I need you to go and bring Damien back. Tell him we need to talk.'

'What's wrong with *you* bringing him back? Why should *I* always do your dirty work for you?'

'Joooohhnn!' she wailed, on a rising note, and once he heard that, he knew he was lost.

'All right... all right! I'll go! Don't throw a fruity. Where did you say this place was – Dark Harbour? I'll have to take a few days off. He might take some finding... not to mention convincing. What if he won't talk to me?'

'He *has* to talk to you... make him!' said Andrea, petulantly.

John put the phone down, speculating how nice it must be to exist in Andrea's perfect little world, where everybody just did as they were told.

III

Damien drove Cherry and himself around to the Port Flint Police Station in the 1996 Falcon Station Wagon they'd just purchased for Cherry at Flint Motors. At $6,800 it had been a bargain, and gave them change from the $8,400 they'd taken from Charlie's wallet. They both entered the Police Station together, and stood waiting patiently at the counter.

'I want to put in a complaint,' said Damien, as Constable Mark Perry fronted them, finally, after a ten-minute wait. There only appeared to be two constables

175

present at that time of day, and both of these looked bored and disinterested.

'What would you like to complain about, sir,' said Constable Perry, sighing heavily.

'It's a Police matter. We want to complain about the police officer at Dark Harbour; a Constable Izzard. We feel we're being harassed!'

'Wait on a minute,' said the constable, and went out the back to see the other officer. 'It's another one for Dizzy Izzy,' he whispered to his off-sider, but loud enough for the two at the counter to hear. 'What shall I do?'

'Just take down the details. Find out what he's been up to this time – the old man's not going to like it!'

Constable Perry reappeared, and began to make notes.

'And the basis of this complaint, sir?'

'He defected Damien's car this morning,' said Cherry, 'just to stop us getting out of town. He ordered us to drive it back to Dark Harbour, when we were halfway to Port Flint.'

Constable Perry shifted uncomfortably on his feet.

'Well, that is standard practice, sir! The law allows you to drive the vehicle back to its place of origin, or to an authorised repair dealer to effect those repairs necessary to remove the defect. That is, as long as the vehicle isn't defected for steering or brakes, in which case it must be towed or carried on a trailer. What were these defects?'

176

Damien told him, but hastened to add that this was just one instance of a number of complaints they had.

'We needed to get to Port Flint, and he ordered us to take the car back immediately, then and there. When we said we intended to continue with our journey by hitching a ride, he threatened to arrest me.'

Constable Perry suppressed a grin.

'He is a little bit officious, sir, but he was probably acting quite within the law as it stands.'

'Well how about this one. He booked me a few days ago for killing a brown snake, then told me I had to be gone, out of town by three o'clock. When I remonstrated with him, he took me aside and threatened me... said that if he saw me around after that time he would run me in. When I indicated that I had no intention of leaving town, he threatened to lock me in a cell, and then intimated that I might just be found to have committed suicide by hanging myself in the cell. It was extremely threatening, constable!'

'Constable Izzard has been known to indulge in colourful language from time to time sir, but I can assure you that he is a respected officer of the law, and I find it hard to believe that he would have made such a statement.'

'Are you calling me a liar, Constable?'

'Not at all sir, not at all! But repeated conversations are often distorted in the memory before being passed on.'

'Well this wasn't distorted. He threatened my life, and I have two witnesses to prove it.'

'I'm one of them,' said Cherry.

'And who was the other?'

'Patsy Donaldson of Dark Harbour.'

'She was there at the time?'

'Yes, we both were, just around the corner of the house.'

Constable Perry stopped writing, and looked up.

'So you weren't, actually, standing within earshot so to speak.'

'We were close enough to hear what was going on,' said Cherry, balefully. 'He'd just told Patsy that Damien here would not be allowed to rent the granny flat at the rear of her premises... something about a Certificate of Habitation.'

'Oh yes... I take it the flat has not been occupied for some time.'

'That's right,' said Cherry.

'In that case, he was just passing on to you the local council requirement. He did you a favour, actually, because if Mister, err... Curtis here had just moved in, the odds are that a council inspector would have come along and turfed him out again.'

'There's more to it than that. It seems that Jack was working in concert with the local publican to try and drive Damien out of town, because the publican had just refused to rent Damien a room. There's something going on in that town, and for reasons best known to themselves, they seem determined to get Damien here out of Dark Harbour.'

'And yet he defected your car this morning… and ordered you to return with it to the town? This is all rather airy-fairy don't you think, Miss Reynolds. Surely, if Mister Curtis was leaving town, and Constable Izzard had wanted him gone, the smart thing to do would have been to just let him go.'

'There's more to it than that. I think it's all concerned with the disappearance of Liz Capel, some months ago. When we challenged him that he might have had something to do with it, his reply was – 'you've got nothing!''

Constable Perry shook his head.

'Now I know that you're building sky castles,' he said. 'Elizabeth Capel returned home about an hour ago. She has been recuperating from a serious illness in a private institution for some months now, and is still very ill. However, she decided that she wanted to return home, and was accordingly discharged. She has just been removed from the Missing Persons Register.'

Damien and Cherry looked at each other, their mouths open.

'Liz….' said Cherry, almost speechless. 'At home! I can't believe it.'

'When did you hear this,' said Damien, who had suddenly gone deathly pale.

'Not half an hour ago, actually! It just came out as one of our regular bulletins.'

Damien nodded, and kept nodding to himself.

'So what are you going to do about… this…' he indicated the constable's notes.

'Well, from what I can see, there's not a single action here that can't be explained within the strictures of the law. If you could only give me something to go on...'

Damien took Cherry's arm.

'Forget it, Constable! I knew it was going to be difficult trying to convince anyone. I didn't know it was going to be *this* difficult! Have a good day.'

'And the same to you, sir!'

As Cherry and Damien turned to go, Constable Perry tore his notes from the clipboard and consigned them, regretfully, to the bin.

Chapter Eleven

Damien and Cherry returned to the car, and sat there in a daze.

'I can't believe it; Liz Capel! I was sure that she was dead.'

'From what you've already told me about the circumstances surrounding her disappearance, I must admit... I thought so too. We have to get back! You need to talk to her, find out what happened to her and whether or not she has any further information about Mary Burton.'

Damien threw the car into drive, waited for the right moment and performed a U-turn in the middle of the main street. They had intended to make a day of it, buy a vehicle, go to lunch at one of the excellent Port Flint Hotels, and wander around the shops, looking for bargains. As Damien had never been there before, he would also have liked to check out real estate prices, and take in the beaches, if any, in the area. While in the car yard, and as Cherry had been finalising the purchase of the station wagon, he had wandered around, looking at some of the caravans on the lot. There were a couple of mobile homes in the yard, and these caught his interest immediately. For a price considerably less than a cottage, he could buy a mobile home and park it wherever his fancy took him. He stole a glance at

Cherry Reynolds, through the window of the office, and decided that at that moment he knew exactly where his fancy took him. She was gorgeous!

'What if Izzard gets there before us? Are you game to go in?' said Damien.

'Jack doesn't worry me,' said Cherry. 'I've known him too long for him to put the wind up me. I'll just go sailing straight past him. I think Liz owes us an explanation, especially after all the worry we've had to bear for the past few months. She could at least have phoned!'

'It depends on what the illness was,' said Damien, musingly. 'That cop reckons she's still very ill, so you'd better tread carefully. Go easy on her! You'll get your answers sooner or later.'

Just past the halfway point heading back to Dark Harbour, Damien slowed down. He didn't want another speeding fine, and half expected Izzard to be waiting along the road as they swept back into the little township.

'Don't go home… just go straight on to Liz's place – that's right, along there!'

Damien followed her directions, and they pulled up outside a little cottage with a badly neglected garden, but one that obviously had once been well tended and outlined. There were little rock gardens, overwhelmed with weeds, and a driveway that had suffered the same fate. Fifty yards along was a second cottage, similarly neglected, and Damien took this to be the late abode of

Mary Burton. Parked on the other side of the road was the Patrol Car.

Izzard was coming out as they walked along the driveway. He held his hand up to halt them as they approached.

'Not a good idea,' he said, as they stopped in front of him. 'Miss Capel needs rest, peace and quiet. She specifically asked me to request people to stay away until she feels better.'

'Did she now? Well, I'll believe that when I hear it from her own lips, thank you Constable,' said Cherry, and pushed past him to approach the front door. Izzard stood in Damien's way, and Damien decided that this time discretion was the better part of valour. If there was anything to discover, Cherry could just as well do it on her own. She didn't need his help.

'Have you moved that vehicle yet,' said Izzard, with a surly look.

'No... not yet! Plenty of time tomorrow,' said Damien, turning his back on him and lighting a cigarette.

'Your time might just be running out,' said Izzard from behind him. There was no mistaking the threat in his voice. Damien spun on his heel.

'Is that so? *Your* time might just be running out, Constable! I've already put in a complaint about you, up the road. No doubt you'll be getting a visit from Internal Affairs next. How do you like those apples?'

'I heard all about that… there's no report going in. You couldn't make a case of it, Curtis! You'll never be able to make a case of it. But I can…'

Damien looked directly at Izzard and saw that he was smiling, a jaundiced, sardonic smile. He was stung to reply.

'You think you're so clever, don't you? Well I happen to know that you're involved in some illegal activity here, Constable, and when it suits me I'll have this place absolutely crawling with uniforms, and not just police ones, either.'

Izzard dropped the smile, and began to shake his head.

'You're determined to talk yourself into a wooden waistcoat aren't you? Just keep going the way you are, Curtis, and Nemesis will strike you down when you least expect it!'

'What was that about Nemesis, Constable?' said Cherry, walking up, unnoticed behind him. Izzard gave a start, and spun around.

'You just keep out of this, Cherry. It would be a shame for you to get involved with this joker, you being a local! If you'll take my advice…'

'I don't need your advice, Jack. I'll do what I want, *when* I want, and *with whom* I want! If anything happens to Damien here I'll be straight down to your headquarters in the city, singing like a bird.'

Izzard stuck his fingers in his belt, and took a pace backwards.

'Get what you wanted from Liz Capel, did you?' he said, tauntingly. 'She give you all the good gear, did she?' Then he laughed, and walked past them down the driveway to his car. They stood and watched as he drove away.

'That arrogant prick!' said Damien, absolutely livid.

'Forget it. Let's go home,' she said. 'There's nothing to do here!'

Damien looked at her questioningly, but kept his peace until they had returned to her cottage, walked in and locked the door behind them. Once inside he had paced the floor a couple of times while she put the kettle on. She seemed loth to start the conversation. Finally, Damien exclaimed in exasperation:

'Okay! What the hell happened in there? Are you going to tell me or what?'

Cherry shook her head, bemused, made the coffee and sat down at the table before she would answer him.

'Patsy was there! I swear to god, she looked at me as if I was her worst enemy. And Liz… God! What a mess. She's in a terrible state, Damien, terrible! She could barely put two sentences together.'

'What's this about Patsy… how do you mean? Worst enemy!'

'As sure as I'm sitting here. I think she's scared, Damien. I think she's frightened out of her wits. She's not the Patsy we've been hanging out with for the past few days!'

'You think Liz has told her something… or someone has warned her off! Which?'

'Damned if I know! I walked in and Liz was lying on the couch, with a blanket over her. She's aged ten years, I swear. I would never have recognised her! If I'd passed her in the street, I swear I wouldn't have known her.'

'What did she say when she saw you. Do you think she knew you?'

'Oh, she knew me all right. When I walked over to her she got all excited and tried to lift herself up on one elbow. She was trying to speak, but she was shaking, Damien, her hands were shaking and her lips sort of quivered. Patsy was sitting beside her and put a hand on her, tried to calm her down. She – Patsy that is – deliberately ignored me at first, wouldn't even look at me. She just stared down at Liz, and kept staring. Liz managed the word 'hospital', then: 'been in hospital...', then 'thank god I'm home!' She tried to say more, but it wouldn't come out. I began to ask her about what had happened to her, why she hadn't phoned, and Patsy glowered at me and said couldn't I see that she was ill? She said there'd be plenty of time for questions when she'd had time to recuperate. 'Just give her a chance,' she said.

'What have you managed to find out, Patsy,' I said, but Patsy just shook her head, and wouldn't reply. I said 'what's come over you, Patsy?', and she looked up at me and bit her lip. But her eyes, Damien, I looked into her eyes and she seemed to be afraid of something. She just wanted me out of there. So I just shrugged, and walked out. No one was going to say anything!'

Damien got up and paced around the room.

'What the bloody hell is going on here,' he said, angrily. 'This is just beyond belief, Cherry… Patsy – of all people! I didn't think they would ever get to her!'

II

At eleven o'clock that night, after going over the sequence of events for the umpteenth time, Damien got up and announced he was going for a walk.

'I think I'll take a walk around the block… clear my head. There's something I'm missing here, and I'll admit it – it's driving me spare! I need to get some fresh air.'

'Do you want me to go with you,' said Cherry, with a worried look. 'I'm not sure that it's safe for you out there, on your own. Someone might come up behind you and hit you over the head.'

'All the more reason for you to stay here, where it's safe! Lock the door behind me. I'll only be gone for half an hour or so, and don't worry, I'll keep to the shadows. I'll avoid all open spaces and I won't let anyone see me out there.' As an afterthought he added, grinning – 'I played commandos as a kid, you know!'

He was as good as his word. There was a line of trees near Cherry's cottage, and some bushy undergrowth, and he disappeared into the shadows within seconds of leaving the house. Spying out the land, he worked out that he could make his way the full length of the road to the main street, without being seen.

It was truly like being a kid again as he sheltered under trees, in bushes, and even lay down in the shadows when the moon came out from behind the clouds, so that if there was anything going on at that time of night he would know about it, but not be seen himself. It was exhilarating, and it sharpened his wits. He went beyond the main street, making a break for it across the road while the moon was hidden, and found himself between the water and a line of bushes. It was then that he saw the lights.

A trawler was coming in, heading towards the old dock, and he decided to get as close to the landing as he could without giving himself away. If there was any funny business going on with these late night trawls, this was the only way he was ever going to find out. By twenty past eleven, he had managed to get in amongst the trees beside the dock, and he now lay down in the shadows while the trawler edged further and further in, finally tying up against the wharf. He was about sixty yards from the three men on deck, and he could vaguely hear them talking to each other as they worked on the catch. One of them was whistling as he worked, a very bad version of 'The Great Pretender', which he interspersed with various warbles that had nothing to do with the song at all. It was a very normal picture of a fishing boat, coming in after a hard days trawling, until something caught Damien's eye and made him sit up, involuntarily, and cause his jaw to drop.

Approaching from his right, and marching slowly but steadily along the boards that made up the dock, was a procession of hooded monks. At least, that's what it looked like. The one out in front trod slowly, and bore in front of him a huge book, about six inches thick, with a leather cover, and held reverently at waist height. Then there was a solitary monk behind him, bearing a rather large bell. Behind him were four more monks, moving in a square, two by two. The master of the boat came to the side to greet their arrival, and didn't seem at all fazed by this strange procession at all.

Once beside the trawler, the monk in front began to speak, some sort of chant, and this was answered by those at the back. The remarkable thing about it was that the lead voice was that of a woman. Damien's sense of excitement at this discovery was so great that he found it difficult to keep himself under cover. He wished now that he had manoeuvred himself a little closer, so he could hear what was going on. The chanting to him seemed like just a jumble of words, and he couldn't make out more than one or two in each sentence. The word 'blessing' came out, as did 'sail', 'catch' and 'give thanks!' At the end of this ritual, a gangway was let down, and the monk with the woman's voice proceeded to mount it, and continue on to the deck. She was followed by the monk with the bell, who stood behind her. The others stayed on the dock. The hooded woman walked over to and past the wheelhouse, where she couldn't be seen by the other 'monks'. The master of the vessel also disappeared behind it, turning to her with a small package. The woman opened the great book and, unseen by the others, the master appeared to place the package on the open book where it promptly disappeared. The book was closed, and the woman-monk walked off the trawler, and led the little procession away along the dock. The whole thing took about seven minutes.

'So that's how they do it,' thought Damien, his brow breaking out in a fine sweat. 'I'll be damned!' The only question was, what was in the packet?

There was no question of making his getaway while they were still working on the trawler. The slightest movement and he felt that he would be highlighted among the trees, and with three on to one, he didn't like the odds. Those odds shortly became four to one, as Frank Kelly suddenly arrived with the refrigerated truck, and backed it up to the trawler.

They began to load the truck with trays and trays of whatever the catch was, but it was obvious to Damien, even at that distance, that these weren't scale fish. Finally he realised that they were loading prawns, iced down in the trays, and ready for shipment to the city. It wasn't until all activity had ceased, and the men had gone home, that Damien finally got achingly to his feet and stretched, to rid himself of the cramp that had set in from the damp undergrowth. He came down to the edge of the tree line, and read the name on the rear of the trawler – 'Sea Horse'. He'd have to ask Cherry about that!

The journey back was more painful than the journey out. He felt his aches and pains, and reflected ruefully that this was a bit different than when he had played the same sort of game with Ronnie Eldridge when they were both eleven. By the time he'd made it back to the cottage, it was almost 2 a.m. Only then did he realise that Cherry was probably freaking out over his disappearance. He *had* said he'd only be gone about half an hour.

He approached the cottage from the rear, made his way around to the side door and knocked, quietly.

'Cherry… it's only me,' he called out, trying to keep his voice down, and yet be heard inside. There was no answer.

Twice more he tried, then he made his way around to her bedroom window.

'Cherry… open up for God's sake! It's getting cold out here!'

A total silence had descended over the cottage, and there were no lights showing. She was probably asleep… it had been an eventful day, after all! Finally he found a window that hadn't been properly secured, and he managed to force it open and climb in. Making his way quietly through the house, he came out into the lounge room, and flicked on the light switch.

'So you finally showed up,' said a voice, and Damien jumped in shock. Sitting in an armchair, facing him, was the local policeman, Jack Izzard. But it wasn't the tone of his voice that put the fear of death into him, it was the ugly snout of the police .38 that Izzard was pointing in his direction.

'What the bloody hell...' said Damien in shock, instinctively throwing his hands in the air at the same time.

'Damien Curtis, I'm arresting you on suspicion of being instrumental in the disappearance of Cherry Reynolds. Anything you say may be taken down and used as evidence in a court of law. Now put your hands behind you, and don't try any funny stuff. This little baby's loaded!'

Izzard got up and motioned Damien to turn around. Before he could get his thoughts together, his wrists were handcuffed behind him, and he was helpless. The policeman walked to the front door, and Damien went to follow him.

'Not so quick, arsehole! I've got somebody out here who's got a bone to pick with you, my friend. You can come in now,' he called out, and in through the front door walked a wild and angry Charlie Fairweather.

'You've got to be joking,' said Damien, turning to the policeman for protection. But Izzard was grinning, and suddenly a blow like an ox hit him behind the left ear, dropping him to the carpet. The last thing Damien remembered was Charlie laying into him with his boots.

III

Cherry had watched Damien disappear into the night, and had then locked the door behind him. She walked back into the lounge and curled timidly up on the couch, hugging herself with apprehension. As Damien disappeared into the darkness she tried to analyse her feelings for him, and suddenly, as if in a revelation, she realised that she cared for him a lot more than she had cared to admit... even to herself. He was growing on her, and the peculiar circumstances in which they found themselves were accelerating the process, pretty much as humidity brings on a tropical plant. He made her feel more secure, gave a rationality to the current extremes that she would not have been able to find without him.

She thought about his face, his kindly eyes, and his occasional outbursts of schoolboy humour. At such times she felt like reaching out to him and giving him a hug, and running her finger carefully along the scar by his mouth, feeling his arms around her and his lips on her neck. Sometimes, she thought of even more tempestuous scenarios, like the night before, when she had lain sleepless in her bed, listening to his heavy breathing out in the other room.

But Cherry was cautious. She'd always been cautious, at least, ever since that one big hurt in her life when she had felt betrayed by the one person she cared about. She shuddered at the thought, and pushed it once more to the back of her mind. That was the one subject she refused to dwell on.

Her musings continued until she realised that the clock had run around to midnight, and there was still no sign of him. She turned out the main lights and went to the window, peered out into the darkness and tried to pick out any moving shadow that might signal his return. There was nothing. The moon peeked out occasionally, giving her a clearer view of the road, but the night was still, and the only movement was the wind in the treetops, along the road.

By twelve thirty, Cherry was beginning to panic. She paced the floor of the lounge room, and continually went back to the windows, biting hard on her knuckles as if the pain from that would keep her from descending into a pit of hysteria. She could feel the panic rising slowly in her throat, and engaged in an imaginative scenario where Damien would arrive back suddenly, safe and sound, and she would attack him with her fists, and claw at his face for putting her through such an ordeal. She alternated between something akin to love, and also hate. Her rational mind continually told her that she was being stupid, that he was just out there playing boys games, and that he would come home soon with skinned knees, looking for sympathy. Then she indulged her other fear, that someone out there wanted him dead, and would take this opportunity to dump his body into the bay.

At ten to one she thought of Patsy. If she couldn't get comfort from Damien, she could at least use her time to challenge Patsy, and find out more of what had gone on during their trip to Port Flint. It was one o'clock in the morning. Patsy never went to bed before one thirty. She'd still be up! Changing into a pair of jeans, a plaid shirt with long sleeves to keep the cold out, and throwing a jumper over the top, she finally ventured to the front door, opened it cautiously and stepped out, pulling it to behind her.

IV

Emily Longstaff walked slowly at the rear of the hooded procession, aware that Igor was beside her in his robes, looking mysterious and very Druidic. They got back to the main road, where they disrobed and placed their robes in the boot of David Owen's car. Then they all dispersed to their various homes, and Ilse marched off with the book safely tucked under her arm. Nobody else was ever allowed to touch that book. It was supposed to be a hand-rendered copy of the Book of Kells, but Ilse was the only one who had ever opened its pages.

To avoid suspicion, Igor headed for home, leaving Emily to make her own way. They had agreed on this, as it wouldn't do for rumours to start getting back to Gordon when he returned. She was unhappy in her marriage, but she wasn't stupid enough to throw it away, and half the property, for the sake of a five-minute fling. She was obsessed with Igor, but wasn't fooling herself that he felt the same way. They would take it slowly, meet every time Gordon went off on a trip, explore and develop their relationship over a long period before making any permanent changes to their lives. That's what they had discussed, and that was what they had decided. There was all the time in the world!

She made her way home, and once inside settled down to a coffee, and to wait. She'd arranged with Igor that she would wait until after two o'clock in the morning, just to make sure that no one was wandering around, then under cover of night make her way to his place and spend two hours with him. At four she would return home, and then sleep for the rest of the day. There was no one to run around after, no one to cook for, clean for, be awake for. She could do what she liked.

To enter more into the spirit of the thing, she sat in darkness, not wanting to attract anyone's attention to the lights in the cottage. She sat and stared out of the window as the shadows slowly changed in the moonlight, and she imagined dark shapes twisting and turning out there, phantoms half seen that ventured out only in that time that humans lay asleep.

It was then that she saw a figure that was most definitely not a phantom - the figure of Jack Izzard, walking rapidly along the side of the road in the general direction of Cherry's place. As he got further along, there was a movement in the bushes, and Jack stopped for a moment, to address what appeared to be another man. For a brief moment, the figure stepped into the road, and pointed to Cherry's place. It was Charlie Fairweather! He disappeared back into the bushes, and Izzard continued on his way until he was lost to sight.

Emily cursed. Tonight of all nights, Izzard had some sort of thing going on. She hoped it would be all over before two o'clock, so she could negotiate her way without being seen. The last thing she needed was Izzard, or Charlie Fairweather getting wind of respectable Emily Longstaff having an affair, or it would be all over town. It was the one thing she had never done, not in twenty years of marriage, and yet she was doing it now.

Just after two she stepped out of the back door, and carefully made her way along to the main street. As she was about to cross the road, a car's headlights lit up the road from Cherry's place and headed towards her at speed. She ducked back around the side of a building, and watched as a car, Ilse's car, pulled up outside the Promenade Hotel. The lights were turned off, and Emily risked craning her neck around the corner to see if she could tell what was going on at that hour of the morning. She saw Craig Mortimer get out of the passenger side, and Ilse from the driver's side. But what made her eyes bulge was watching them drag someone out of the rear seat of the car, and bodily carry that person in through the entrance to the Hotel. Even at a distance, she could see it was Cherry Reynolds. And even at a distance, she could see that she was unconscious.

It was ten minutes before they reappeared again, and when they did they drove away quickly, returning in the general direction of Ilse's cottage. Emily was shaking with apprehension. It was like a bad dream. She waited a few more minutes, and then took off at a trot along the main street, heading for Igor's cottage, which was situated opposite the Police Station in Third Street. No sooner had she got in through the gate than she heard another car approaching. She ducked down behind Igor's hedge, but the patrol car pulled up outside the station, and she watched as Jack Izzard and Charlie Fairweather lifted an unconscious and blood-spattered Damien Curtis out of the back seat, and dragged him, legs trailing, into the station. By the time Igor let her in through the front door, Emily was almost in hysterics, and had to be calmed down with a stiff brandy before she could explain what she'd seen.

Igor listened to her story, nodded sympathetically, and then went out the back and surreptitiously phoned Ilse Hirsch.

Chapter Twelve

John had been meaning to call around at the house the following morning, but Andrea beat him to it. She was standing in the doorway of the flat at seven thirty, a pensive look on her face, and an irritable twitch at the corner of her mouth. She took one look at the flat, and scowled.

'I thought you said you were coming back here to clean up?' she said. 'Look at this place – it's like a tip!'

John staggered around, scratched his head and looked guiltily around him.

'Yeah, it is a bit of a mess, isn't it? I must have fallen asleep on the couch. Sorry doll!'

'I just came to make sure you got off early to Dark Harbour. I should go with you, but if I saw Damien with that bitch, I know I'd lose my cool, and do something I might regret.'

'Well maybe you'd better not come then. It's not her fault, you know. She didn't tell you to ditch him!'

'That's not the point! She must know he's taken. Men like Damien never stay single for long!'

'Which is exactly her point, I suppose. She's probably aiming to be the next Mrs. Curtis.'

Andrea clenched her fists and stamped one foot in temper.

'That's *not* going to happen! You get up there and tell her in no uncertain terms, that Damien is *married... married!*'

John looked at her in disbelief, and shook his head, as if to indicate that she must be at least two sandwiches short of a picnic!

'Have you listened to yourself lately,' he said, exasperated. 'Have you stopped and considered what it is you're asking me to do? I'm the man that ran off with his wife, and you, his wife, want me to go back to him and tell him that he's not allowed to get involved with anyone else, because you might not like it? Are you even on the same planet as everyone else, Andrea?'

'There's no need to be insulting, John!'

John raised an eyebrow, and flopped back down onto the couch.

'There's every need from where I'm sitting! You're still sleeping with me, still telling me you love me - *when clutched in love's warm embrace,*' he said sarcastically, ' – but every other statement you make shows that you haven't any intention of giving up on Damien yet. Just what is your intention, Andrea? Do you intend going back with him or not – if he's silly enough to return, that is!'

Andrea pursed her lips, and attempted to manoeuvre around the pit she was digging for herself.

'I'm just worried about him, worried sick if you must know. You don't know women like I do. There are a lot of sharks out there, just waiting to get their claws into him, spend all his money and then dump him. I don't want to see him hurt, John!'

'Yeah, yeah, yeah! All right – I'll give work a ring and take a week off, though it's against my better judgement. It means a week less on my holidays this year.'

'You'll be doing Damien a favour, John!'

So it was that by ten thirty that morning, John Inglis found himself heading north along National Highway Number One, a couple of suitcases in the boot, and his spare uniform packed just in case he might need it. Once away from Andrea's influence he cursed his own stupidity for becoming involved in what would no doubt turn out to be a most unpleasant experience. He dropped his speed to eighty, and stopped at every small town along the way, trying to put off the inevitable for as long as possible.

At Longvale, the last town south of Dark Harbour, he pulled in to a café and ordered cappuccino and a couple of toasted beef and tomato sandwiches. By the time they were delivered to his table, another couple had wandered into the café and ordered, and to John's dismay he realised it was Veronica Watson, one of Damien and Andrea's erstwhile friends. He put his head down in hopes that he wouldn't be spotted, but it was to no avail. Veronica homed in on him like a beacon.

'Well, look who it is! John Inglis! Hello John – what on earth are you doing in this neck of the woods? The last thing we heard about you was that you and Damien had come to a parting of the ways. How's Andrea?'

John groaned inwardly, but tried to put a brave face on it.

'Oh, she's fine. I'm just off for a short holiday up north.'

'Yeah, we heard! Dark Harbour isn't it? Andrea got me on the mobile about half an hour ago. We got the whole story.'

John pulled a face and shook his head.

Veronica smiled. She couldn't help herself.

'If you'll take my advice, John, you'll go and make it up with Damien, and tell Andrea to take a jump. She's a control freak at the best of times, and will only make your life a misery.'

John raised one eyebrow in surprise.

'I thought you and she were mates?'

Veronica grinned.

'We are! But that doesn't mean that I can constantly overlook all the appalling things she does to people. When I heard about you and Damien, I couldn't believe it. I mean, you've been friends since Adam was a boy. Believe me; that friendship is worth far more than anything you might get from Andrea. She's selfish, arrogant and out for one thing – Andrea! It's different for me, because I don't have to live with her. If she starts to piss me off I can just hang up on her. But once she gets her claws into you, boy, then you'll begin to see what I mean. Get out while you still can!'

'I've got a feeling that I'm out already,' John said, glumly. 'I've been sent on a mission to entice Damien back to her. She can't seem to let go.'

'Exactly my point,' said Veronica. 'Did I tell you we gave Damien a lift to Port Flint… yesterday, wasn't it darl?' She turned to her partner, and he nodded. 'He was with a woman called Cherry, late twenties! A good looker, too! They were going to buy her a car, a Ford Station Wagon wasn't it?' Her partner nodded again.

'Well, if they were there…'

'They'd just driven up for the day. It seems that Damien was staying with this Cherry at a cottage in Dark Harbour. He seemed as happy as a pig in poop!'

'Did he say how long he was going to be there?'

'No, but he didn't seem to be in any hurry to move on. I think he may have found someone… you know what I mean. A soul mate! They make a good-looking couple. I hope so for his sake, anyway.'

'How big's this place, this Dark Harbour?'

'Put it this way; if you blink, you'll miss the turn-off. It's a tiny little place with one pub and a little main street, and a few scattered cottages with a deep-water harbour. They run a few trawlers out of there.'

'So you don't think he'd be hard to find!'

'No – just go in and ask around. Ask for Cherry and the new fellow, Damien. The locals would know. They know everything in these little towns.'

John nodded, and pulled a face.

'I don't suppose he said anything about me… like he'd like to break my neck, or anything like that, you know, that could be injurious to my health.'

Veronica laughed.

'I think you'll be surprised. Damien isn't the type to normally hold grudges. Mind you, having said that, it might be a little different when you're talking about his woman. Just tread warily, and he shouldn't come down too hard on you.'

'I don't know why the hell I'm doing this! If he goes back to Andrea, that's me out of the picture anyway.'

'Going by what we saw yesterday, I don't think there's much chance of that. They might not know it yet, but those two are made for each other.'

Veronica got up to go.

'Anyway, best of luck! Oh – there is one thing though. Don't fall foul of the local copper. Damien was saying what a pig he was, and that he'd harassed him since arriving there. He said he'd even tried to run him out of town.'

'What – Damien? God, he *must* be a pig. Damien's harmless!'

'He's not exactly your bikie type, is he,' laughed Veronica. 'Say hello to him for me when you see him, will you?'

'Yeah, no worries,' said John, and waved them off.

Three quarters of an hour later he was driving along the turn-off into Dark Harbour, and wondering what Damien's first words would be when he saw him. He had a bet with himself, and that bet amounted to a sentence filled with exclamation marks, and the two words... 'fuck off!'

II

Cherry Reynolds woke that morning with a doozey of a headache, and found that she couldn't seem to get her eyes open. Everything was strangely silent as she rubbed her eyes, finally opening them to the dim light of a dark green room that she'd never seen before. She lay for a moment, bewildered. Then she sat up suddenly.

There was an overpowering smell of Dettol, and it was coming from a bucket and mop standing up against the far wall, while she lay on a dingy divan, the only furniture in the room. There was an old sink and a toilet, and above the smell of the Dettol was another smell, that of stale sweat and beer. There were no windows, just one ventilator near the ceiling, and a solid metal door on the far wall.

Getting to her feet she crossed to the door and tried the handle; it was locked! The air was stale, and she pulled a face, wondering how the hell she had fetched up here, when she couldn't remember a thing about the night before.

She sat on the edge of the bed, and put her head in her hands. Where was she? As her head cleared, images of the night before began to return to her, and she thought of Damien and his head-clearing trip into the night. When he hadn't returned, she had decided to go and knock Patsy up, and try to discover what she had found out about Liz Capel. She remembered leaving the cottage and making her way along the road to Patsy's place, finally knocking at the door and being greeted by a stony silence.

'Patsy – I know you're in there. Answer the door, bugger you! Come on, let me in… we need to talk.'

After knocking and calling out for three or four minutes, Cherry heard a movement on the other side of the door. Then she heard Patsy's voice.

'Go away! It's late, and I've already gone to bed.'

'Come on, Patsy; open the door! You and I need to talk… about Liz. What the hell's going on?'

There was a pause, and then a whispered reply.

'For god's sake Cherry, if you value your life, get away from here. You don't know how dangerous it is for me to even be seen talking to you.'

Cherry stood back, and put her hands on her hips.

'Right! That's it, Patsy. If you don't let me in, I'm going to create a disturbance out here, and everyone will know I've been here. Do you want that?'

'No, for god's sake….'

There was the sound of a bolt being drawn back, and the door opened a fraction. Patsy put her eye to the opening, and pleaded with Cherry, an agonised look on her face.

'Cherry, you're in terrible danger… so is Damien! So am I if it comes to that! Take my advice and get out of Dark Harbour, take Damien with you. Don't come back for at least three months, and everything will have settled down by then.'

Cherry put her shoulder against the door and heaved. On the other side of the door, Patsy buckled, fell backwards and lay sprawled in the hallway. Cherry went in and shut the door firmly behind her, then reached out to pick Patsy up off the floor.

'You crazy bitch! What are you trying to prove?'

'I want some answers, Patsy, and I want them now. You've been acting really bloody strangely since we dropped you off yesterday. When I saw you today over at Liz Capel's, you acted like a total stranger! What's happened to you since yesterday to make you act like this?'

'You really don't want to know, Cherry. Believe me, it will only make matters worse for you if you know. No one was more shocked than I was when Liz Capel showed up again. She was in such a terrible state… and I knew, the moment I saw her, I knew!' Patsy burst into tears and put her head in her hands.

'Oh, for god's sake, Patsy! How can I help you if you won't talk to me? We're friends, aren't we… We've been friends since we were kids. Tell me what's going on, even if it's just for old time's sake.'

Patsy shook her head, and continued to cry. Cherry continued:

'If I'm in danger and Damien's in danger, then you're in just as much danger, simply for the fact that we hang around together.'

'That's why I want you to go! Can't you see… if I open my mouth, I'm as good as dead. At the best, I'll end up like Liz Capel.'

'Well, tell me about her. Tell me how she happened to turn up again, out of the blue. When did you find out she was back?'

Patsy tried to recover herself, and went to sit at the small dining table. Cherry sat down opposite her.

'It was yesterday morning. I was walking down along the harbour front, trying to get a feeling of normalcy back into my life. All that aggro with Izzard had really upset me... I know I look tough, and I act as if I'm tough sometimes, but people like him really overwhelm me. I'm really highly strung where it comes to violent arguments or violence in any form. That's why I decided, after that fight with Charlie Fairweather, that I'd better stay home for a bit. If Charlie came around to my place in the night, like he did to you, I think I'd just collapse in a heap. Anyway, as I said, I was just walking, and I looked along the road and thought I saw a movement over at Liz's place. As I got closer I could see someone in the front garden, staggering about as if they hadn't any balance. There was no one else in the vicinity, just this one person, so I hurried along and it was Liz. I couldn't believe my eyes. She looked so old and... and disoriented! She looked at me as I approached her, and then she suddenly fell; sat hard down in the middle of the garden as if she couldn't keep her balance. She reached up towards me, this terrible pleading look on her face as if she was begging for help, but from a total stranger. She didn't know me at first. It took me some time to convince her that I was

Patsy, her old friend, and then she burst into tears and I helped her inside.'

'But where did she come from? If she was in that much of a state, she couldn't possibly have got there on her own. She must have been dropped off by someone.'

'That's exactly what I thought, and I looked around to see if there was any sign of anyone in the vicinity. But there was no one. I got her inside and made her a cup of tea, and I could see that she wasn't well… I mean *really*… not well!' Patsy looked at Cherry pointedly.

'What does that look mean, Patsy? Not well! Was she zonked out on something?'

'I must admit, that was the first thought that came into my head. I thought 'you're stoned!' But I think it's more serious than that. Still, she could have been drugged.'

'So what did she tell you?'

Patsy sighed and shook her head.

'I didn't really get that long to talk to her. Jack Izzard turned up after about five minutes and went through all this rigmarole about where had she been, didn't she realise that she was on the missing persons register, and that people had been worried about her. She just shook her head, confused, and didn't manage to answer him at all. What's more, I'm not all that certain that he wanted answers, either. It was a bit like a charade, as if he was playing a part. The whole speech might have been staged just for my benefit.'

'That wouldn't surprise me in the least,' said Cherry. 'He's probably known where she was all along. He certainly knows something, but what?'

'Then after you left, Ilse Hirsch came over to have a look at 'the patient', she called her, though why she would call her a 'patient' straight off, just like that...'

'Doctor Ilse?' said Cherry. 'Who told her?'

'Izzard, obviously! Still, that's fair enough; she *is* a doctor! The funny thing, I thought, was that she'd come prepared, hypodermic and all. She gave Liz a shot – didn't say what it was – and Liz just fell asleep on the couch. So that was that!'

'Did Ilse say anything to you about her condition?'

'No – just asked me if I'd like a shot, too. Joking! She did say not to sit too close, it might be contagious.'

Cherry shook her head.

'I don't know what to make of all this. I'm just going to go home, try and find Damien and drag him into bed. Stuff it!'

'What do you mean... try and find Damien. I thought he was with you!'

'Oh, he is! Or was. He went out for a walk at about eleven, and hasn't been back. I was getting worried so I thought I'd come over here and see you. I don't suppose he called in?'

Patsy shook her head. She had a haunted look about the eyes.

'So you've got something going with Damien, have you? Oh well, best of luck.'

Cherry got up to go.

'It's not that far advanced. Just a feeling I've got, that's all. I think he's there for the asking.'

Patsy looked agitated.

'I'm glad. Look – you'd better go! If someone sees you here…'

'That someone being Izzy? Don't worry, he doesn't venture out after eight o'clock at night.'

'No, I was thinking more of Ilse.'

Cherry looked surprised.

'Now why on earth would you say something like that? Ilse's a mate of ours. We all go drinking together. This conspiracy theory's really getting to you, isn't it!'

'It's just something that Liz said, that's all. She mentioned Ilse.'

'Oh yes,' said Cherry, waiting for the rest of it.

'She's seen her… over the past few months – while she was missing,' Patsy hissed, trying to keep her voice down. 'I think Ilse's been looking after her!'

Cherry's jaw dropped, and she could only shake her head in disbelief.

'I don't believe it,' she said, shocked. 'All these months… and us worried sick!'

'I know,' said Patsy, not wanting to pursue the matter any further.

Cherry had let herself out, and begun to walk back along the road. After that, her memory failed her. Had she returned home? She really couldn't remember. She sat on the bed and tried to penetrate the mist that surrounded those last few minutes of consciousness, but failed. Whatever had happened, it must have been sudden.

She put her hand up to her head, and felt her skull. It was bruised. The moment she touched it she realised that the dull ache she had woken up with came from a crack on the head. Somebody had hit her from behind.

About an hour after she woke up there was a fumbling on the other side of the door, and the sound of a key in the lock. Cherry sat up on the divan and waited. The door opened, and a woman with a headscarf walked in, shutting the door behind her.

'Ilse! What the hell's going on? Where am I and what are you doing here?'

The doctor looked at her with a wry expression, and took a hypodermic out of her bag.

'I thought you'd still be out to it. That was a pretty hefty whack you got last night. How's your head?'

'It's bloody terrible, but that doesn't explain a thing. What are you doing here, and why was I locked in?'

'Give me your arm, Cherry. You need this jab.'

'What do you mean; I need a jab? Just keep that thing away from me and tell me what's going on. Where's Damien? And what's going on with Liz Capel?'

Ilse stood back, the hypo still in hand, gauging the situation.

'First things first, Cherry! You've got yourself into a bit of a fix, and unless you cooperate, things could get nasty. Damien – never heard of him! And neither have you... got it? There is no Damien! And Liz Capel died at 10.15 this morning. She's dead, Cherry. Dead! So if you want to survive this, you'd better give me your arm. I promise it won't hurt!'

Chapter Thirteen

John drove slowly along the sea front, noting the picturesque cottages on his right, and the trawlers lying at anchor in the harbour. Overall there was the shape of a high knoll that rose above grey cliffs on the northern side of the township. He drove until he came to the main street, turned along it and saw how small it was. There were a couple of streets running off it, one of which housed the Police Station, the blue sign high on a post outside. A good place to avoid, he thought, as he did a U-turn and travelled back the way he'd come. The first thing that struck him was the apparent lack of activity in the street. There was nobody to be seen, absolutely no one! Maybe they all took a siesta at this time of day. A quick glance at his watch told him it was coming up for three o'clock. He'd held off for as long as he could, and had then driven slowly to his destination. He was in no hurry to get a black eye.

Stopping outside the hotel, he decided to stick his head into the bar and sound a few of the patrons out. He locked the car and ventured in.

'Excuse me,' he said to the barmaid, who was busily washing glasses. 'Pretty quiet around here,' he said, nodding at the empty bar.

She stopped and looked at him, sizing him up as he approached.

'It's always quiet at this time of day,' she said, putting the tea towel down.

'I wonder if you can help me? I'm looking for a friend of mine, Damien Curtis.'

The girl shook her head, doubtfully.

'He's a newcomer to the town. I believe he's hanging about with a woman called Cherry.'

There was a momentary glint of recognition in the barmaid's eyes, then the shutters came down.

'No, sorry!' She went to turn away.

'Do you mean 'no' to Damien, or 'no' to Cherry? Surely you must know Cherry!'

'Yep! I know Cherry. She's gone away... on holiday. So people tell me, anyway. Never heard of this Damien though!'

John looked at her suspiciously. For a liar she was totally unconvincing. He walked slowly out of the bar and out into the road. As he did so, the barmaid went out the back to find her boss, and see if she'd done the right thing.

John climbed back into his car and turned right at the end of the street, then drove north. He pulled up outside a cottage on his right, then wandered over and knocked on the door. After a few minutes he knocked again, and was just about to give up when the door opened, and a blonde woman with a worried expression appeared in the doorway.

'Excuse me,' John began, 'I'm looking for a friend of mine, Damien Curtis. I believe he's with a woman called Cherry.'

Patsy looked at him suspiciously, then darted glances up and down the road.

'You wouldn't be John, by any chance,' she said, an air of caution in her tone.

'Yes, that's right, John Inglis. You've obviously heard of me!'

'Yes – and it's all bad,' said Patsy, thrusting out an arm and dragging him inside. John was taken by surprise.

'Gee – you don't waste time on introductions, do you,' he said, as she slammed the front door behind him.

'Haven't got time for that. Are you a friend of his, or not?'

'Yes, I'm a friend of his, though he probably doesn't think so at the moment.'

'I know all about it… you ran off with his wife. My name's Patsy Donaldson, and I'm a friend of Cherry's. Come through into the lounge, we need to talk.'

John sat at the table in the lounge, and suddenly felt very uncomfortable.

'Look, I know what you're thinking, and I probably deserve it, but…'

'We haven't got time for all that right now,' said Patsy, sitting opposite him. 'You'll have plenty of time to go over all that when you see him. Anyway, that's between you and him. The fact is that Damien has disappeared!'

John looked at her, puzzled.

'You mean he's left town!'

'No, I mean he's disappeared, and his life's in danger – if he's not already dead, that is.'

'But… how do you know that? I mean, what makes you think that,' John replied, trying to work this woman out, who was so dazzlingly attractive that his heart had missed two beats when she dragged him in through the door.

'Cherry's disappeared as well, and that means that they've got her too. I tell you, this is serious. I tried to warn her last night!'

'I think you'd better begin from the beginning,' John said, 'you've got me totally confused.'

Patsy looked at him intently, as if trying to suss out whether he could be trusted or not. In the present circumstances, she didn't have much choice.

'Damien met Cherry a few days ago. Actually, they had an accident… that's how they met. Cherry came out of the pub one night, pissed, and collided with his trailer, knocking it over the seawall. All his stuff floated away. The next day I went with her, and we met him. He was charming about it… about the accident, I mean! I think we both fancied him, actually, but then we found out that his wife only left him the week before. That sort of put a dampener on it, because he was still pining for his wife. We went to dinner with him at the Promenade – that's the local hotel, and discovered that he had been attacked by some bloke the night before, and told to get out of town. The following morning some idiot had scrawled 'Piss Off!' on the windscreen of his car. Well, you know Damien! I think that only made him more

217

determined to stay. Then the publican refused to rent him a room for the next few nights, and tried to put him off renting or buying in the area. It was really weird, as if someone here had something against him, though he'd never been here before in his life.'

'It does sound a bit strange,' John conceded.

'When I tried to rent him the old granny flat at the back here, the local policeman turned up, and he told him to get out of town. Then he started harassing him, booked him for killing a brown snake that he'd killed in the bedroom of the flat – and I'll swear that snake wasn't there only hours before. It was as if someone was trying to frighten him off. Then the cop threatened to run him in if he wasn't gone by three that afternoon.'

'Did he give any reason for this,' said John, bemused.

'Nothing! Not a thing. The next day we took Damien up the Knoll to show him the view from the top, and this local deadhead called Charlie Fairweather came up in his jeep, let the brake off Cherry's car and let it run away down the hill and smash into a tree. Damien went running down there and flattened him – much to Charlie's surprise, I think. He fancies himself as the local hard man. Anyway, Damien knocked him out, then searched him and found over $8,000 in Charlie's wallet, so he took it and gave it to Cherry to replace her car. He said that was the only way she was going to get it. I'd had enough by this time, so I decided to stop hanging around with them until the heat died down. I'm not too good with confrontation.'

'No one could blame you for that,' said John, sympathetically. 'But I still don't see why you think his life is in danger.'

Patsy briefly went into the disappearance of Mary Burton, and the further disappearance of Liz Capel a month later. Then she got to Liz's reappearance in unusual circumstances the day before.

'She was a real mess. A real mess! She was hooked on heroin – I knew it from the moment I saw her. I used to have a cousin who was a junkie, and you can always tell. Besides, she had tracks up both arms. While she was away, someone had got her hooked on heroin. I hadn't been with her long when the local cop turned up, Jack Izzard. He went through this rigmarole about where she'd been, but it all sounded false somehow. Then the local doctor turned up and gave her a shot. I'd swear she gave her a shot of heroin!'

'The local doctor! So you think the doctor was involved.'

'I hate to say it, because Ilse Hirsch has always been a friend of ours. She's not just our doctor; she's our mate. We go out drinking together and get sloshed. To find out that she's been involved in something as threatening as this is horrifying. It's unbelievable! But I'm convinced that she was seeing and treating – or injecting – Liz Capel all the time she was missing. So where was she?'

'This is starting to sound really weird,' said John. 'It's like some sort of conspiracy theory. What do you think is behind it?'

'Well originally,' Patsy replied, 'we thought that they might be smuggling large quantities of illegal fish or abalone, something that brings incredible prices on the black market. We very rarely see Fisheries inspectors here, and when they do turn up, the trawler masters seem to know exactly when they're coming.'

'Well that certainly sounds suspicious,' said John. 'I'm not in Fisheries, but I am in Customs and Excise, and smuggling in its various forms is a major problem in this State.'

Patsy sat back and did a double-take.

'Customs and Excise! Is Damien in Customs and Excise too?'

'No, no, he's just a small trader, a bit of a whiz in sales, actually. He makes more than I do.'

'I just wondered, that's all, because of the reaction around here. I thought maybe somebody might have recognised him.'

'I doubt it,' said John.

'The other idea we had was that maybe they were smuggling drugs, bringing them ashore on the trawlers.'

John sat bolt upright. All of a sudden his professional instincts began to kick in.

'We've had a massive problem with heroin, ecstasy and dope for the past couple of years. It keeps on turning up on the streets despite all our efforts. We search every ship that arrives in every port in Australia, as much as it's possible to do so. But we've had very little success overall. You might just have stumbled onto something here.'

Patsy nodded.

'If it's drugs, that would explain where someone like Charlie Fairweather would get over $8,000. As far as I know, he's on the dole.'

'Yes, you're right. Where the hell would he get that sort of money? So who else do you think is involved in this little conspiracy?'

'The publican for one, Frank Kelly! Then there's the local constable, Jack Izzard. Charlie Fairweather, almost certainly, and his mate Lionel Jury, the newsagent. Then there's Igor Morris, a Welshman who drives the fish to market overnight. They all call him Rigor Mortis around here. He's a bit strange. Then the doctor, Ilse Hirsch.'

'What about the fishermen? There would have to be someone on the trawlers.'

'True! I'd go for Craig Mortimer. He's a deckhand, but he's always got his fingers into every sticky pie around. Just mention money, and he comes running. He works for whoever calls him out first, but if anyone's a bit fishy it would have to be Katie's father, Wilf Carstairs. He always seemed to be struggling to make ends meet until a couple of years ago, then all of a sudden he'd got money. I'd put him down for sure. I don't know about the others. Erin Lachlan, the guy Katie's marrying, I'd say he was as straight as a dye.'

'So there's quite a few! This would have to be smuggling on a grand scale, just to keep them all happy with their cut.'

'Yes, when you think about it, multiply that $8,000 by ten and you're starting to look at big money.'

John nodded, thoughtfully.

'That still doesn't tell me why they would want to kill Damien!'

'I haven't come to the end of the story yet. I went over to see Liz Capel this morning, to find out more if I could, and to see if she needed nursing. She was in a terrible state yesterday. So when I got there, at about ten o'clock, there was no one else around. I let myself in through the back door, walked through and found her still lying on the couch. But she was dead! Whatever that shot was that Ilse gave her yesterday, it finished her off! I didn't know what to do, so I just left. I didn't dare go to Jack Izzard, and I don't dare let on that I suspect anything, because I think she was killed for what she knew.'

'God almighty,' said John. 'That is serious! If they won't stop at murder, and if what you say is right, that this Mary Burton before her was murdered as well, then Damien could be in deep trouble.'

'Cherry's disappeared as well,' said Patsy. 'I went to see her after going to Liz's place, and there was no sign of either her or Damien. The bed hadn't been slept in.'

John stood up, walked over to the window, and looked out.

'My car's out there, standing out like a beacon. I should move it out of sight.'

'You can drive it around the back of the cottage if you like, though it's probably been spotted by now.'

'Okay, I'll do that. Then maybe I should wait until after dark. If you're right, then we need to find those two, and quickly! Where could they be keeping them I wonder.'

Patsy walked over and stood beside him.

'I've been thinking about that. There's really only the pub, the police station, or one of the trawlers that I can think of. There are guest rooms in the pub, and I think there's a beer cellar. No one ever gets to go there, of course, except Frank Kelly.'

'Surely they wouldn't take the chance of using the police station?'

'They might! Jack Izzard is an arrogant pig. No one goes there unless they have to, and there are cells out the back.'

'And what about these trawlers,' said John, turning to face her. 'Is there anywhere on board that you could keep someone locked up?'

'There is usually a cabin below deck, a galley, and somewhere to sleep. If someone was drugged, they could hide them down there, no sweat.'

'It looks as if we've got our work cut out for us, doesn't it. I don't suppose you've got a gun in this place?'

Patsy shook her head.

'No, never had need of one.'

'Well, you might now,' said John, grimly.

II

Cherry sat back on the divan and stared at Ilse, hanging over her with the hypo.

'There's no way you're going to stick that in me, Ilse. You'd better tell me what's going on. What have you got against Damien? He's never done anything to you.'

Ilse took a pace back, and leant against the wall. There was no point in pushing it. The door was locked, and Cherry wasn't going anywhere.

'Your Damien has got some unfortunate friends. It would have been healthier for him to have got out of town when he was told. It's too late now, he's upset too many people.'

'All your compatriots, no doubt,' said Cherry, sneering. 'What the hell is a doctor doing in the company of people like Charlie Fairweather, Frank Kelly and Jack Izzard, Ilse? For god's sake, how did you get mixed up in this... whatever it is?'

Ilse shook her head and pulled a strangely malevolent face.

'Oh, you think you're so clever. You have no idea, do you, of what's been going on around here. You're just one of nature's little innocents. Well, I'll tell you. This is a prosperous little community, more prosperous than most. Why do you think that is?'

'The fishing,' said Cherry, trying to get behind those eyes that were now less than friendly.

'That's right, the fishing! What do you think would happen to this place if the fishing was suddenly suspended, indefinitely.'

'I suppose a few fishermen would go broke.'

'Not just a few fishermen, Cherry! The whole township! This place would be devastated. Every man and his dog would be thrown onto the dole, and all those fishing dollars would dry up. Have you any idea how much those trawlers contribute to the local economy, Cherry? Hundreds of thousands! Hundreds of thousands a year! That could disappear overnight.'

Cherry looked puzzled.

'But why on earth would it? This has been a fishing port for over a hundred years. Why now? What could cause something like that?'

Ilse shook her head.

'If you're so clever, why don't you work it out? I'm certainly not going to tell you, because then you'd be in the same boat as your friend, Damien.'

'You mean, the same boat as Liz Capel, Ilse. You said she's dead. Well she wasn't dead yesterday, so what happened?'

'Liz happened, that's what! Liz and her multitude of occasional boyfriends, Cherry! She did it to herself. Officially, she died of complications arising from double pneumonia.'

'But in actual fact, she died of a drug overdose – isn't that it? A drug overdose that you administered in the presence of Patsy Donaldson, yesterday.'

Ilse shook her head, as if trying to decide what to do.

'Liz Capel was a junkie, Cherry. She always needed a fix of one thing or another. She was also a walking dispenser of everything from herpes to syphilis. She was a danger to the town. The trouble was that she was in the position to create huge problems for us, so she had to disappear. We didn't intend to kill her, just keep her out of harm's way for a while. The heroin was to keep her quiet.'

'You got her hooked on heroin, so you could control her,' said Cherry, looking at the hypodermic in Ilse's hand. 'What happened to Mary Burton, Ilse? What did she do that was so terrible?'

'Mary Burton was a thief! She was just a petty thief, Cherry, and she stole something that was of great importance to the livelihood of this town. She got what was coming to her.'

Cherry felt the hairs on the back of her neck beginning to rise. The look on Ilse's face was sullen, and angry. There was something not quite right about her, and Cherry sensed it.

'If you really want to know, I played croquet with Mary Burton's head. After the boys had finished with her - and they had a bit of fun, I can tell you... I had her buried up to her neck in the ground, and then I came along like the figure of death, and sliced her head off with a sickle. Have you ever seen a head come off its shoulders, Cherry? It's amusing! The lips and eyes keep moving for a good minute after parting company with the body. Mary Burton was still mouthing 'Help!' for a good minute after she was officially dead.'

Cherry shrank back, away from her.

'You're fucking mad,' she said, her voice shaking.

Ilse suddenly made a dive for her, and Cherry brought her legs up, catching Ilse in the chest. With a

226

great heave she threw Ilse back against the wall, jumped off the divan and had hold of the needle before Ilse hit the ground. Then she raised it like a dagger and jabbed it down into Ilse's thigh, pressing down on the plunger as she did so. Ilse let out a moan, and knocked it away before Cherry managed to inject the contents. The hypo flew under the bed, and Cherry wasn't about to waste her opportunity in trying to retrieve it. She looked up and saw blood on the wall where Ilse's head had contacted the plaster.

Going through her pockets, Cherry found the key and went for the door. It took a minute for her to unlock it, by which time Ilse was starting to come around. She was moaning, as Cherry exited and locked the door on the other side. Then she dropped the keys on the ground.

Once out, she found herself in a cellar full of barrels and cartons of wine. The hotel! Suddenly she realised what a predicament she was in. If she were to be intercepted before she got out of the door, they'd kill her. She walked around the barrels and made her way to the other door. Opening it slightly, she peered through to see if there was anyone else about. Only the stairs in front of her, the stairs from the cellar! She mounted these as she heard the first few thumps on the door she'd locked behind her. Ilse had come around, and was beating on the door to get out. The sound of it gave Cherry wings, and she flew up the stairs and out into the passageway.

Slowing down, she made her way along to the entrance and out into the street. There was no point in going back to her cottage, they'd just pick her up again. So she headed off in the other direction, towards the cottages of Liz Capel and Mary Burton.

Instead of heading out into the road, she sought the cover of the trees that backed up to the cottages, and hid herself firmly in the wood. If she remained under cover until dark, perhaps she could get hold of her car and head out of town, find a larger town with a decent sized police station and report Damien's disappearance. At the same time she could report her suspicions about Liz Capel's death, about a group from Dark Harbour smuggling drugs, and about Ilse's confession regarding the murder of Mary Burton. Even as she considered all this, she could imagine the looks of disbelief she would get from the officers there. It all sounded so far fetched – even to her.

Sitting in the shadow of a tree, her back to the trunk, she realised that she would be more likely to succeed if, under cover of darkness, she could locate Damien's whereabouts and help him to escape. In the meantime she could only wait.

Chapter Fourteen

When Emily had calmed down, Igor sat opposite her and got the gist of what had upset her so much. Making some excuse he had then gone to the phone out the back, and quietly phoned Ilse Hirsch who was still up and about after her escapade with Craig, kidnapping Cherry.

'What is it now, for god's sake? Don't you know it's nearly three o'clock in the morning!'

'I wouldn't be phoning if it wasn't serious,' said Igor. 'I've got Emily Longstaff here, and she saw you, with Cherry, dragging her into the pub!'

'Oh, shit!'

'What's more, she saw Izzard and Charlie dragging that new bloke into the police station, all covered in blood. She's freaking out, wants me to drive her to Port Flint to put in a police report.'

'Well, that's not going to happen, Igor! You're going to have to detain her there until we can figure out what to do with her.'

Igor looked pained.

'How the hell am I supposed to do that,' he whispered. '*I* can't go hitting her on the head.'

'You'll have to drug her, and then stick her down in your cellar until tomorrow night. We've got too much on our plate at the moment. I haven't decided yet what we're going to do with Cherry when we finally get hold of her. I think she's for the high jump, along with that boyfriend of hers. We might even have to include Patsy.'

Igor shook his head, wildly.

'Don't you think this is getting out of hand. You're talking about bumping four people – four! If they ever get onto us, they'll throw away the key!'

Ilse grimaced at the other end of the line.

'Don't be a wimp, Igor. There are always accidents, you know! Lots of accidents out there! Don't forget, we've got the local constable onside, and I'll sign any death certificates. How could it go wrong?'

'I still don't like it,' said Igor, his hands beginning to tremble. He hated violence, and had only agreed to go along because he needed a regular income to fund his library of rare books.

'You don't have to like it,' said Ilse, harshly. 'Just do it! You've got a few sleeping tablets there… grind them up and put them in her drink. When she's asleep, take her down your cellar and tie her up. Oh…you can have your wicked will of her first, Igor! I don't mind. Like Mary Burton… remember Mary Burton, Igor?'

The sweat broke out on Igor's brow. Yes, he remembered Mary Burton all right. It was wicked what they'd done to her, just for mistaking two packs of heroin for icing sugar. It was a stupid mistake, but Frank Kelly had insisted on getting rid of her, and Ilse had come along with the sickle idea.

'Yes, I remember!'

'Make sure you do. Because we all hang together in this!'

'Very well,' he said, and put the phone down.

'I'm really frightened,' said Emily, when he'd reappeared with a hot drink, laced with sleeping pills. 'I don't know what that man has done, but I had heard that he was being hounded by Jack Izzard. Veronica Watson was telling me the other day how Jack had defected him and Cherry on the way to Port Flint, and Cherry was complaining of harassment then! I tell you Igor, he was absolutely covered in blood. They'd beaten him up dreadfully. Now I'm worried about Cherry! When I saw Ilse Hirsch and Craig Mortimer, of all people, carry her into the Hotel she was totally out of it. What's going on around here? I think we'd better go and see the police at Port Flint. I think Jack's gone crazy or something!'

Igor made soothing noises in his throat, but didn't commit himself to any specific course of action. Underneath his placid exterior he was scared out of his wits. He knew what Ilse was capable of; he'd seen it! He'd helped Frank Kelly and Charlie Fairweather dig a hole, and watched as they buried Mary Burton up to the neck. She'd been reduced to a gibbering wreck by that time, after being raped four times and questioned unceasingly about the heroin they'd found in her kitchen. She'd admitted taking it, said she thought it was icing sugar, and she was going to make lamingtons or some such foolery. The moment Frank Kelly discovered it was missing, he knew it was Mary! It could only be her! Four hundred thousand dollars worth of heroin, at street value! They obviously couldn't let her get away with that. So Ilse had appeared on the Knoll like some medieval figure of Death, and had scythed away the grass in front of Mary's face until Mary was literally frothing at the mouth in terror. Then she'd calmly sliced her head off at the neck. After angrily kicking her head about between them – an activity Igor didn't participate in because he was too involved in throwing up behind a tree at the time – Ilse carried the head to the edge of the cliff, and heaved it into the harbour. Being mostly bone, there was no fear that it would float. Then they'd covered Mary Burton's protruding neck with a heap of earth and leaves, and left her to fertilise the forest.

Igor had no doubt that Ilse was mentally unbalanced, but he was in too deep to cut and run now. If they broke ranks, everyone would go down!

'Well, what do you think,' said Emily, interrupting his reverie.

He shook his head, and looked confused.

'Sorry, I was miles away. I think you should finish your drink first, and then we'll work out a plan of action, Emily.'

Those were the last words she remembered him speak.

II

Damien finally woke up tasting blood in his mouth, and feeling as if his head had swelled to unreal proportions. Everything ached, from his kidneys to his chest to his legs to his head. He put his hand up to his face and flinched. It was battered and bruised, and painful beyond anything he could ever remember. He'd been in a few fights when he was younger, but had never suffered this badly. The one positive was that the cuffs were off. He could move his hands.

When he finally managed to get his eyes open, his view of the world was bloodshot and dim. But he did manage to make out that he was in a cell of some kind, and it didn't take a rocket scientist to work out that he was locked in a cell at the rear of the police station. Luckily the watch on his wrist was still intact, and that told him that the time was 2.20 p.m. He'd been unconscious for about twelve hours. Anything could have happened in that time, and he wondered how Cherry was faring. God help them if they'd got her too!

He rolled off the bunk and ended up on his hands and knees, on the floor of the cell. He was by no means certain that he would be capable of getting to his feet from that position, but he gritted his teeth and attempted to stand upright. Aided by the bunk, he finally managed to pull himself up, and stand in what was approximately an upright position, but the pain in his back was intense. That bastard Charlie Fairweather had certainly done for him.

Damien made a mental note that if he got out of this, Charlie Fairweather would live to regret that one-sided bashing. So would Jack Izzard, cop or no cop! He wouldn't be so potent without a gun to back him up, and

Damien was determined to turn the tables on both of them.

Looking through the bars of his cell, he noted that there was a narrow corridor with a door at the end. That door was closed. Damien guessed that it led through into the front of the police station, and although it was only a one-man station, it was obvious that they wouldn't be able to keep him there for too long just in case Izzard received a visit from some other member of the force. No doubt they did periodical inspections of the premises, so the fact that he was there at all was quite surprising. Izzard must feel very sure of himself.

In the cell itself there was nothing but the bunk beds, enough for two prisoners, and there was a toilet in the corner. Above the beds there was a small window, fitted with the usual bars for security. Damien braced himself, climbed up and looked through the window. Nothing but an empty block of land, with someone's side fence about forty metres away. Away to his left he could see the side street that the police station fronted. There was no one in sight.

After that he climbed down and tried to exercise to overcome the aches and pains in various parts of his body, and get it functioning again. It was painful work, but the stiffness caused by the bruising soon began to loosen up. At least his hands were all right. If he had to swing a punch, it wasn't exactly going to put him through the roof.

Over the next hour or so he exercised each part of his body, and meanwhile checked out the bars on his cell.

They were old and partly rusted under the grey paint, but still too solid to hope to bend or break. The door was fitted with a huge old-fashioned padlock, so there was no getting around that. Picking locks was not one of Damien's specialities, even if he'd had the tools – which he hadn't. By five o'clock he was beginning to feel his old self again, battered and bruised though he was, and he wondered how long it would be before one or the other of his tormentors was going to turn up and try to put his lights out for good.

What was it Izzard had said? 'Don't be surprised if you end up the victim of a horrible accident. You might even take it on yourself to hang yourself in your cell.'

Damien smiled grimly at the thought. Let them try it! They might just be surprised at how much fight he had left in him. And if Izzard pointed that gun at him again, he'd call his bluff. The last thing Izzard would want would be a dead prisoner with a police bullet hole in him.

Damien carried on with his exercises, thinking furiously all the while. He was so badly knocked about, cut and bruised, that they wouldn't dare try the hanging trick anyway, because the coroner would call foul, and there would be an investigation. All hell would break loose. He smiled to himself. Things weren't as grim and one-sided as he'd thought.

At just on six thirty, the door at the end of the corridor opened, and Charlie Fairweather came through, grinning and holding a brown paper bag. He stopped outside the cell and stared at Damien, a sardonic expression on his face.

'Feeling a bit battered, pal? There's plenty more where that came from. I hope you enjoyed spending my money, because it's the last money you'll ever spend. You should have got out when you were told. Here…' he threw the bag through the bars. 'The dying man's last meal! Don't say we didn't look after your creature comforts.'

'You're pretty handy with your fists when you're beating up an armless man. Not so hot when he can defend himself though, eh?'

Charlie muscled up to the bars.

'I can take you anytime, you shit! You were just lucky that day on the Knoll. You had the slope in your favour!'

'I didn't need the slope. You're just a bag of wind that likes to think he's tough. Come in here and I'll sort you out, right now!'

Charlie backed away, and just laughed.

'You must think I'm simple, mate. You're going on a trip tonight, one way, to the bottom of the harbour. I'm hardly likely to open that door and give you a crack at leaving us so soon. No, you can stay where you are until Jack gets here. Don't worry, we'll wait until after dark, so you've got plenty of time to enjoy your meal.'

'I knew you were gutless… and that proves it!'

The door at the end of the corridor opened once more, and this time a woman came striding along to the cell. Damien didn't recognise her, but he could see that under the headscarf she was wearing, she also had a bandage around her head.

'What proves what?' she said, as she approached. She stopped outside the cell and stared in. 'So you're the one who's been causing all the bother! You should have got out of here while you still had time, Mister Curtis. It's too late now, and even if we were inclined to be lenient, we couldn't be. There's too much hanging on the next few days for it to be upset by Customs and Excise! You should have taken your holidays elsewhere.'

Damien stared at her in bemusement.

'And who the hell are you? Surely you're not mixed up with this lot of shysters!'

'I suppose it won't hurt you to know who I am. Doctor Ilse Hirsch, and I'm not pleased to see you at all!'

'The feeling's mutual, I'm sure. And while you're at it, I'm not in Customs and Excise, never was! I sell novelties for a living. I'm a salesman!'

Ilse stared at him through the bars, and shook her head.

'If that's right, how come we found a photograph of you, in the company of another man in the uniform of Customs and Excise? Don't tell me you haven't been sent here to spy on us.'

'That's an old mate of mine. I've known him since we went to school together. Now I begin to understand. I thought it was strange that that particular photo was missing when your friend returned them.' He paused for a moment. 'So I was right... this *is* a smuggling racket. You're smuggling drugs, aren't you? You're all in it together!'

'A good guess, Mister Curtis, but you'll never know now, will you?'

'More than a bloody guess. You were the one in the hood... I recognise the voice! I watched you pick up the dope and drop it into the book. It's hollow, isn't it? Clever, but not clever enough.'

Ilse stepped up to the bars, her face transformed with anger.

'How the hell could you know that? You couldn't possibly have seen us.'

'Oh, I saw you all right. What are you... Druids? Welsh Bards? A fairly handy disguise to have if you don't want to be recognised.'

Charlie grabbed the bars, and looked as if he was going to reach through and grab Damien by the throat. Damien stepped back. Ilse looked at him in sudden amusement.

'So you were hidden in the trees by the dock! What would a novelties salesman be doing spying on an ancient ceremony at that time of night? You've just blown your own cover, Mister Curtis. Why don't you just admit it?'

Damien wiped his lip, and considered his options. Either way, it wouldn't make much difference.

'All right! Yes... Customs and Excise have had their eye on you for some time. In a few hours this place will be crawling with uniforms, and you lot will have a lot of explaining to do. What with you and Charlie here, that Craig, and Jack Izzard… and don't let's forget our publican friend, Frank Kelly. Oh yes, they've got a whole list of you back at headquarters. The game's over, lady!'

Ilse seemed to relax, stepped back and smiled.

'You knowing is one thing. Them, another! You didn't have time to pass that information on before going back to Cherry's place last night. It's a good job that I put Jack on your case, isn't it? You could have spoiled the whole thing. In actual fact, all you've managed to do is to ensure that you won't live out the night, and that Cherry Reynolds and Patsy Donaldson will be joining you in a small boat disaster. It happens all the time in these parts. Stupid people going out at night in a boat, no lights, then being run down by one of our trawlers. Once you've been through the props of a trawler, there won't be any questions about the state of the bodies. They make a terrible mess of flesh and bone.'

'What the hell's it got to do with them,' said Damien, angrily grabbing the bars. 'They don't know anything!'

'They've been seen with you! All three of you, driving around the town! It won't seem out of place for the three of you to have decided to go out late night fishing together. Then Patsy won't be able to spill anything she knows about Liz Capel, will she? And neither will Cherry.'

'This is just bloody murder,' said Damien, his face paler than usual.

'No, Mister Curtis, not murder. I prefer to call it expedience,' said Ilse, and turned to walk away.

Charlie grinned, and went to follow her.

'See you later, pal! Make the most of your hamburger – it's the last one you'll ever get.'

III

Cherry sat in the gathering gloom and watched the various protagonists driving back and forth along the main road, obviously looking for her. First of all it was Charlie Fairweather. He drove down to Liz Capel's cottage in Lionel Jury's car, and stormed inside. After a few minutes he came out again, and instead of going back to the car turned and looked over at Mary Burton's place. Then he turned and walked the fifty metres or so to the cottage and entered by the back door. When he obviously didn't find anything, he came half running out of the cottage and headed straight back for the car.

Then Jack Izzard coasted slowly along the road in his patrol car, stopping occasionally to look around, and then continuing on his way, right out to the turn-off. Minutes later he would be back again, still slowly checking out the areas each side of the road. Later still Craig Mortimer came looking, this time on foot. He walked all the way down to the dock, went through the trees and back out onto the road again. One thing remained common to their features; utter frustration.

At seven o'clock the patrol car appeared again, this time with a passenger. Ilse Hirsch was with Izzard this time, and they drove directly to Liz Capel's place, both of them going in. After five minutes or so they reappeared, and Izzard made a great show of locking the front door. They'd obviously made the place secure, and Cherry wondered if Liz's body was still in there.

Cherry had never been that close to Liz, but she had been shocked, nevertheless when Liz had disappeared. Patsy was closer to Liz than anyone, and had shared in her secrets. Liz had confided her various conquests to her, and even though Cherry was Patsy's best friend, Patsy would never pass on these choice tit-bits for general discussion. Her friendship with one was exclusive of her friendship with the other. Cherry had a general idea that Liz was fairly accommodating where it came to the men in her life, probably encompassing the majority of the men in Dark Harbour, but she was not the type to point the finger, or to moralise on such issues. If Liz wanted to live her life on her back, that was her decision, and Cherry would have been the last person to cry foul.

Now she was dead, after some months of being god-knows-where, of being chronically ill, and tended by another friend of Cherry's whom she obviously knew less about than she'd thought. Ilse Hirsch! What was her story? She'd seen a side of Ilse in that room that Ilse had never revealed before, a ruthless, uncaring streak that had been kept well hidden. Not just that, however, but a genuine strain of madness that had not only admitted to, but gloried in, murder. Cherry shuddered at Ilse's description of taking Mary Burton's head off her shoulders with a sickle. That had both terrified her, and fired her determination to escape. It was the thought of that that had galvanised her into action, and that had powered her legs to fling Ilse against the wall. Now Ilse was cruising around with Izzard, looking for her.

At just after eight o'clock it was finally getting dark. Cherry was restless and upset by this time, and had a number of bouts of weeping silently in the gloom, thinking variously about her own fate, and that of Damien. She was just getting to the point where she thought she could safely make a move, when she heard footsteps in the undergrowth behind her, and froze. Whoever it was, they were moving cautiously through the trees, but the dead leaves and twigs on the floor would give anyone away.

Cherry's heart went into her mouth, and she could feel the terror rising in her throat. If it was Frank Kelly, or Izzard, either man would have been too powerful for her to resist. She put her hand to her mouth, as if that action alone would stop her from screaming, but when the man stumbled around her side of the tree, they both jumped in shock, and Cherry let out an involuntary shriek.

She jumped to her feet, and stared in horror at someone who turned out to be a total stranger. John Inglis stared in horror back.

'Oh shit! I'm sorry. Did I startle you,' were the first words that came to mind, as he stood there on tenterhooks, his hand outstretched in hopes that she wouldn't set up a screaming fit.

Cherry didn't know whether to be relieved or alarmed.

'God! You nearly gave me a heart attack,' she said, putting her hand over her heart. 'I'm sorry, I shouldn't have jumped like that. But this is a funny place to be walking. Are you lost, or something?'

John looked at her enquiringly, taking in her features and colouring,

'You wouldn't be... you wouldn't know a woman called Cherry by any chance?'

Cherry coloured slightly. Who the hell was this? Had he been sent by the others?

'Why... who wants to know?' she replied, defensively.

John hesitated for a moment. He could be in deep trouble here.

'Look; I'm looking for a friend of mine, a Damien Curtis. I understand he was in the company of a woman called Cherry, but she's supposed to have gone away on holiday, and Damien's disappeared.'

'John! Oh thank god you're here,' said Cherry, tears in her eyes. 'You're Damien's friend, John!'

'That's right! So you are... you are...?' he said, prompting her.

'Cherry, that's right. Oh, for god's sake, keep your voice down. If they find us here they'll kill us!'

John motioned her to sit down again, and he sat down himself. They made smaller targets, seated. They looked at each other through the gloom, neither knowing quite where to begin.

'I've been at Patsy's place,' John began.

'Is she all right? I've been worried sick about her,' said Cherry. 'She's going to be next if she's not careful.'

'She's fine... at the moment, anyway. What happened to you? What are you doing out here,' said John, his voice a bare whisper.

'The same thing as you! Hiding, and looking for Damien.'

Cherry briefly told him of the events of the previous evening when Damien went out late for a walk, and never came back. Then she told of her subsequent visit to Patsy's place, and how she must have been attacked on her way home, because she had woken up in a room next to the cellar in the hotel. She told him about the doctor, and her confession, and by this time John was alarmed.

'Have you any idea where Damien could be? I was heading down to the dock, to see if I could get onto that trawler and check below decks.'

'He could be there,' said Cherry, 'but it's not very likely. I think they've got him at the police station, probably in a cell out the back. I was going to go and check it out at midnight, when no-one's around.'

'I think we'd better stick together,' said John. 'We'd stand more of a chance then, if there's only one of them. We should arm ourselves. I don't suppose you know where we could get hold of a gun?'

Cherry shook her head. Guns were not common around Dark Harbour, especially since the government had called them in. The only gun that she knew of was kept by Katie's father, on his trawler. He used to fire at porpoises if they looked like going through his nets. A porpoise could put a hole in a net the size of a bus. It was highly illegal, but that didn't worry people like Wilf Carstairs, not once he was out on the open water.

'The only gun I know of is on that trawler at the dock. I think it's an old .303 rifle.'

'Well that's worth a try,' said John. 'At least we could protect ourselves. Do you know exactly where it is?'

'I think it would be in the wheelhouse. If you could get on it without being seen, you'd find it easily enough. There's no security.'

'In that case, I'm going to try for it. This cop has a gun, right? That's probably how they got Damien. It's the only way he'd give in to anyone, if they were waving a gun in his face.'

'I'll come with you,' said Cherry. 'There's safety in numbers.'

'I think it would be better if you hung back until I actually got hold of the gun,' said John. 'Then we'll go together to the police station and break Damien out. Where does this cop live… is it a residence attached to the station?'

'Not exactly! The house is alongside, but on the opposite side to the cells.'

'Well that's one thing in our favour! We might be able to get in from the rear.' John looked out through the trees, over towards the dock. The trawler lay in darkness, a shapeless hulk in the gloom. He looked back at Cherry, speculatively. 'How close are you two? I mean, would you say you've progressed to a relationship, or are you just friends?'

Cherry smiled in the dark.

'Are you worried about Andrea? He told me all about it. Let's put it this way; Damien won't be going back to his wife, not if I've got anything to say about it. I think I've finally found the man I've been looking for all my life.'

John nodded, and smiled in satisfaction.

'Thank god for that. After Andrea, you're like a breath of fresh air. I don't think I'll be going back to Andrea, either, if the truth were told. She's vastly over-rated.'

'In that case I'll have to introduce you to my friend, Patsy.'

'We've already met,' he said, and then looked at her, meaningfully. 'I could really fall for a woman like that!'

'Really,' said Cherry, smiling.

'Yeah, really,' said John.

Chapter Fifteen

Damien checked out the contents of the brown paper bag, and found a soggy hamburger, and a small box of orange juice. The box was double sealed with a straw attached, and Damien inspected it carefully for any leaks. He looked especially for any pinpricks that would indicate it had been interfered with. It would be easy to inject some soporific through the cardboard. Finally satisfying himself that the drink hadn't been tampered with, he opened it and took a sip. It tasted all right. He knew he was becoming dehydrated, so the drink was important, more important than the food.

After that he opened up the hamburger and inspected each layer thoroughly. Between the tomato and the lettuce, he found some telltale grains of a white powder, so shoved it back into the bag and threw it on the floor. He wasn't that stupid!

The drink revived him somewhat, and he turned once more to the problem of the cell. The bars were too thick to bend, the lock was too solid, and the walls must have been over a foot thick. The place had been an old stone building, and it would take a jackhammer to get through those walls. He climbed onto the top bunk, and discovered that the ceiling was lower than he'd thought. He could only kneel, stooped on the bunk, otherwise he would hit his head on the ceiling.

He lay back and stared at the plasterboard above his head. By following the nail heads he could work out where the rafters were spaced, and there was a good gap between them. Raising his feet from a prone position, he braced himself against the plasterboard, and gave it a shove. There was a satisfying crack above his head, and as he continued to push, the plasterboard began to tear. It was the old-fashioned plaster and horsehair board they used to use in the old days, before gyprock became the standard. This board had been affected by damp where the roof leaked, and was subsequently weakened. It didn't take too many shoves before Damien broke though it, and it was the work of minutes to widen the hole enough for him to get head and shoulders through, and up into the ceiling.

The roof was iron. Damien tested it, to see if he could force a sheet off, but the noise was horrendous. A nail began to squeal as he pushed, and he was forced to stop. Looking towards the edge, he could see where the iron tapered down to the outside gutter, and just before that, there were the eaves. These were merely some sort of fibrous panelling, without a great deal of support. He rolled along the rafters to the eaves, and attacked the panelling with his feet. Four swift kicks broke a large section away, and Damien pulled himself through and hung from a rafter, gauging the drop to the ground. Ten seconds later he had landed on the waste land beside the police station, and was making his way off the block and around the back of the main street.

It was dark outside! He'd been out of action for about twenty hours, and his first priority was to find Cherry. All other considerations paled beside the necessity of finding the woman that, he suddenly realised, meant more to him than the wife he had been so decimated to lose. But he needed to arm himself. He had no intention of being bailed up again by Izzard's .38, or falling foul of Charlie Fairweather's fists and feet. Next time they met, he would go for the jugular.

He was briefly tempted to make for Cherry's cottage, but remembering what had happened there the night before, he knew that it was highly unlikely that he'd find her there. What had Izzard said? 'The 'disappearance' of Cherry Reynolds!' If she had disappeared in the three hours he was away, then he knew who it was down to, and he mentally ticked off the names that had been mentioned as members of the 'Klan'. Izzard, Fairweather, Craig Mortimer, Frank Kelly, and one he'd never met, the newsagent. There might have been more.

Damien racked his brain to try and work out where he'd be most likely to get a gun, and after a few moments, nodded to himself, and turned towards the dock.

II

Wilf and Meg Carstairs had been finishing their tea when Jack Izzard knocked at the door. Meg got up to answer it, and came back, a worried look on her face.

'It's the policeman, Wilf! You haven't been getting into any trouble have you,' she whispered, anxiously.

Wilf looked up in surprise, shook his head and wiped his mouth with a napkin. Then he got up and putting his finger to his lips to indicate silence, he pushed past his wife and shut the door behind him. He didn't want Meg worried with whatever it was Izzard had come about.

At the door, Izzard stood back in the shadow, and beckoned him outside.

'Shut the door behind you, Wilf. We've got a little job for you.'

Wilf followed him out to the patrol car, and was surprised to see Ilse Hirsch sitting in the back seat. He was told to get in beside her.

'What's all this about, Jack?' he growled, not comfortable next to the local doctor.

Izzard sat in the front, and swivelled around to face them over the back of the seat.

'Meet Ilse Hirsch, Wilf! She's got something to tell you.'

Carstairs didn't look impressed.

'We've met! Last night, in a hood if I'm not mistaken! I hope you're not going to discuss our business in front of...,' he broke off, and indicated the woman next to him.

'I *am* your business, Mister Carstairs,' Ilse said, sharply. 'You just haven't dealt with me before, that's all. But now you have to, because we have a job for you... one you might not like!'

'What the hell's she talking about, Jack?'

250

Izzard grinned.

'Who do you think has been keeping book for us for the past two years, Wilf? All those payments! Meet your benefactor.'

Wilf looked at Ilse again, in shock. She wasn't in the mood to waste words.

'Eighty seven thousand four hundred dollars! Not bad for a tax-free sideline, Carstairs. Over forty grand a year! Just so you know I know!'

Wilf looked at her, uncertainly. He'd always considered her to be one of those snobby types, who wouldn't get her hands dirty in their sort of business.

'Are you telling me that she's behind the whole thing,' said Wilf. 'If I'd known that, I would never have become involved.'

'Why – because I'm a woman? You haven't got much time for women, have you! If I remember rightly, I've had to treat your wife for a few involuntary bruises over the years,' said the doctor, sharply. 'Anyway, that's not why we're here. We need you to take your trawler out later on tonight with three passengers aboard. Jack here will follow you in a sixteen-foot fibreglass speedboat. Five miles out you will dump your three passengers overboard, then run over them a few times until you've chewed them up pretty well with the prop. Then Jack will come on board, and you can do the same with the boat – run it down! We want a believable boating accident with gruesome results. Three dead and a half sunken fishing boat! As long as it looks like an accident.'

Wilf looked at her as if she was speaking in a foreign tongue.

'Are you fucking mad? That's murder!'

'That's right, Wilf. And that's exactly what you'll do,' said Izzard, not smiling now. 'You have to take the good with the bad, old pal. You've taken the good, now comes a bit of bad. So what? Even if they sheet it home to you, you can just say you didn't see them at all – you were down in the galley, taking a piss. Anything! You never saw anything; you never felt anything, you never heard anything! It's a mystery of the sea.'

Wilf shook his head.

'I don't know what you take me for, but murder is out! I didn't mind picking up the drugs for you. I took the risks for that – and I'd have gone a row if I'd been caught. It was worth that for the money. But murder…'

'There are worse things,' said Ilse. 'Far worse! What if I were to tell you that neither you nor your wife were likely to live for more than another three years?'

Wilf swivelled in his seat and glared at her.'

'Is that a threat? Don't you fucking threaten me, lady!'

Izzard waved his hand over the top of the seat, to tell Carstairs to cool it.

'It's not a threat, Wilf! It's a promise! If we don't finish what we started here, then we're all going to die, mate! All of us… and it won't be pleasant!'

Carstairs looked at him, uncomprehendingly. Ilse took over.

'I'll explain it in words of one syllable. You're HIV positive, Carstairs, so is your wife! So is Jack here, and so are over half the men and a lot of the women in this town. Do you remember Liz Capel? I can see you do!'

Wilf went all shades of red at the mention of Liz Capel. He had thought that his little fling with Liz had gone un-noticed. Ilse nodded.

'What about her… she disappeared!'

'She's back! Arrived back yesterday. Or should I say, she never really went away!'

'What the hell are you talking about?'

'You made the mistake of bedding a woman that was HIV positive, and well on the way to full-blown AIDS. She finally died yesterday… of AIDS related symptoms.'

'Died? Are you telling me that I got AIDS, and then infected my wife?' said Wilf, aghast. He buried his head in his hands in anguish. 'Oh, God help us!'

'Not AIDS, Carstairs, HIV! That's one step short of AIDS. Over a period I have been secretly blood-testing most of the adult population in this town; every time someone caught a cold, I took blood. Everyone who had relations with Liz – and there were many – came away HIV positive. I didn't know it was her at first, I had to narrow it down! Then they all had affairs with each other, and relations with their wives, spreading it everywhere. You're all heading for AIDS, Carstairs, and when that hits you, it will be too late. The reason we need you to do this little job for us, is to buy us time. There's a cure on the way… literally, on the way! If this guy, Damien, brings his Customs and Excise buddies up here, it will be all over. The same goes for his two confidants.'

'And who would they be,' said Wilf, his hands shaking on his lap.

'Cherry Reynolds and Patsy Donaldson! We don't know how much they know, but they're a risk. We've got to move one more shipment of heroin, and harvest and sell a crop of dope. The money we get for that will top up our fund.'

'She means for the cure,' said Izzard. 'It doesn't come cheap! It's going to cost an average of a hundred and sixty thousand per person to get hold of sufficient quantities of this new drug. It hasn't even been released yet, and it comes from the States. That means that it has to be smuggled out of the laboratory, and as our currency is only worth seventy percent of U.S. currency, it means we have to pay twice as much, plus a premium for smuggling it out. $160,000 Australian per person, and at last count there were forty seven people in this town with HIV.'

'My maths isn't that good. How much are we talking about here?'

'Over seven and a half million dollars! Why do you think it's taken so long to raise the money?'

Wilf shook his head in exasperation.

'Why have you kept this hidden? Why haven't you let us get treatment through the normal channels? We could be halfway on the road to recovery by now!'

'There is no recovery, Carstairs, don't you understand that,' said the doctor. 'The best we can hope for is to stop the disease developing into full-blown AIDS. No drug on the market to this point can guarantee that. I happen to have a contact in a research facility in the U.S. that has developed an entirely new drug over the past two years, called Fureonn. I won't go into the medical details; you wouldn't understand them anyway. All I can say is that this drug prevents the AIDS virus from invading white blood cells. With this treatment, it's possible that the HIV infected will never progress to full-blown AIDS.'

'But why have you kept this such a bloody secret,' said Carstairs, mortified. 'I mean, my wife, for chrisesake!'

'Because… you dolt,' Ilse snapped back, 'if this got out, what do you think would happen to the market for your catch? What if the world out there discovered that all the fish, and prawns, and crayfish, caught and processed at Dark Harbour, were being handled by people who were all HIV positive? Work it out!'

Wilf Carstairs complexion suddenly turned grey.

'Good God,' he said. 'I never thought of it in that light. That would be the end of it… the end of us all! The industry would collapse!'

'Dead right, mate,' said Izzard. 'Which is why you're going to do this little job for us – tonight!'

Wilf nodded slowly. He could see it now, ruin for them all! He'd sailed close to the wind financially, most of his life, and he had no intention of ever getting back into that bind again. He could see he had no option.

'I thought we were just doing the drugs for the money,' he said. 'I had no idea!'

'We knew that no one would cooperate if they didn't get paid,' said Ilse, 'so we split the proceeds 30/70. Thirty percent for payoffs, and seventy percent for the fund! We need another $600,000 and we're there. The first shipment of this AIDS drug is due in two weeks, and we'll be picking it up the same way... offshore, in a craypot!'

'So you'll do it?' said Izzard, noticing Meg Carstairs peering curiously through the curtains.

'You don't give me much choice, do you?' said Wilf.

III

John decided that their first move should be to secure the rifle from the trawler, and then go on to try and break Damien out, if he happened to be in the police cells.

'Look... why don't you wait here while I go over and check out the trawler? It shouldn't take me too long, and I'll come straight back here and collect you.'

Cherry shook her head.

'Not in a fit! I'm coming with you. If we get into trouble, then at least there will be two of us to contend with. They've got to be better odds!'

John smiled in resignation.

'Okay, but keep down for chrisesake! We need to stay in the shadows. Keep close, and when I run, you run too!'

It took them ten minutes to circle around and approach the dock through the trees at the rear. The most hair-raising part was crossing the main road, and they took that at a run. They just hoped upon hope that they hadn't been spotted.

Cherry stayed undercover at the edge of the dock, while John, picking his shadows, clambered aboard the 'Wavefarer'. It was pitch black, and he couldn't help stumbling over ropes on the deck as he made his way to the wheelhouse. There were four steps up to the wheelhouse, and he climbed these carefully, grasping the handle on the wheelhouse door and opening it carefully. He had only taken two steps into the wheelhouse when suddenly his feet were taken from under him, and he found himself on the floor, on his back.

'Don't you fucking move, or I'll put a bullet through your head!'

John lay there confused, looking up into the barrel of a .303 rifle. Behind it there was a shadow, but it was so dark that he could make out no features. He knew the voice, however.

'For chrisesake, Damien! It's me, John!'

There was a moment's silence while this information was assimilated.

'What the…. what in bloody hell are you doing here? I thought it was Izzard!'

'No mate, it's me! And I've got your lady friend in the trees out there, Cherry!'

'Cherry! Thank god for that. I thought they'd got her!'

'They did, but it seems she broke out. She was out looking for you when I ran into her. I see you've got the gun, anyway. Let's get out of here.'

'Yeah, let's move – though why I'm even talking to you, I really don't know. How's Andrea?'

They made their way down the steps and onto the deck, still whispering.

'She sent me to get you. She wants you back, mate!'

Damien choked off a laugh.

'What… couldn't you keep her satisfied? You should have known she only wanted a fling, John. Relationships are a bit beyond her, even *I've* learnt that much.'

They skirted around to the side of the vessel and clambered over onto the dock. As they did they could see headlights approaching along the main road. They had only just gained the anonymity of the trees when the headlights turned and headed down towards the dock. By the time the car pulled up, Cherry was in Damien's arms and they were otherwise occupied.

They watched as a man got out of the passenger seat and walked over to the light pole, hit the switch and lit up the dock. It was Wilf Carstairs. In the drivers seat was Charlie Fairweather. Damien raised the .303 and took a bead on Charlie's head through the widow of the car. The temptation to pull the trigger was almost overwhelming, but John laid his hand on Damien's shoulder, and the moment was lost.

'Not worth it, mate,' John whispered. Cherry nodded her head in agreement.

'Don't do it, Damien. I want to see that bastard stand trial, along with Ilse Hirsch, Izzard, and all the others. If you kill him, we lose all credibility.'

Damien put the rifle down, and they watched as Charlie got out and went over to talk to Carstairs. They were within earshot.

'You get it set up, and we'll be back with the three 'accident' victims in about an hour. If we can't find Cherry, we'll bring someone else in her place. There will still be three!'

'Who's the other one,' said Wilf, turning as he gained the deck.

'Emily Longstaff! She's under the gun too. Don't worry, her old man's at sea right now!'

'Don't fucking worry,' Wilf exploded. 'Are you fucking mad? Emily Longstaff is a respectable long-term resident of Dark Harbour. What could she have done?'

'Don't you worry about that! She's for the high jump anyway, so just do your job.'

Charlie jumped back into the car before Carstairs could put forward any further argument, and backed off the dock. Wilf sat down on the deck of his trawler, and put his head in his hands, in an attitude of abject despair.

IV

'They've got Emily! Oh my god, this is a nightmare! They must have Patsy, too,' said Cherry, clinging to Damien's arm. 'What on earth would they want Emily for?'

'She must have stumbled onto something,' said Damien, 'pretty much the way we have.'

'I think we ought to take that guy out of the formula,' said John, indicating Carstairs on the deck. 'He's obviously not happy about things.'

'Fairweather told me that I was going to the bottom of the harbour tonight,' said Damien. 'That's probably what he meant. Out on the trawler, miles from anywhere, then dumped over the side. It now sounds like they intended the same for Cherry and Patsy. So now what do we do?'

'Get rid of the trawler,' said John. 'If that's gone, they'll have to think again!'

John and Damien crept to the edge of the dock, and John headed for the switch on the light pole, while Damien covered Carstairs with the rifle. The lights suddenly went out, and Carstairs jumped to his feet, shaken out of his misery on deck.

'Who's that?' he called out, looking around him in the dark.

'Shut the fuck up and sit down,' a voice rang out. 'I've got you covered, and one little move and you're dead meat.'

Carstairs sat down again, his hands shaking. Damien climbed up onto the trawler, and walked towards him, rifle at the ready.

'You're in deep trouble, aren't you mate,' said Damien, taking up a stance in front of him. 'We know what you intend doing, and we're here to offer you an alternative option.'

'What might that be?' Wilf growled, but somewhat subdued.

'Take your trawler out into the gulf and stay there for at least twenty-four hours... two days if possible. By that time we'll have sorted these swine out.'

'You don't know the half of it,' Wilf said, wringing his hands. 'It's not that simple.'

'Well maybe you'd better tell us all about it,' said Damien, 'because we're sick of being kept in the dark. You've been smuggling drugs, haven't you? You're the pick-up boy, and Ilse Hirsch has been running the show.'

'Yes, but I didn't know that until tonight. I thought it was just Igor Morrris, Izzard and Frank and Craig Mortimer... and Charlie and Lionel. I didn't know the doctor was involved until the Bards came along and did the pick-up in their robes last night. It's usually Igor Morris. I usually pack the drugs inside a large snapper, and hand him that separately. I thought it was strange when they told me about this procession idea! Tonight they told me what I'd got myself into. I had no idea!'

'And what exactly have you got yourself into, Wilf?' Cherry had swung her legs over the side, and now approached him, grimly determined to get the truth.

'Oh, it's you Cherry! Look, it wasn't my idea. I've got nothing against you, you know that. But they've got me over a barrel.'

'Well spit it out, Wilf. What the fuck's going on?'

Wilf shook his head, and put his head down into his hands.

'We've all got AIDS! Liz Capel had AIDS, and she's passed it all around the town. I was stupid enough to screw her myself, and now I've passed it on to Meg. I could kick myself.'

Both Cherry and Damien stood there, stunned.

'AIDS! Good God, Wilf! Who's got it? Have I got it?'

'I don't know, Cherry, but I think your mate Patsy has. All the main players around here have got it... HIV anyway. They're smuggling some new drug in from America that's going to cure everyone. It's due in two weeks, and the drugs... well, that was just to raise the money to buy the AIDS anti-virus. It hasn't been released yet, so the doc's got someone over there who works in a lab producing the stuff.'

'That would be her cousin,' said Cherry, biting her lip. 'But why didn't they just go through the normal healthcare channels?'

'They reckon that the drugs on the market so far can't stop it, only slow it down. This new one actually stops it entering the white blood cells, or some such thing. It all sounds double-dutch to me, but no doubt the doctor knows what she's talking about. They reckon there's forty seven people in the town that are HIV positive.'

Cherry gasped.

'But that's half the population of the place!'

'Right! And they all work in the fishing industry.'

Damien stamped one foot, as the light of understanding finally filtered through.

'Well, I'll be stuffed! So that's what it was all about. Fish!'

'Food,' said Cherry. 'Of course! Everyone's so superstitious about how people catch AIDS that despite the fact that you wouldn't be able to catch it by eating a product handled by an AIDS sufferer, common sense goes out the window.'

'And they're willing to kill us to keep this under the carpet,' said Damien, angrily.

'The trouble is, it wouldn't be the first time,' said Carstairs. 'They killed Mary Burton for stealing two packets of heroin, in mistake for icing sugar.'

Damien's jaw dropped.

'So that was what it was about!'

'That's what Ilse meant when she said Mary was a petty thief,' said Cherry. 'It's all so clear now!'

John came over from the dock.

'I hate to interrupt you lot, but it's time we made a move. Make your minds up!'

Damien waved the rifle in Wilf's direction.

'Okay! What's it to be? Are you going to take this trawler out and disappear for a few days, or are you going to get involved in more murders?'

Wilf got to his feet.

'There's nothing for it now, I suppose, except to get the hell out. I expect you to put in a good word for me at the trial.'

'If you do as we say, then we'll do our best for you,' said Damien. 'Now, get the hell out of here!'

With that, the three of them clambered over onto the dock, while Carstairs made for the wheelhouse.

'Cast her off for me,' he called out, and then they heard the big Perkins diesel start up.

John threw off the bowline, and Damien got the stern. Then the three of them melted back into the trees.

Chapter Sixteen

At nine o'clock that night, a small car pulled up outside the front of the Promenade Hotel, and a smart, well-dressed woman got out and went in through the entrance to the lounge. She walked up to the bar and tapped urgently on the little bell to attract the barmaid through from the bar. Instead of the expected barmaid, a thickset middle-aged man appeared behind the counter, and looked at her, quizzically.

'Excuse me,' she began. 'I need a room for the night. What do you charge?'

'Are you on your own,' said the publican, 'or with your husband?' He pulled out a guest book from under the counter, and opened it at the appropriate page.

'No, just me,' she said, looking around the empty lounge.

'Forty dollars for the night, vacate by ten o'clock tomorrow morning. Name?'

'Andrea Curtis.' She pulled out her purse and extracted two twenty-dollar notes, placing them on the counter.

'Curtis! I seem to have heard that name before,' the publican murmured as he wrote her name in the book.

'Have you… around here? I've come looking for my husband, actually. Damien Curtis! Perhaps you've heard of him, or run into him over the past few days.'

Frank Kelly shook his head, slowly. His eyes took on a sharper glint as he looked down and completed the entry in the book.

'No, can't say as I have. But I can ask around for you if you like. I'll put you in room six. Will you be wanting breakfast – that's an extra eight dollars.'

'No thanks; I'll get something later in the day. If you can find out anything about my husband's whereabouts, I'll be very grateful.'

Kelly handed her the key and escorted her to room six.

'If you need anything, just give the barmaid a call on the phone,' he said. 'It's hooked directly through to the bar.'

Andrea walked into the room, and shut the door. She took off her coat, kicked off her shoes and breathed a sigh of relief. Then she sat on the bed.

It had been a last minute decision to follow John Inglis to Dark Harbour, partly because she was impatient to find Damien and salvage him from the clutches of this woman, and partly because she didn't trust John to do what he'd been told. He hadn't exactly been enthusiastic about going, and that could mean that at the first rebuff he might turn tail and run back home.

Andrea had no intentions of letting Damien go that easily. She had miscalculated before, that was true. Initially, she had expected Damien to be so decimated by her decision to leave him that he would chase and pester her for weeks before she would, reluctantly, agree to return home. In the meantime she expected to be able to enjoy a fling with John, quite openly, and continue to maintain that she was the injured party. It hadn't worked out like that. For some reason, Damien had refused to play the game by her rules. That had been a shock in itself. The second shock was in discovering that the only thing she had in common with John was sex, and that he was a slob of the first order who could not possibly replace Damien in any other area of life.

Since John's departure, Andrea had been on the phone regularly to Veronica, discussing the pro's and cons of the case, and trying to ascertain how Veronica herself would tackle this particular problem. Veronica finally snapped.

'That's really a question for you to work out, Andrea. After all, it's your life, and only you know what you want out of life. I've never, personally, experienced a situation like you find yourself in, and to be honest, I hope I never shall.'

'You're not being very helpful, Veronica,' Andrea had snapped. 'You're supposed to be on *my* side!'

'To be quite honest, Andrea, I think you're an absolute idiot!'

'You *what?*'

'An idiot, Andrea! Yes! From what I can make out you've jeopardised a loving relationship with Damien for the sake of a few cheap thrills with his best mate, and now that things aren't going as planned you've cried foul, and expect to be able to turn back the clock. It will serve you right if you've lost him for good!'

'Veronica! How dare you…'

'Oh, don't give me that outrage crap, Andrea. You've brought this on yourself, now you're just going to have to wear it. When I saw Damien with his new lady, they looked a picture. If ever anyone looked made for each other, they did. Give it up, Andrea, let Damien make a new life for himself. You blew it!'

Andrea slammed down the phone in anger at that point, and then burst into self-indulgent tears. It was then that she realised she was going to have to go to Dark Harbour herself. Damien had taken their main car, the Falcon wagon, but she still had access to the second car, a two-door Datsun that they kept for emergencies. Andrea rarely drove herself anywhere, but she steeled herself to the task, packed a bag and left almost immediately.

Now she looked around at the dingy hotel room and felt a wave of apprehension pass through her. She looked down and noticed that her hands were shaking. If she'd lost Damien for good, she didn't know what she was going to do. Surely, once he saw how upset she was his resolve would crumble, and she would condescend to forgive him. Yes, that's what she would do. She'd bring him back with his tail between his legs. Andrea tossed her head and caught a glimpse of herself in the mirror. She was a fine looking woman, she thought to herself, and that thought gave her renewed confidence.

'Can't you people be trusted to do anything right,' Ilse snapped. She was standing in front of the cell at the rear of the police station, staring at the tell-tale hole in the ceiling, and stamping her foot in rage. Behind her stood Izzard and Charlie Fairweather, both looking rather embarrassed at this turn of events. 'Well, you'd better get out there and find him. I don't care if you have to shoot him, weigh his body down and dump it in the harbour. We have to shut his mouth. That goes for Cherry too!'

'What about Emily Longstaff? Igor's still got her in the cellar.'

'Stuff Emily! She can lie there and rot until we sort the others out. Jack, you go and pick up Patsy Donaldson, and take her up on the Knoll. That will flush Cherry out.'

'You don't mean…'

'Yes, I do mean! I want her buried next to Mary Burton. I don't know what she's told Cherry, and that makes her dangerous. We can't have any loose mouths out there, especially now, when we're just waiting for the first delivery of the new drug. You have to find them before they manage to get out of town.'

'I've already ripped the leads out of Cherry's new car, so that won't be going anywhere,' said Charlie. 'And *his* car is still halfway along the road to Port Flint, isn't it, Jack?'

Izzard nodded. He was just going to speak when there was the sound of someone barging through the door into the police station, and presently Frank Kelly appeared in the doorway, looking grim.

'I can see everything's under control as always,' he said, sarcastically, nodding up towards the hole in the ceiling.

'We don't need feeble attempts at humour at this hour of the morning, Frank. What's the problem?' said Ilse.

'I think we've just had a stroke of luck,' said Frank. 'I've got a new guest in the hotel, and you'll never guess who it is.'

'Well, don't keep us in suspense,' said Izzard, abruptly.

'That guy's wife – Curtis! She's come up looking for him, so it looks as if they had a split before he came here, and now she's come after him.'

'I thought he was single,' said Ilse. 'He's been coming on strong to Cherry!'

'So did I,' growled Charlie Fairweather. 'That bastard! He stuffed any chance I had of going out with her.'

'There was never any chance of that, Charlie,' Izzard grinned. 'She's had your number for years!'

'Well, thanks for those words of support,' Charlie replied, aggrieved.

'So the bitch is at the hotel, Frank! You're right, that is a stroke of luck.'

'There's just one problem,' Frank replied. 'I only just found out about it, but Betty says that some guy came in last night looking for this Damien. Supposed to be his mate. I showed her that photo of the guy in Customs uniform, and she said it looked like him, though she couldn't be a hundred percent sure. It was taken some time ago. But if it is him, he's another one we'll have to deal with.'

'Let's hope that he hasn't caught up with his friend. That could make things a bit sticky,' said Izzard. 'I think we'd better arm ourselves. I can give Charlie here a spare .38. Has anyone else got a weapon?'

'I've got a shotgun,' said Frank. 'I keep it behind the bar!'

Ilse frowned, then made a decision.

'Well you'd better get it out, and load it. Then go with Jack here and get Patsy and Emily, take them both up the Knoll and dig three holes.'

'Three...?'

'Yes! One for this wife of his! When it's done we'll sedate her and take her up there too. That will be the bait to get this Damien, Cherry, and his mate out of hiding, and up to the Knoll.'

'What about Carstairs, waiting down by the dock?' said Izzard.

'Change of plan,' snapped Ilse. 'If we haven't got them, we can't send them out in the trawler. No, we'll just have to play it by ear. Get going you two, and we'll go out and try to communicate with this Damien. He'll have to approach us in the end if we make it known that his wife's here.'

'I don't know how you're going to do that,' Izzard remarked.

'I'll work something out,' said Ilse.

III

'What do we do now?' said John, as he, Cherry and Damien headed through the trees.

'How the hell should I know,' said Damien, savagely, carrying the rifle at his side. 'I'm just a lowly novelties salesman. I sell candles, for god's sake. I chat up office girls! This is like wandering into Alice in Wonderland – take this, and grow bigger, take that and get AIDS. Take something else and we'll cure you, but we've got to pay for it so we'll smuggle drugs, and if you open your mouth we'll murder you, like Mary Burton.'

Cherry grabbed at his arm and gave him a squeeze.

'Let's get my car and make a run for it. If we stay here, either they'll get us or you'll end up shooting someone, then *you'll* be on trial.'

'Oh yes... leave Patsy to her fate! Leave Emily - your mate, Emily - to be disposed of. Because they're gonners, regardless of what we do! No, we can't! We've got to get them out as well or we'll never forgive ourselves. This is bullshit!'

'Calm down, mate! Keep focussed,' John puffed, coming up in the rear and trying to keep up. 'Don't go losing it now!'

Damien spun around in the dark and confronted his erstwhile friend.

'Have you seen my bloody face? Have you any idea how it feels to get seven bells kicked out of you with your hands cuffed behind your back? If nothing else, I'm going to get Jack Izzard for that, and that slimy little toad, Charlie Fairweather. I'm going to kick the living shit out of both of them, give them a taste of their own medicine. If I have to shoot the bastards first, then so be it.'

'If you don't keep it under control, you'll do for the lot of us,' said John, coming to a halt. Damien turned back to face him.

'Keep it under control? If you'd kept it under control we wouldn't be in this mess. You're a great one to talk!'

John nodded. He looked resigned.

'I knew this was coming. Okay, so I deserve it, I should have had more sense. But you're better off now anyway. Look at you; you've got Cherry! She leaves Andrea for dead.'

'Who says he's got me,' said Cherry, not sure that she wanted to be included in this argument between old friends.

Damien looked at her, and suddenly all the anger and frustration seemed to leave him. He was quiet for a moment, then held his hand out to Cherry.

'Yeah, she's right. You're taking things for granted. Cherry and I haven't had time to even discuss a relationship yet, and yet you've already got us paired off. But I don't mind telling you that if I get my way – and if we survive this – Cherry and I will be together for a long, long time.'

Cherry smiled at him in the darkness, moved in and kissed him.

'That goes for me too,' she said, softly.

'Yeah, well... right!' said John, not knowing where to look.

'That's okay, you can have Andrea,' said Damien, 'with my best wishes. You'll be able to bring her to dinner, and we can all reminisce about old times.'

John looked somewhat embarrassed, and shook his head, slowly.

'I... er... don't think so, Damien. She's fixed on you! I should have realised that she wasn't looking for a long-term relationship. I don't think she even likes me, to tell you the truth. She thinks I'm a slob.'

'And so you are,' said Damien, grinning in the darkness. 'You always have been!' Then he punched John playfully on the shoulder, and John knew it was going to be all right.

By this time they were across the road, into the trees on the other side, and making their way towards Patsy's cottage. The house was in darkness, but something wasn't quite right, and as they approached from the rear they could see that the side door was open.

'I don't like the look of that,' said Cherry, and Damien motioned them to wait while he took a look. He was back two minutes later, shaking his head.

'Gone! They must have picked her up already. But there was this…' He held out a note, written in black marking pen, that he'd found stuck on the door. It was addressed to Cherry.

'Cherry – if you want to see your friends again, you'll find them up on the Knoll. Bring your new friends with you, and she won't come to any harm. Otherwise – they're dead! PS – tell your friend Damien that we've got a surprise for him - his wife Andrea!'

'Oh, for chrisesake, they've got Andrea! What the hell did she want to come up here for, poking her nose in? That complicates things!'

'Don't worry about Andrea,' said John. 'She'll get up on her high horse and tell them all what she thinks of them,' said John, grinning. 'We'd better get up there, though, and sort this out!'

'Oh, sure,' said Damien when he read it. 'We're just going to go walking into the jaws of hell and give ourselves up. Not bloody likely!'

'Damien!' Cherry protested. 'Keep the language down.'

'We might just have to do that,' said John. 'If I hold back and cover you with the rifle, at least we'll be able to find out what the odds are.'

Damien looked at the woman beside him.

'I'm not going to expose Cherry to that sort of danger. We'll get the car, send Cherry off to get help, then you and I can go on up the Knoll and find Patsy and Emily.'

'Like hell,' said Cherry. 'You're not getting rid of me that easily. I'm sticking with you two! Why don't we just take the car and get help together. If we go straight away, maybe we'll be able to get back in time to save them both.'

When they got to Cherry's, the bonnet was open on her new car, and the spark plug leads missing. To cap it off, someone had slashed all four tyres.

'So much for that,' said Damien. 'What about your old car? It's battered, but it still goes.'

The old car was around the back of the cottage, and through an oversight had been left untouched. Cherry was all for them getting out of town and going for help.

'I think we ought to even things up a bit. Before we go anywhere, let's check out the doctor's house. If she's there we'll take her along with us, at gunpoint. We can do a swap.'

'That sounds reasonable,' said John. 'Where else would she be at this time of night, anyway? She'd have to be in bed.'

'She could be up on the Knoll with the rest of them,' said Cherry. 'For god's sake, let's just go. Let the police worry about it.'

'That's not very charitable, Cherry,' said Damien. He looked at her and saw the fear in her eyes, so didn't push the point. 'I still think you should take the car and head south, go to the city where they'll be more likely to listen. We'll go to the Knoll and sort things out there.'

'No,' she said, stubbornly. 'Where you go, I go! Look what happened when I let you go out for a walk - you just about got yourself killed. I'm not going through that again.'

Damien shrugged. He couldn't win this one.

'How far is the doctor's cottage from here?'

'About another half a mile further along the road! You'll see it back among the trees off to the right. It's got a blue porch; you can't miss it. But be careful, she keeps snakes there. It's her hobby.'

'Oh, is it,' said Damien, raising an eyebrow. 'You didn't tell me that before, when that bloody brown snake nearly got me in the flat.'

'I never thought of it,' said Cherry. 'Who would ever have suspected a respectable doctor?'

'Well, I want you two to wait here. There's less chance of me being seen if I'm on my own. Give me half an hour, then get in the car and drive up, no lights, and pick me up. With any luck I'll have the good doctor subdued.'

'So you're taking the rifle?'

'Yes, I'll have to if I want to subdue her ladyship. Once we've got her, we'll go up onto the Knoll.'

Damien disappeared into the darkness, and Cherry and John settled down to wait. A car briefly went past them, headed north, and turned off up the track they had taken to the Knoll, on that one occasion that Damien had seen it.

'Could you see who was in it,' John whispered.

Cherry shook her head. Her thoughts were taken up with Damien, and how they were going to come through all this without getting themselves killed.

'I wish to heaven that Damien would just listen to sense,' she said. 'We stand a much better chance of getting out of here if we go now. We could have the police here in a matter of hours. They should be dealing with this, not us!'

'Well, if you know Damien,' John sighed. He knew from bitter experience what it was like trying to deflect Damien from a course of action once he'd made up his mind.

'If we go up on that Knoll, we're as good as dead,' said Cherry, fearfully. 'I know these people! I always thought there was something a bit ruthless about them. The big surprise to me is Ilse. I can't believe how she's turned on me. We've known each other for years.'

Half a mile further on, Damien was silently making his way around the back of what seemed to be a deserted cottage. It was in darkness, but that didn't mean anything. It was the middle of the night after all, and people were usually asleep at that hour.

He crept around the back and found himself alongside a Perspex enclosure, full of rocks and small shrubs. The moon came out from behind a cloud and lit the area up, and a movement in the enclosure caught his eye. He looked again, then shrank back against the cottage wall. Inside the enclosure, slithering purposefully in his general direction, was a six foot brown snake. Damien felt the hairs rise on the back of his neck. A typical city dweller, he had rarely seen a snake close up and the sight of them gave him the creeps. Killing that brown at the flat had taken every bit of raw courage that he could muster, and he hadn't managed to replace it yet.

The back door was unlocked. It was the work of only minutes to ascertain that there was no one in the cottage, but he realised he had some time to spare, and found himself going through a desk in the study, hoping to find something incriminating that he could use. After forcing a locked drawer, he inadvertently found what he was looking for, a diary. A quick glance showed him that it had been written up like a journal, with entries spaced sometimes weeks apart. The important thing to him was that it started three years before, and continued up until the present day. Tucking it under his arm, he made his way outside, and slipped into the car as it came slowly along the road.

'Look what I've got,' he said to Cherry. 'The good doctor's journal! And I can tell you, the first few entries will blow your mind!'

Chapter Seventeen

22 March 1999

Roland arrived up here for the first time last week. I thought that at last we might be able to overcome our differences, and sort out our relationship. But he was offhand with me from the start, said I was too cold and indifferent to his needs for him to reconsider, and that he had met someone else. I couldn't believe it when he told me that he was seeing Liz Capel... Liz, of all people! She's the slut of the town, though he hasn't realised that yet. Typical male, he thinks that she's fallen for his charm. He's in for a rude awakening. As for that bitch, well, I've got plans for her. If I can't have him, neither will she!

2 April 1999

I've been raging around this cottage for three days now – Roland hasn't bothered to contact me at all, and he's lying low over at Liz Capel's. At times like this a cold hard rage takes over, and all I can see is blackness and hate. I can't stand the idea of him together with that slut, probably talking about me as well, which makes it even worse. I know that it won't last, none of Liz's affairs ever do. But it's different this time. He's mine, and whether I want him or not, no one else is going to make him happy while I feel so miserable.

I threw his dog into the snake pit yesterday, and took great solace from its dying yelps. Goebbels put paid to it with three or four swift strikes, and then Axis Sally came in for the kill. Well, he should never have left the damned pooch with me if he wanted it looked after. He should know me by now. When I was at med school they called me Killer Ilse, because I used to joke when I was cutting the heads off live mice and rats, and again during the autopsies of accident victims. I'll say that much... when I want to be I can be cold and unemotional, and focus on any living thing as just another object to be experimented on. It never bothers me in the least. In fact, I would much rather have been involved in medical experiments than be stuck in a one-horse town, doctoring for idiots. If he doesn't call me shortly, I shall go mad!

11 April 1999

It's over, and I shouldn't be making this entry because I know it will come back to haunt me one day. But my training has always been to make notes, record observations, and I don't see why I should stop now. Roland came home with his tail between his legs two days ago, like the mongrel he is... or should I say, was! Just like his little dog! I was elated at first, but after the first few hours, that feeling gave way to a white rage when I discovered that he was only here because Liz had kicked him out. I felt a sudden contempt for him, and the more he tried to make his peace with me, the more I resented him; hated him in fact. He tried to get me into bed, but I resisted. Sex is a reward for making *me* feel better, not for someone else to use to manipulate my feelings. Fuck him!

I cooked the evening meal, and mixed a liberal dose of purgative in with his portion, and before long he was vomiting and running at both ends. It made him as weak as a kitten, and he still didn't realise that I'd done it deliberately. How dense! I made him go in the shower to clean up, and afterwards, as he was stepping out I made him bend over the sink so I could check his hair out – or so I said! I made out I thought he had nits, and that these could be affecting his system. He still didn't suspect.

Then I went out to the kitchen and came back with the meat cleaver, and held him down by the hair. Just before I did it I said – 'This is just to let you know how much I hate you! – and then I hit him with the cleaver, and took his head off with three swings.

God, the blood! He fell on the floor and I dropped his head into the sink. It fell face up and was looking at me, and his mouth was open and making an attempt to speak. The last thing he saw of me was *me*, laughing in pure jubilation. It was like a rush of pure adrenalin, and I was surprised to find that I not only wet myself in confusion, but I had an orgasm that lasted for about three minutes straight, until I could hardly stand up.

Luckily the floor is tiled, otherwise I would never have been able to clean up the blood. As it was it took me over an hour to get rid of the mess, flushing it down the drain. Late that night I dragged his headless body out and put it in the boot of the car, wrapped in plastic of course, so there are no tell-tale bloodstains in the boot. I drove out to Mission Point and shoved him over a small cliff there into the sea. The tide was in, but I could see the body getting carried out into the bay, and with any luck it will drift out there and eventually sink before it's discovered. I don't care anyway. Nobody knew anything about our relationship together – except maybe Liz Capel – and I've got plans for her. He'd never been to this town before, so knew no one else, and without a head he'll be difficult to identify.

Do I feel remorse? No, and again, No! I'd do it again. I intend to bury the head up on the Knoll when I can be sure there's no one around.

13 April 1999

Bloody disaster! Erin Lachlan, one of the trawlermen, found the body floating out in the bay, about two miles out he said. The only one that worries me is Liz Capel, but I understand she's now having some torrid affair with a vacuum cleaner salesmen, so she probably won't even think twice about Roland. She never remembers the last affair; she always concentrates on the affair of the moment. The word around town is that the body is probably from anything up to a hundred miles away, the way the tides operate around here. Anyway, if I'm questioned at all I'll just act surprised. There's nothing to tie me in to it at all, except his head. That's still sitting in a cupboard, wrapped in a towel. It makes it all the more important to get it out of here, however.

5 May 1999

The talk about the body has all died down. There was a brief splurge in the Adelaide papers, but the police are generally scratching their heads. I buried the head about three days after the last entry. It was starting to look a bit desiccated by then, but I buried it near an ants nest, so there won't be anything left of the flesh by now.

Liz Capel came in for a pregnancy test about a week ago, and that was the opportunity I needed. Under cover of giving her a blood test, I infected the bitch with the HIV virus. She doesn't know it, but she's under a death sentence for what she did to me. It will be interesting from a research point of view, anyway, to see just how far the virus will spread in this town. Anyway, she's a slut of the first order, and any man that takes advantage of her services will deserve everything he gets.

At least I feel now that I'm accomplishing something useful. If I keep strict records of all my patients, and record those who get HIV, it might give some indication about how quickly this virus can spread in a small community like this - where there's a lot of partner swapping and one night stands going on - due to the isolation of the place. I might even be able to write a paper on the subject, and get it published in a Medical Journal. I wouldn't, of course, give away my part in the commencement of the epidemic, but I could write it from a historical point of view, going around afterwards and questioning all those infected as if to find out who they've slept with, and when. This could be quite interesting. A bit more interesting than colds or flu in a small town, anyway!

23 July 1999

I've been pretty busy for the last month or so, and this journal has suffered. But I'm keeping my patient records on the computer anyway, so it's not as if I'm not observing and recording. Liz Capel continues to screw her way through the male idiots of Dark Harbour – how apt that name is now! Dark Harbour! And the darkest harbour is between Liz Capel's legs! From my own personal knowledge she's screwed about six men since the last entry, one of them being the good local constable here, Jack Izzard. He's one of the few that I would have warned off if I could, but how can I warn anyone? It would just compromise the experiment. Luckily I'm not the sentimental sort, or I'd be absolutely useless for this type of research. As far as I'm concerned, if these guys are stupid enough to follow their dicks around to Liz's place, then they deserve all they get. I tested Jack Izzard a couple of weeks ago, and yes, he's HIV positive. Serves him right! Also Lionel Jury – he was the first confirmed victim, and I'm pretty sure that Igor Morris has been sniffing around there too whenever he's been sober enough to think about it. But I'll confirm that in due course.

I'm just going to have to be patient though. The progression from HIV to full-blown AIDS can take years in some cases, and I'm going to have to hope that none of these people decide to consult another doctor outside Dark Harbour. I've got all the time in the world. There's no way that I'm going to be jumping into bed with anyone who is even remotely attracted to Liz Capel. The fact that she's not showing any symptoms just yet means nothing. She's like a little factory, producing the virus and spreading it around wherever she goes. It's a pity I can't tell her, and gloat over it. But I might just do that in the end – the day before I kill her off for good!

II

Cherry sat in the driver's seat, listening to Damien reading, aloud, the first few entries of Ilse's journal, and struggling to comprehend.

'My God, Damien! She's mad! This Roland she talks about… I've never even heard of him. There again, Liz never told me anything. She might have confided in Patsy, but she certainly never did in me. If Patsy did know about him, she kept it to herself.'

'From what I can make out,' Damien mused, 'this Roland was someone she'd had a relationship with somewhere else, not in Dark Harbour. How long had the doctor been here?'

'She arrived here in about '95.'

'So it's possible that they broke up just before she got here then.'

'It's possible, I suppose. She was always going off to town and disappearing for a few days, here and there. Maybe she stayed with him when she was down there, and maybe they argued about him coming up to live in Dark Harbour. If he worked in the city, he would hardly be likely to want to throw it all up to come here.'

'So finally she convinces him,' John put in, 'and then she finds that he hasn't come up for her at all, but that he's met Liz Capel – I suppose it's possible that he could have met Liz in Adelaide?'

'Oh, hell yeah! Liz used to make regular trips as well, mainly for shopping purposes in her case. Maybe she met him in a hotel one night. Knowing Liz, she would have quite happily gone off with him on the first night, if she were attracted to him. She was pretty well available in that sense.'

'What does it say about Mary Burton,' said Cherry, watching Damien turn the pages of the journal.

'When do you reckon it was – about a year ago?' said Damien. 'Oh, here! Listen to this!'

13 February 2002

There's been a hitch with our little stash of heroin. Frank Kelly went home last night to find that there were two packs missing from a box he was keeping it in, in the spare room. It's disguised as Icing Sugar, in clear plastic bags, and we had eight packs, ready for delivery. Now there's only six! $200,000 a pack! That's a major disaster! Whoever did it is dead – dead!

15 February 2002

Everything works out in the end. It took Frank less than a day to find out that it was his house cleaner,

Mary Burton, that had stolen the H. She was so stupid, she really believed it was icing sugar, and was in the middle of trying to make icing with it when Frank and Craig picked her up, outside her cottage. They were so mad that they took her down the cellar of the hotel, and stripped her off and raped her. I went down later, and watched as Igor and Lionel Jury, and Charlie Fairweather took it in turns. Izzard came in halfway through, and had his go as well. It was quite a turn on, actually, and she screamed her head off. Every time she screamed, I came close to a climax. Then they asked me what I wanted to do with her – thinking that I was the only one that had missed out, being a woman – so I told them to take her up to the Knoll, and bury her up to the neck. Later on, I got Frank to sharpen an old sickle that I'd found, out in the back shed, and I went up there and swished it around in the grass in front of her until she was literally frothing at the mouth. When I finally took her head off, I was surprised at how easily it separated from her shoulders. Then we all went a bit mad, I think, and kicked her head around between us, all except Igor, the mutt, who was too busy throwing up behind a tree. Weak!

Later on, I carried it up to the edge of the cliff, and dropped it into the harbour. No doubt, someone will go diving there one day, and find a human skull, and there will be a scandal. But that won't happen for years.'

'Let's just flick on through this thing,' said Damien, totally intrigued by now. 'Here! Another piece about Liz Capel:

2 June 2002

Liz Capel has finally pushed us to the brink. I was for killing her at first, but Izzard was a bit more cautious this time. He said we should keep her alive, just in case we had to produce her at any time in the future. She'd been mouthing off about Mary Burton again, and was about to head off to Adelaide to try and interest the authorities in mounting a full-scale investigation. She never would shut up about it, especially after we had the furniture removalists take Mary's furniture away one morning, and drop it at a second-hand shop in Adelaide. Dangerous! So Izzard went around and asked her to call in at the police station over some trivial matter, and when she did she was knocked out, and carted down the cellar in the pub. The only way to control the bitch was to get her hooked on heroin as soon as possible, so I began a series of injections, and for the past two weeks we've been shooting her up twice a day. She's well and truly hooked. I only have to threaten to withdraw the drug, and she's grovelling on her knees down there, so I don't think she'll give us any problems, even if she does manage to get out one day. It will be shut up, or go cold turkey.'

Damien put the diary aside, and looked grimly up at the looming shadow that constituted the Knoll.

'Well at least we know what we're dealing with here. A complete nutcase who also happens to be a mass murderer, if you take the HIV virus into account! Then there are her faithful minions like Jack Izzard and Charlie Fairweather who obviously don't know that the reason they got HIV in the first place was because she was conducting a sort of vengeful experiment, using her rival, Liz Capel, to spread the seed. And she's got Patsy and Emily up on that Knoll, and maybe even Andrea. Good God!'

'She's going to kill them,' said Cherry, in a sudden burst of anxiety. 'Oh, Patsy!'

'Give me the rifle, and I'll watch your backs,' said John. 'Once we get up there, I'll hang off in the bushes and see what's happening. Then I'll follow you at a distance. If this Izzard character pulls his gun out, I'll take him out.'

'But you can't kill him,' said Cherry, anxiously. 'We'll all be for it.'

'Don't worry about my friend here,' said Damien, nodding towards John. 'He can pick off a five cent piece at a hundred metres on a good day.'

'With my own rifle,' John demurred, 'not this heap of crap. And in daylight, not in the middle of the night! But I'll do my best,' he acknowledged.

Cherry started the car, and they drove slowly towards the Knoll, which looked like a black abyss in a cloudy sky. It was like a black hole in space, and they drove right into it, lights out, and almost feeling their way along the old track.

'It's a good job that I know the way up here. I could just about do this with my eyes shut,' said Cherry, negotiating her way through the trees.

'You'd better let me out about fifty metres before you hit the top,' said John, 'or wherever you intend to stop. I'll come along behind you so I'm not seen.'

'Well don't you lose us, for chrisesake,' said Damien, peering blindly through the windscreen. 'We're relying on you!'

'Don't worry,' said John. Cherry stopped the car, and he slipped silently out of the rear door, and was instantly gone in the darkness. Then she continued on for another fifty metres, and stopped again. They both got out and started to walk.

They'd only walked thirty metres when a voice rang out ahead of them on the track. It was Charlie Fairweather.

'Lucky you saw sense! We've got some of your mates up here, and a bit of a surprise for you, Mister bloody Curtis. Your wife's been asking for you!'

He indicated that they should follow him, and took them through dense undergrowth towards the military fence. Once there Damien could see that they'd cut a hole through the mesh, and they were told to pass on through and keep walking for another fifty metres, dead ahead. They'd only walked ten metres when there was a thud behind them, and Damien looked back, squeezed Cherry's hand, and grinned in the dark.

'That's one out! John just flattened Charlie with the butt of his rifle!'

They kept walking and presently the land began to clear. Suddenly they were walking alongside a plantation of bushy plants, some six feet high. Damien was in no doubt about what they were.

'Marijuana,' he whispered. 'There must be millions here!'

Shortly they came out into a small clearing.

'Stop right where you are!' Jack Izzard was standing some thirty metres away, pointing his .38 at them across the clearing. Craig Mortimer stood a few feet away. Nearby was a hooded figure, holding the long, wooden handle of a sickle. Down on the ground were three pale faces, staring directly at them from where they were buried up to the neck. One of them was Andrea! The women's eyes rolled in their heads, they were so drugged out that saliva was running out of their mouths, uncontrollably, and they were incapable of speech.

Despite himself, Damien made a sudden movement towards them, and a bullet whistled past his ear and thudded into a tree behind them.

'Don't even think about it, Curtis! Next time I won't miss.'

'If you dare to harm any of these women,' Damien spluttered in rage, but Izzard waved his gun, and both Damien and Cherry were made to stand off.

The hooded figure suddenly spoke.

'Have you ever seen someone beheaded, Mister Curtis? It's most entertaining! Take your wife for instance. This is so much cleaner than divorce, quicker, and more lasting. There is no appeal, and no property settlement!'

Andrea was facing Damien, the hooded figure behind her. Her mouth was open in shock, but she couldn't seem to utter a word.

The sickle moved ominously, cutting a swathe through the grass behind Andrea's horrified features. She could hear its hiss as it came closer through the grass.

'Don't!' yelled Damien, holding his hand up, as if that would be enough to stop this madness.

Izzard's gun came up and suddenly there was an explosion behind them in the trees, and Izzard shrieked as the gun flew out of his hand into the bushes. Two of his fingers were missing, and he fell to the ground, nursing his bloodied hand. Mortimer stared at him in shock, and began to back away. Before Damien could move, the sickle sliced along the ground in a wide arc, and Andrea's head magically lifted away from the ground and rolled noiselessly towards Izzard, writhing on the ground. Then there was the awful sight of blood, spurting in steady bursts into the air where Andrea's head had been. It continued to spurt a good two feet into the air for about twenty seconds, then just spread wetly about the ground nearby while Damien stood transfixed in shock, his mind unable to accept what he had just witnessed. Cherry, meanwhile, had collapsed onto the ground, and fainted dead away.

Another shot rang out, and the sickle sprang away from the hooded figure's grasp, blood spattering the forearms of the green gown. There was a scream, and Ilse Hirsch turned and sprang away through the trees, doubled over with the pain. Mortimer raised his hands in the air and got down onto his knees.

'Don't shoot me! For god's sake, don't shoot! They made me come here, it was nothing to do with me!'

Behind him, a figure came crashing through the undergrowth from the other direction, and burst out into the clearing, a shotgun at the ready. Frank Kelly! Another shot rang out, and Kelly crashed to the ground, a spreading patch of blood above his left knee. He bellowed in pain and tried to raise the shotgun to fire, but another explosion from the cover of the trees took it effectively out of his hands and flung it six feet away.

Damien was in shock! He watched the ongoing slaughter as if in a dream, totally unable to move from the spot. His eyes were riveted on Andrea's head, which lay on its side, staring off into the distance.

'Any more fucking surprises,' John yelled from cover, and then slowly advanced into the clearing, covering Mortimer, now cowering on the ground.

He went over and grabbed Damien by the shoulder, and shook him.

'Snap out of it, Damien! Take this.' He thrust the butt of a .38 into Damien's limp hand, and made him grab hold of it. 'I frisked it off your mate Charlie out there,' he said, as Damien began to come back from wherever his head had been.

'She murdered Andrea,' he groaned. 'Took her head clean off. I can't believe it… Andrea's dead!'

Suddenly Damien lurched away to the side and threw up.

'That's it; get it out! I need you, Damien. Get yourself together!'

Ten feet away Patsy and Emily stared horrified from their ground level positions, staring straight ahead, but drugged out of their minds. They were not even capable of screaming! John waved the rifle towards Mortimer.

'Dig them up – now! And make sure you don't even scratch them, or I'll take *your* fucking head off!'

Mortimer got to his knees, then warily walked over to pick up one of the shovels that had been used to dig the holes in the first place. He began to loosen the dirt around Patsy's shoulders, and John stood back and watched.

Cherry moaned and sat up, then began to weep uncontrollably.

'Get yourself under control, Cherry,' said John. 'We're not out of the woods yet.'

Cherry gulped twice, then went over and began to help Mortimer free, first Patsy, and then Emily.

'Where is that bitch?' yelled Damien, suddenly back in the land of the living. 'And that fucking Charlie Fairweather?' He caught a sight of Izzard on the ground, hanging onto his mutilated hand, walked over and kicked him in the gut. Izzard grunted in pain. 'How does it feel, you bastard? How does it feel being on the receiving end?'

'Fuck you!' said Izzard, looking up.

Damien kicked him fair in the head, and laid him out.

'Don't kill the prick, Damien. He's going to jail for life!'

Damien spun around, intent on finding Charlie Fairweather. While John kept his eye on proceedings in the clearing, Damien crashed back through the undergrowth to the fence and looked around for Charlie. But Charlie had woken to the sound of gunshots, and had well and truly flown the coop.

Chapter Eighteen

Without even turning back to check on the others, Damien began to run down the hill, the .38 grasped tightly in his fist. He had one thought in mind, and that was to stop Charlie Fairweather making a break for it and getting clean away. When he got as far as Cherry's old car, he was surprised to find it still there. He'd thought that Charlie would have taken it and fled. When he checked the dash, however, he realised that the keys were missing. That was why Charlie hadn't taken it! He would still be on his way down the hill, no doubt, on foot.

Damien was just about to follow him when he suddenly remembered that Cherry was in the habit of throwing the keys under the front seat. He walked back and groped around, and sure enough, there were the keys. It was a matter of moments to start the car, turn it around, and head back down the hill.

No caution this time! He put the lights on high beam and lit his way through the trees as the car careered along, bouncing and lurching along the track. If he'd expected to catch up with Charlie on the way down the hill, he was disappointed. He must have been moving a lot faster than Damien had thought. He turned the car along the main road back to the town centre, and seconds later saw a figure half running and half limping along the grass verge at the edge of the road. Moments later he was sure it was Charlie.

As he approached, Charlie looked fearfully over his shoulder, and began to make a beeline for the trees some hundred metres back off the road at that point, but Damien had no intention of being thwarted at this stage of the game. He mounted the grass verge and gunned the motor, and Charlie threw one last despairing look over his shoulder before the car lunged at him from the road, and ran him down, knocked him to the ground and then rolled excruciatingly over his legs. Damien brought the car to a halt fifteen feet further on, and got out, gun in hand.

Charlie was screaming in agony and clutching his twisted and broken legs. He wouldn't be going anywhere.

'Now it's my turn, you prick! How do you like being helpless for a change?'

Damien ran at the screaming form on the ground and took a kick at his head. He laid open Charlie's forehead with the first blow, and Charlie fell back and looked dazed and confused. Driven by pure rage, Damien set about his kidneys, his legs and his torso until Charlie was throwing up on the grass, then he knelt down and smashed his fists into Charlie's face, knocking three teeth out in the process. When he was totally unconscious, Damien felt at last avenged for the beating he'd taken, and returned his thoughts to the main culprit of the group – Ilse Hirsch. She had disappeared through the trees, hit in the forearm by a .303 bullet. The question was, where was she?

Damien's guess was that she would have returned to her cottage, bound up her arm, and then high-tailed it out in her car before all hell broke loose. No doubt she had someone in Adelaide who would shelter her until she could change her identity, or leave the country. So he headed for her cottage.

The place was in darkness when he got there, though the door was shut. He wasn't going to stand on ceremony this time, so took a run at the door and kicked it open, shattering the lock in the process. As he stormed in through the door, he heard a shriek and a whimper towards the rear of the house, then he heard a rear door open, and he followed the sounds to the back of the house.

There was a movement outside, and he followed the sounds out through the back door. As he walked out, he hit a light switch on the wall, and the back yard lit up. There, standing whimpering in the middle of a large, Perspex enclosure was a most remarkable sight. Ilse Hirsch, still in her blood-stained, hooded gown, was standing on a rock in the centre of the enclosure, holding her bleeding arm out in front of her.

'You'll never take me alive,' she whimpered, from somewhere inside the all-enveloping hood.

'I think I've already got you, don't you?' said Damien, grimly. 'You might as well come out; it's all over! I've got your diary, and I know all about the HIV you infected Liz Capel with. You're a twisted bitch, murdering my wife like that, and god knows how many others. I've a good mind to chop your head off too, just to let you know how it feels – only that would be too quick, don't you think?'

'I'm glad I did it… glad! It was worth it just to see your stupid face!'

At that moment, something stirred in the enclosure, and a head appeared from behind some foliage.

'Don't look now, but there's a bloody great brown snake heading your way,' said Damien. 'You'd better get out, now!'

Ilse looked around and squealed in terror. She was under no illusion that just because she had fed these monsters for years, that they felt any kinship with her.

'I told you, you won't take me alive,' she babbled, then began to moan in terror as the second head appeared, that of Axis Sally.

They both struck at once, darting their heads at the long gown, and trying to find a way through it. Ilse began to dance frantically on the spot, suddenly looking for a way out. She launched herself at the Perspex fence, but Goebbels saw his opportunity as the gown lifted, and quick as lightning his great head darted underneath the gown and disappeared up between her legs. She let out a shrill scream, half fell, and then screamed again as Axis Sally rose up and bit her on the face, through the folds of the hood. Damien could only stand back and watch, though afterwards he realised that he'd had the .38 in his hand, and could have dispatched both snakes long before the damage was done.

They struck again and again, Goebbels doing his damage somewhere underneath her skirt where he couldn't be seen. Ilse fell backwards into the enclosure and after a few short screams lay quietly twitching with the poison's rapid advance. Damien waited until the body lay still, and then turned, walked back through the cottage and out to the car.

II

Cherry was in the shower by six thirty, valiantly scrubbing at herself in an attempt to remove not only the dirt from the previous night's carnage, and the blood of Andrea Curtis, but also all memory of the horror they had experienced on the Knoll. She was under the shower for half an hour, and when she got out she passed through into the bedroom, and gratefully dressed herself in clean, fresh clothes, then sat and stared at her image in the mirror. She looked tired and worn, but knew that a good night's sleep would fix that problem.

She looked down at the dressing table, and frowned. There was a new container of talc there that she hadn't seen before, the brand being, ironically, *'New Beginnings'*. She called Patsy in.

'Hey, Patsy, did you leave this here the other night? I don't remember seeing this before!'

Patsy picked up the unopened container, and shook her head.

'Not one of mine! Maybe you bought it at one of those parties, and forgot about it!'

Cherry shook her head.

'I'd remember it if I'd bought it. Still – never look a gift horse in the mouth. We've got Katie's wedding coming up, and after that her baby shower. I'll stick it aside and wrap it up for the babe. She'd like that!'

'God! Katie's wedding. Do you know, I'd almost forgotten all about that over the past few days. Once I've had a good sleep, I'd better get out and pick up a new outfit,' she said. 'It's only a week away.'

'A lot can happen in a week,' said Cherry, looking at her friend in the mirror.

'You're not wrong. The past week was the longest week in living memory,' Patsy replied.

They went out into the lounge, and smiled at the state of their partners in crime.

'I could sleep for a week,' said Damien, staggering to the table, where Patsy had just lined up four coffees for the haggard looking group.

Outside Cherry's cottage the town was a hive of activity, with police cars going backwards and forwards along the main road between the main street and the Knoll, and the occasional ambulance turning up to collect the various injured around the town. Customs and Excise were down at the dock, checking through the trawlers and the fish processing plant, while their vigilant servant slept, exhausted, on Cherry's couch.

The police had taken Igor Morris and Craig Mortimer into custody, and had collected Wilf Carstairs the moment his trawler docked. Lionel Jury had disappeared. Frank Kelly, Charlie Fairweather and Jack

Izzard had been spirited off to hospital in Adelaide under heavy guard, and there was a STAR Force team up on the Knoll, chopping down a forest of marijuana plants and filming them for evidence.

Patsy dragged herself over to the table and grabbed a coffee, dropping into a chair and taking a sip as if it were some sort of divine nectar of the gods.

'I didn't think I'd ever get to drink another coffee,' she mumbled, flashing Cherry a thankful smile. She looked over at John, spark out on the sofa, and smiled again. 'He's cute, isn't he,' she said to Cherry, who looked at her ruefully, and raised one eyebrow.

'Just give it time, Patsy. We're going to have all the time in the world after this!'

'What happened to your friend, Emily,' said Damien, who had been instrumental in driving ten kilometres down the coast until his mobile suddenly sparked into life, at which he had then pulled over, and alerted the authorities.

'She's off to Port Flint Hospital, recovering from her ordeal and getting an HIV check,' said Patsy. 'They wanted to take me as well, but I said no! I just wanted to be back with my friends.'

'And so you are,' said Cherry, putting her arm around Patsy's shoulder. 'And we'll never be separated again!'

'I don't know,' said Patsy. 'I think Damien might have something to say about that!'

Damien looked up blearily from over the top of his coffee, and shook his head.

'As far as I'm concerned, it's up to Cherry where we go from here. If she wants to stay in Dark Harbour, I suppose I can still operate from here. I'll just have to go on the road, cover all the country towns up and down the coast. I don't have any great desire to return to Adelaide.'

Cherry sat down beside him and held his hand.

'I'm really sorry about Andrea. It must have been appalling to have to witness something like that.'

Damien looked down at the table, a pained expression in his eyes. He lifted her hand, and put it to his lips.

'I shall never forget it for as long as I live. But there again, neither will you! It's a sobering thought that Andrea will be a part of our lives forever.'

'When's the funeral,' said Patsy, 'or haven't they worked that out yet?'

'I think they'll be storing the bodies until the coroner's hearing. I understand that they've found Mary Burton as well. She was only a few feet away from where they buried you.'

Patsy shuddered, and took another sip of her coffee.

'When I heard that sickle swishing through the grass, I thought that all my birthdays had come at once. I would have been next... if it hadn't been for John there.'

'Did he say why he didn't take Ilse out before she had a chance to kill Andrea?' said Cherry.

'Yes... we were in the way,' said Damien. 'It seems that from where he was standing, we were right between her and him. It was only when you collapsed, after… you know what… that he could get a shot in!'

'So where's the bitch,' said Patsy, grimly. 'I hope she's rotting in hell!'

'I think the body's still lying in the pen. They're getting someone up from the zoo to take care of the snakes, before they can get her out. No one's game to go near her.'

'It's a pity we didn't get to read the rest of that journal,' said Cherry. 'What we saw was incriminating enough, but it might have been interesting to know the rest of it.'

'The police grabbed it, and no doubt it won't surface now until long after this whole business is over. Can you imagine Jack Izzard and Co. finding out, finally, at the trial, that Ilse had deliberately infected Liz Capel with the virus. They'll go berserk! It's lucky for her that she's dead.'

'What about this cure that's supposed to be coming from America?'

'Well, they won't be getting that now, will they? I should imagine Interpol will be picking up Ilse's contact in America at the first opportunity. End of story!'

'Not quite,' said Cherry. 'You haven't asked me yet!'

'That's right… I knew I'd forgotten something. Will you be my lawful wedded wife, Cherry Reynolds, to have and to hold, and protect me from crackpots that try to run me out of town for no apparent reason?'

Cherry smiled at him, and nodded.

'I will, Damien Curtis. That I will!'

III

Lying unread in the Police evidence room, and locked up securely until the trial, was Ilse's journal, its final entry waiting to strike a chill into the coroner.

23 April 2003

Why is it that something so simple can be screwed up by incompetents? With the willing support of my victims, I've managed to amass nearly seven million dollars, supposedly for this new anti-virus coming from the States. Which just goes to show that some people will believe anything! Idiots!

Everything was going along just fine, when this nobody turns up in town, and suddenly my entire operation is compromised. If it hadn't been for that stupid photo, none of this would have happened. Customs and Excise, for God's sake! He's a nobody, this Curtis, a nothing! And yet he's managed to turn this place into a mare's nest. We're lucky the police at Port Flint didn't take him and Cherry Reynolds more seriously, or we'd all have been for it, and I would have been sucked into the vortex.

However, I've got my tickets to Rio – I leave on the 28th of May. The seven million will be going with me! But this Curtis... he's going to pay for this, and so is Cherry! Just as a little goodbye gesture, I've infected a container of talc with anthrax, and after Cherry knocked me down and took off from the hotel cellar the other day, I went back and left it on her dressing table. It's not the brand she normally uses, but sooner or later curiosity will get the better of her, and she'll open it and douse herself in the powder. That's all it will take! If she's still in tight with Curtis, he'll go down as well.

Serve them bloody right!